"Hard to match for subtlety and understanding....A sharply focused study rather than a broad exploration of adolescence, written wittily, lucidly, and with great respect for the resources of the language."
—*The New Yorker*

"Miss Stafford writes with brilliance. Scene after scene is told with unforgettable care and tenuous entanglements are treated with wise subtlety. She creates a splendid sense of time, of the unending afternoons of youth, and of the actual color of noon and of night. Refinement of evil, denial of drama only make the underlying truth more terrible."
—*Saturday Review*

"Miss Stafford holds the reader spellbound throughout the narrative. She creates an intense atmosphere with a few simple phrases and characterizes her figures in a masterly manner through the eyes of the children."
—*Catholic World*

belisk

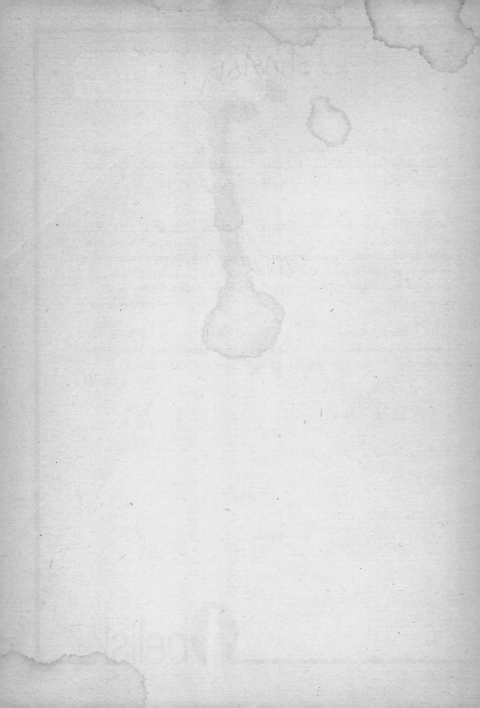

The
MOUNTAIN LION

Jean Stafford

The

MOUNTAIN LION

A Dutton Obelisk Paperback

E. P. DUTTON, INC. / NEW YORK

This paperback edition of The Mountain Lion
first published in 1983 by E. P. Dutton, Inc.

Published in the United States by
E. P. Dutton, Inc., 2 Park Avenue, New York, N.Y. 10016

Library of Congress Catalog Card Number:82-73904

ISBN: 0-525-48031-5

Published simultaneously in Canada by
Clarke, Irwin & Company Limited, Toronto and Vancouver

10 9 8 7 6 5 4 3 2 1

TO CAL AND TO DICK

A friend loveth at all times, and a brother is born for adversity.

PROVERBS XVII, 17.

AUTHOR'S NOTE

THE LAST SENTENCE OF *The Mountain Lion* WAS WRITTEN on a misty April day in 1946 in Damariscotta Mills, Maine, while a local carpenter was screwing handles on the drawers of a desk he had made for me. He had lived in Maine for most of his life, but originally he was "from away" and was not graced with the autochthonous Down East taciturnity. He was the gabbiest workman I have ever had on any premises anywhere. But he was an excellent artisan, so I put up with his homespun wisdom ("Like the feller says, never rains but it pours." "Can't count on only two things in this life, them being death and taxes") and his disgraceful politics and his totally incomprehensible jokes (I either laughed too soon or failed to laugh at all and, thinking I had been listening to a misfortune, would say, "Oh, what a pity!"). His head was just below my typewriter and his breath was strong (he chewed, but mercifully forebore to do so in his clients' houses; I *did* own a cuspidor but it was small and made of milk glass and I kept straw flowers and bittersweet in it) and as usual he was twaddling on, sixteen to the dozen.

But I was so deep in my remorse for what I had done to my heroine, Molly Fawcett, that I heard not a word he said and cared not a pin that he was there.

The desk has been moved ten times. At it, I wrote another novel and a great many short stories and essays and reviews. It is too big for my present study, but it is up in the attic and in its well is the Royal portable on which I wrote *The Mountain Lion*. I bought that typewriter, paying for it in installments, in 1937 when I had a salary of $100 a month for teaching Freshman English to pretty, featherheaded girls in Missouri. The typewriter has long since been replaced by a series of standards which reach obsolescence in early nonage. It antedates the desk by eight years, but it is still in working order (it is stiff in the joints from disuse and its touch is heavy, but I can limber it up with a little workout) and it served me valiantly until its retirement: on it I wrote several novels that weren't any good and abide, yellow and crumbling, in my files; and on it I wrote all three of my published novels. Every now and again, I go up to the attic on a cool day and, removing the Royal's shabby cover, I write what I always write when I am trying out a new typewriter or a new pen: "This is the day when no man living may 'scape away."

Good Deeds says that in *Everyman*. I can't remember when this announcement of Doomsday is made—probably toward the end of the play when the grim reaper lets it be known that Everyman's number has come up—but I should know, because I used to have that particular Morality by heart. At least I knew by heart what Good Deeds had to say because I played the role one time when I was a student at the University of Colorado. Good Deeds is one of Everyman's men friends, and I was a girl at the time—now I am an old lady with a crocheted hug-me-tight around my shoulders and a tatted cap upon my nodding head—but I was chosen for the part; I suppose it could be argued that out there, in those olden, golden days, we were already on to the treacheries deriving from Male Chauvinism and this was a little bitty protest. I think it is more likely, however, that I spoke his lines because I had (and have) the voice of an undertaker. And Good Deeds, while well-intentioned (he is, in fact, a real brick and goes, as you recall, along with Everyman to the hereafter when all his other fair-weather friends have ditched him), is melancholy.

And up there in the attic, amongst the hornets and the cobwebs, in my house at the eastern end of Long Island, across the continent from the Pacific Seaboard where Molly was born (and, by curious coincidence, so was I) and far from the Rocky Mountains where she died (and I was stage-struck for a couple of weeks), I grow as melancholy as Good Deeds. Poor old Molly! I loved her dearly and I hope she rests in peace.

JEAN STAFFORD

The Springs
Long Island
September 21, 1971

The
MOUNTAIN LION

CHAPTER ONE

RALPH WAS TEN AND MOLLY WAS EIGHT WHEN THEY HAD
scarlet fever. It left them with some sort of glandular
disorder which was not malignant, but which kept them
half poisoned most of the time and caused them, frequently,
to have such bad nosebleeds that they had to be sent home
from school. It nearly always happened that their nosebleeds came at the same time. Ralph, bleeding profusely,
would stumble into the corridor to find Molly coming out
of the third-grade room, a handkerchief held in a sodden
bunch at her nose. Their mother could not bear the sight
of blood and her distress, on seeing them straggle up the
driveway, never lessened even when these midday home-
comings had become a habit. Each time, she implored them
to telephone her so that she could send Miguel, the foreman,
in the car. But they never did, for they liked the walk home,
feeling all the way a pleasant superiority to their sisters,
Leah and Rachel, who were still cooped up in school with
nothing at all to do but chew paraffin on the sly.

In the September following their illness and on the day
Grandpa Kenyon, their mother's stepfather, was to arrive for
his annual visit, they met with gushing noses outside the

art supply room and seeing Miss Holihan through the open door at the paper cutter with a sheaf of manila paper, they walked on tiptoe, giggling silently until they reached the stairs and then they ran. Once outside in the empty school-yard, they congratulated each other; Molly would not have to draw an apple on Miss Holihan's paper and Ralph would miss both Palmer Method and singing. Actually, they would gain nothing by getting home some hours before the school bus since Grandpa's train did not get into Los Angeles until the middle of the afternoon and then it was another hour before Miguel brought him up the driveway in the Willys Knight. So they dawdled more slowly than usual, not certain that they would find anything to absorb them at home, but certain, on the other hand, that their mother, fussing and chattering as she always did when they had company, would be as cross as sixty when she saw them.

It was a narrow, winding country road they walked along. On either side ran clear small ditches, making a mouth-like sound. Now and again they stopped and dipped their hand-kerchiefs and wiped the blood off their hands and arms. On their right was an orange grove from which, at all seasons of the year, came a heavy fragrance and where they sometimes saw flocks of such bright, unusual birds that they thought they must have flown up from the South Seas or westward from Japan. Some of the little pyramidal trees were always in bloom and some were always bearing fruit. There was a man on a ladder in the grove today and he turned when he heard them coming. He took off his hat and wiped his forehead on the sleeve of his black shirt and called, "Hello, you kiddoes," but as he was a Mexican, they

4

did not reply and scuttered on, terrified, until they no longer heard his derisive laugh.

Next they passed Mr. Vogelman's huge clean dairy. Mr. Vogelman was a fat German who wore a white coverall and who had once been stoned by a group of second-graders when they learned what the Huns had done to the Belgians. Their mothers, fearing that he might take his revenge by treating the milk with tuberculosis germs, had written him an apology. But as the demonstration had taken place on Hallowe'en, Mr. Vogelman had misconstrued it and did not understand the letter at all. He had Guernseys whose hides gleamed in the sun like a metal, not so yellow as a banana and not so blue as milk, but something in between. Today there was a new calf near the fence, its fawn-like face wearing a look of melancholy surprise when it saw the human children staring. Its outraged mother bellowed at them, her great black nostrils hugely dilated, and they ran away for, although they would never have admitted it, they were afraid of cows. They knew a joke about a cow which they had read in *The American Boy,* and when they were safely beyond the pasture, they recited it as a dialogue:

Ralph: What are shoes made of?
Molly: Hide.
Ralph: Hide? Why should I hide?
Molly: Hide! Hide! The cow's outside!
Ralph: Oh, let the old cow come in. I'm not afraid.

They laughed so hard that they had to sit down in the road holding their stomachs and the laughter made their noses bleed twice as fast so that, convulsed and aching, they dabbed desperately with their handkerchiefs, screaming with pain, "Oh! Oh!" Finally, when they were sobered, Ralph said, "I

5

guess I'll tell that joke to Grandpa," and Molly said, "Me too." Of late, Ralph had had moments of irritation with her: often, when he had finished telling a joke or a fact, she would repeat exactly what he had said immediately afterward so that there was no time for people either to laugh or to marvel. And not only that, but she had countless times told his dreams, pretending that they were her own. He did not want the joke about the cow to fall flat and so, after a reluctant pause, he agreed to let her tell it with him as they had recited it just now. It was not as long as one of the darky pieces Leah and Rachel spoke together, but it was so much funnier that they were sure Grandpa could not fail to laugh in that big, roaring way of his, slapping his knee and saying, "By George, that's a good one."

They proceeded, thinking of Grandpa, joyfully scuffing the white dust of the road until their oxfords were all powdery, even the shoelaces. Next to the dairy was a deep, dry arroyo called "the Wash." It had been hollowed out by a flood that had come in the spring of the year Leah was three, but they had so often heard the details of its devastation that they were certain their impressions came from memory and not from their mother's and her friends' talk when there was nothing new to discuss and they had to return to the thrills of the past. Mr. Fawcett had gone across a raging creek on a horse named Babe, long since dead, to rescue an aged woman whose house was later washed away. He brought her home flung over his saddle like a gunny sack of feed and gave her artificial respiration on the kitchen floor. Thousands and thousands of finches came out of the pouring rain to perch on the front porch; there were so many Father said it looked like a regular bird sanctuary;

6

Fuschia was baking a cherry pie and Father asked her if she wanted four and twenty finches to put in it. A grapefruit tree came floating right down the driveway, roots and all, and Father planted it beside the solar tank. Every year it bore one grapefruit, which was smaller than a golf ball and almost as hard.

On the floor of the Wash, Ralph and Molly could find bright-colored stones, pink and green and yellow and blue. After a heavy rain, there was sometimes fool's gold in the puddles. Strange harsh shallow-rooted flowers grew all over the steep slopes and clumps of mallow that yielded bitter milk. There was one place where the mud dried and cracked into wedges like pieces of pie and when Molly was very small, she thought that this was where the sandwiches lived. All mystery and evil came from the Wash. Those smooth colored stones they gathered were really stolen jewels and the thief was a coal-black Skalawag who slept in the daytime in Mr. Vogelman's cornbin but kept watch at night. They did not venture down into the Wash when they had nosebleeds because the Skalawag could smell blood, no matter how far away he was, and he would get up and come legging it after them. So they passed it quickly with sidelong glances. Last autumn, when they had taken Grandpa Kenyon to see the Wash, he had said, "Well, now, that's something like it. There's too damn much green in this here California. But that dried-up little old crick bed down there makes me think of a place that *is* a place." He swept his black eyes round the scene and breathed shallowly as if the sweetness of the orange blossoms offended him and he said, "To think there ain't any winter here! Why, I'd as lief go to hell in a handbasket as not to see the first snow fly."

The children were a little angry and shy and sensing this he explained to them—though they did not understand what he meant—that Nature here offered a man no real challenge. "You take that place of mine in the Panhandle. Nature ain't any ornrier anywhere in the world than she is right there, but she's a blooming belle of a fighter." When he had bought the land, there had not been a drop of water on the whole forty-five thousand acres of it, not a stream, not a pond. Everyone said he was a boob to buy it. But he turned in and bought it anyhow and then he took a little forked switch of holly and he chose a place on a rise just to the west of where he meant to build his house. He stood there with his holly wand, holding a fork of it in either hand. By and by, the rod bent down: where she showed him, there was a deep clear spring that had never yet gone dry.

The Wash, after that, had a new meaning for Ralph and Molly and they came to believe that the Skalawag was so watchful because he feared someone might come with a divining rod and once water was found, all his gems would be washed away. And now, too, whenever they went past, they thought of Grandpa's ranch in the Panhandle and Ralph, sighing, would say, "Golly *Moses,* I'd like to go out West." For they believed Grandpa Kenyon when he told them that California was not the West but was a separate thing like Florida and Washington, D. C.

For example, out West you would not find such falderal as Miss Runyon went in for. Miss Runyon lived next to the Wash in a little white house with green shutters and begonia in all the windows and Molly had loved it before Grandpa called it "a devil of a note." The flower garden came straight down to the road and standing among the

8

beds of phlox and bachelor's buttons and oxalis were all sorts of curious creatures: a huge green frog, three brownies, a duck and four ducklings, two bluebirds as big as cats, a little Dutch girl in a sunbonnet, and a totem pole. There was a sign over the front door of the house which said "Dew Drop Inn." Next to the house was a doghouse built exactly like Dew Drop Inn and over its door was a sign that said "Dun Rovin" because Miss Runyon's sheep dog was named Rover. Under the eaves on the front porch was a bird house built like the other two but its name was not so ingenious: it was simply called "Jennie Wren, Her House."

Miss Runyon was the postmistress and was known as a character. She drove an automobile herself which she called "Mac"—short for "Machine" which she humorously pronounced "MacHeinie." She ate neither meat nor spices, for she was a follower of Dr. Kellogg. She occasionally invited the Fawcetts to a picnic supper on her lawn and served them hamburgers which were really made of Grape Nuts agglutinated with imitation calves'-foot jelly. She always came on Sunday afternoon to read their paper and made no secret of the fact that she liked the funnies as well as any child, reading them with the same unamused absorption that Ralph and Molly and Leah and Rachel did. Once she said that she was tired to death of Elmer Tuggle and his everlasting baseball mitt; Happy Hooligan was her favorite. In spite of her aggressive good nature, she was very timid and could not sleep alone in a house, so she had living with her a little Japanese woman named Mrs. Haisan. If ever Mrs. Haisan had to be away, Leah and Rachel went there to sleep, although they never wanted to, for the first time they stayed with her, she suddenly looked up from *McCall's* in the middle of the evening and said tensely, "Hark! I heard a human swallow!" Ralph and Molly thought it was likely that it had been the Skalawag swallowing and the possibilities of *what* he had been swallowing were so numerous and terrifying that they could not hear the word without trembling.

It was thought, jestingly, by Mrs. Follansbee, the pastor's wife, that Miss Runyon had set her cap for Mr. Kenyon, part of this supposition being based on the rhyming of the two names; and it was true that several times during his visits she had invited them all to come and take "pot luck" with her but they never went, for as Mrs. Fawcett said in the bosom of her family, "I am sure I don't know what a hearty eater like Mr. Kenyon would do if he had to have an evening meal of cereal, I don't care how she disguised it."

Ralph thought perhaps he could tell Grandpa a funny story about Miss Runyon, not a true one but one in which he just used her name, and he stood leaning upon the picket fence, pondering and allowing his nose to drip on the palings so that two of them looked like spears that had struck home. Or maybe he could tell one about Mrs. Haisan. Mrs. Haisan had two children about his and Molly's age who lived with their aunt, a tiny little thing who was Mrs. Fawcett's washerwoman. Their names were Maisol and Maisako and one of them had been born on the Fourth of July and the other on April Fool's Day. One terrible day they had come with Hana and had made Ralph and Molly go down to the watermelon patch with them and not only had they cut up an unripe watermelon with a putty knife but they had said things and hinted at others so awful that Ralph and

Molly had to fight them. They won very easily, of course, because the Jap kids were much smaller.

Ralph could not think of a single joke except the one about the cow. He thumbed his nose at Miss Runyon's house and chanted, "Runyon todunyon tianigo sunyon, tee-legged, tie-legged, bowlegged Runyon!" And then, seizing his sister by the hand, he ran like the wind because simultaneously Mrs. Haisan had appeared at the door of Dew Drop Inn and Rover at his door, and while Rover was as harmless as a ladybug and Mrs. Haisan more than likely had only wanted to give them a candied kumquat, it was pleasanter to think that they were rushing out in anger like the Skalawag, and as soon as the house was no longer in sight, Ralph knelt down and put his ear to the road and jumping up cried, "Hey! They're a-gainin' on us!" and they did not stop running until they had turned down their own road.

When they had gone a hundred steps, they could see the palm trees that marked the boundary of their land. On this last stretch, Molly always thought for some reason of Redondo Beach where they went for a few weeks at the end of the summer. Looking up into the blank blue sky, she could feel that she was barefoot in the hot sand, hunting starfish and sand dollars, hearing the cries of the frightened ladies to their wading children who petulantly cried back that the waves were not high. The thought of the beach made her restlessly nostalgic and sometimes made her whimper, because she always remembered a feeling of queer and somehow pleasant horror when once a gull had winked at her and she had seen that his lower eyelid moved and not the upper one. But today she did not cry: Ralph was too gay, she knew, to comfort her and that was the only pleasure in crying, to be embraced by him and breathe in his acrid smell of leather braces and serge and to feel, shuddering, the touch of his warty hands on her face. It was always possible for her to will herself not to think sadly of the beach but to think instead of her dead father, of whom she had no memories but only the knowledge that he was up in the sky with Jesus and would miraculously recognize her when she came to heaven even though she had not been born when he died. This was the most thrilling thought she ever had and it had made her almost delirious ever since the day she and Ralph agreed not to die until he was ninety-nine and she was ninety-seven so that when they got up there they would look much older than their father who had died at the age of thirty-six.

As soon as they turned in the drive, Ralph began the game of Dead Horse. He said, "I saw a dead horse lying in the road." Molly answered, "I one it," and they went on: "I two it." "I three it." Just as they got to the side of the front porch, Ralph cried out, "I eight it," and Molly screamed hysterically, "Mother! Ralph ate a dead horse *again!*" But their mother was not sitting on the front porch as she usually was, and they looked at each other in numb embarrassment.

They should have known that she would be in the kitchen, preparing for Grandpa. Now they could hear her bustling across the front hall in her French-heeled slippers, anticipating what she would see and crying, "Oh, I declare I just don't know!" And then she stood in the screen door, arms akimbo at her small waist in her pearl-gray skirt, unable to decide whether to be angry or worried, too upset for a moment to utter a word. The children waited on the bottom step like well-mannered dogs and their mother, seeing their humility, chose to be anxious and flew down the steps, embracing them but carefully so that she would not stain her white smocked shirtwaist. She smelled of orris root and gingerbread and the children, sniffing, sensed the arrival of company even more than they had when they saw Miguel drive out this morning to meet the train. He had gone early to shop for delicacies in the Los Angeles markets; among other things, they were going to have black cherries and Turkish Delight.

"Oh, the poor chicks!" she cried, her blue eyes quickly full of tears. "Oh, dearies, *why* didn't you telephone? *Why* must you aggravate your mother?"

Molly said, "If we had telephoned it would have been silly because Miguel isn't here and neither is the car and even if the car was here it would still be silly because nobody but Miguel can drive it."

Molly's logic always made Mrs. Fawcett angry and now she drove them into the house and upstairs to the bathroom, ejaculating unfinished sentences: "I simply never . . . !" "No matter how hard I try . . . !" "Today of all days in the year . . . !"

The nosebleeds almost always stopped as soon as they got home, a phenomenon that obscurely vexed Mrs. Fawcett, and she had spoken of it in their presence to Mr. Follansbee, who had replied, with a catarrhal chuckle, "Well, you know, Rose, that puts me in mind of my sainted mother who was stone deaf *except* when she wanted to hear something." Neither Ralph nor Molly had any idea what he meant but they caught an undertone of ridicule in his voice, and fearing and hating him, they went up to Ralph's room where each of them printed "Rev. Follansbee" seven times on sheets of drawing paper and then burned the papers in the gilt Buddha incense burner.

Washed and dressed in their company clothes, they went outdoors and sat under the umbrella tree playing mumbly-peg, hurriedly concealing the knife when their mother came to the door to call some warning about their clean clothes or getting too much sunlight. Mumbly-peg was forbidden as everything was that was attended by the least possibility of danger, for Grandfather Bonney, their real grandfather, had died of blood poisoning. José, the gardener, was trimming the palm trees, and as he deftly wielded his banana knife he sang songs which they knew were bad although they could not understand a word of them since he sang in Spanish. They knew, because he was a bad man. Once Rachel had dreamed that he pursued her on a bicycle without holding his hands on the handlebars, that same banana knife between his teeth, one hand brandishing a monkey wrench and the other the Civil War saber that had belonged to Great-uncle Harry Fawcett, about whom not another fact was known. And once José had called Ralph a son-of-a-gun and threatened to burn his eyes out with a red-hot poker if he took any more berries off the bittersweet for his pea shooter.

Budge, the kindly cat, lay sleeping on the rim of the frog pond, and the only kitten that had been spared her out of her last litter gazed fixedly down into the slimy green water. Mrs. Fawcett, who did not like animals even in their own place, believed that Budge had brought the scarlet fever germs to Ralph and Molly, for goodness only knew what sort of houses she visited in her search for food and tomcats, and she would have had her destroyed if Ralph had not heard her talking with Miguel under his windows one morning when he was thought to be asleep. Weak with fever, he tottered to the window and called down the stern promise that if Budge were not still on the place when he got well, he would leave at once for the Panhandle and would never come back in a thousand million years. There were times when Mrs. Fawcett feared for the reason of her two younger children: they had natures of such cold determination that she trembled to think what they might do if they were crossed in a matter very close to their hearts. She could never imagine where they had got this streak, certainly not from her side of the family, and although Mr. Fawcett had by no means been a mollycoddle, he had been very mild-mannered and had always been able to see the other fellow's side of an argument. Budge remained. And then the astonishing Molly had literally read her mother's mind one evening. Mrs. Fawcett was looking at Budge asleep on the hearth and Molly said, "If anything ever happens to Budge, like poison or something, I'm going to set the pumphouse on fire."

From the cool-looking house—the dark green blinds were drawn to keep out the sun, though the turquoise berry was so dense it admitted little light—came the dulled sounds of Mrs. Fawcett and Fuschia as they made the dinner. They had been cooking for two days. They had made pineapple upside-down cake, boiled dressing, potato salad, beet pickles, baked beans, brown bread, sugar cookies, lady fingers, Sally Lunn, and temperance punch. Fuschia had brought in the new Schmierkäse that had been swinging for three days in its muslin bag in the icehouse and she had got six bottles of grape juice from the preserve closet to put in the refrigerator.

Ralph and Molly, the afternoon before, had cracked a bowl full of last year's walnuts from their own grove and today Fuschia had glazed the whole meats and put the broken ones into penuche. The duck was in the oven, baking in a bath of orange juice. Before school, Leah and Rachel had polished the Bonney silver and had laid out the morning-glory tablecloth.

The afternoon seemed to have no end to it and yet the children were not really impatient to have it pass, for looking forward to Grandpa was in some ways as pleasant as having him there in the house. The sun appeared to remain in exactly the same position and the shadow of the umbrella tree to be unalterable. The bees, restless in the blossoms of the lippia lawn, and the humming birds, lancing the turquoise berries, worked at top speed as though eternity were not time enough to accomplish all they had to do. Mrs. Fawcett and Fuschia were forever softly banging things and chirping in muted screams, and José was forever at his palm trees. It was very quiet. The Mexicans harvesting the walnuts in the grove were silent. Once a dog began to bark and stopped so suddenly it was as if someone had seized his jaws and held them together. "That's Schöneshund," said Ralph. Schöneshund was a mean and hideous mastiff owned by the German family next door and Mrs. Fawcett was never willing to allow that the name had been chosen ironically; she preferred to think that the Freudenburgs simply did not know any better, for they were not "our sort." "If I could not have a carpet in my parlor," she said, "I would have some sort of inexpensive grass rug, or I would leave the floors bare. I certainly would not have linoleum." Ralph, identifying Schöneshund's bark today, wondered suddenly if Grandpa had any dogs on any of his ranches and he regretted that in the years past he had asked the old man so few questions that he knew very little about him. The two weeks he was here were always so short. Too many new impressions were crowded into the dazzling days, the smells of school that he had forgotten during the summer, the frightening complexities of the new arithmetic book, the surprise of finding in his lunchbox a hard-boiled egg colored magenta with beet-pickle juice, and over it all, the wonder of the rich old man who was different from anyone else in the world. Always before he had been too unbearably excited to plan a way to catch one of these bright hours, but he promised himself that this year he would gather facts to think about in the winter: the kinds and the names of Grandpa's dogs for one thing, whether he had ever been to a prize fight, if he had always had a beard, the name of the town in England where he had been born, and how many silver dollars he could carry in his money belt at one time.

The sun, in time, brutalized even José, and he stopped singing and worked more slowly. The children's game was languid and they had given it up long before the school bus came and Leah and Rachel trudged down the driveway, swinging their schoolbags in one hand and their lunchboxes in the other. They were cross at Ralph and Molly for coming home early and did not speak but went directly into the house and appeared half an hour later, bathed and dressed in the new Scotch plaid tissue gingham dresses that Aunt Kathleen had sent them from Marshall Field's. They came out to pick dahlias for the parlor and for the table. They walked past without looking at their sister and brother.

Rachel said, "I *was* going to give Molly my extra Cashmere Bouquet just out of the kindness of my heart, but I'm not going to now." And Leah said, "I know. I was going to give Ralph my Colgate's shaving soap, but now I wouldn't give either of them anything but a swift kick." Ralph and Molly ignored them, but when they had gone on, Ralph, looking after them with scorn, said, "If I didn't have anything better to do than send for free samples, I'd go jump in the lake." And Molly, agreeing (she and Ralph sent for gun catalogues and booklets on things like "How to Care for Your Glenwood Parlor Burner"), said in a whisper, "Do you think they're going to be sassy to Grandpa?"

"I guess they'd better not," said Ralph. "If they do you and I will make them a pie-bed that'll be so tight they'll both break both their legs."

Leah and Rachel, almost young ladies, had, along with many other people and many habits, outgrown the soiled and rumpled old gentleman and looked with the same disfavor their mother did upon his table manners, his rough and ungrammatical speech, his clothes, and his profession, even though it had netted him three million dollars. He had four cattle ranches: one in Missouri, where he lived, one in Oklahoma, one in Texas, and one in the mountains of Colorado which his son, Claude, Mrs. Fawcett's half-brother, ran for him. How Leah and Rachel could imagine their mother's distress when her mother married this second husband! What a contrast he was to Grandfather Bonney, that noble person in the portrait over the fireplace in the parlor! And how different the life must have been for her and her sisters on his ranch in the northern part of the state when they had been used to the hustle and gaiety of St. Louis!

Last September, when Grandpa left, Leah, watching the car go down the drive, put her arm around her mother's waist and said, "I could simply *cry* for you, Mother, when I think how you must have missed St. Louis." Mrs. Fawcett, who was wonderfully plucky, smiled fondly down upon her perceptive child and answered, "Well, dear, you know we can't have everything in this life." From that time onward, the two older children heaped upon the absent Mr. Kenyon an articulate and savage ridicule, commingled with resentment which was at once aimless and precocious: shortly after he had left the Colorado ranch last October, he had gone to Europe, as he frequently did in the winter, and while heretofore these casual trips all over the world had been something to admire and to refer to in conversations with other children who had no such traveled relatives, the girls this year were angry, realizing fully for the first time that their mother had never been abroad. And their anger was inflamed when Mrs. Fawcett from time to time remarked that often in the years she had lived in his house, taking charge of his child, he had taken these long journeys, not giving a thought to her. And you can imagine what those lonesome winters in the country were like for a girl who had been brought up in the city!

But Ralph and Molly, in a smaller world, would rather go to reform school than live in St. Louis. The one time they had been there they had been in tears half the time at all the poor old men selling shoelaces and lengths of elastic and at all the homeless dogs with sore eyes and limping legs; the smell of smoke and the horrid noises and the terrifying pace of the trolleys had almost made them sick. Their mother, introducing them to Mrs. Waite, their hostess, had said, "And these are my two little country bumpkins. They already want to go home. Can you feature it?" They had not really wanted to go home; they had wanted to go visit Grandpa Kenyon, but their mother wouldn't let them, falsely declaring that they would be bored to death for there would be nothing there to do. There was certainly nothing to do in St. Louis and all summer long Mrs. Fawcett and Mrs. Waite had had whispered conversations about Fatty Arbuckle so that Ralph and Molly were in a temper the whole time because, when they asked, the ladies only said, "Little pitchers have big ears."

At Grandpa's place they could have done what they pleased. Their mother didn't know anything. She said that she knew from experience that there was nothing to do. Had she not spent her boarding school holidays there with Aunt Rowena and Aunt Kathleen? All those long, still summers when there was nothing to distract their thoughts from the heat! The immense lawn, going down to the river, was bare of trees so that one had an unobstructed view of the Mississippi: one of the Bonney girls' few amusements was to watch the barges and the steamers going down toward Hannibal. Sometimes the sound of a banjo was carried to them on the motionless air, making Rowena, the least controlled of the three, so restless that she would cry, "Oh, why doesn't something *happen!*" Behind the house was an apple orchard, kept as formally as a garden, and in the center of it was a clearing with a little summer-house where they sometimes sat through the airless afternoons, fanning themselves with palm leaves, homesick for St. Louis. It was ten miles to the nearest town, and once you got there there was nothing to look at or to buy and no one at all congenial to call on. Aunt Rowena and Aunt Kathleen amused themselves by riding horseback and driving the buckboard, but their sister Rose would not join them. She would not because Grandfather Bonney's blood poisoning had been the result of a scratch from a nail in the railing of a paddock when he was watching her take her first jump, and ever afterward, feeling that she had been the cause of his far too early death, she vowed she would have nothing to do with horses.

If the Bonney girls had not all been great readers, they would have been half out of their minds with boredom. Fortunately, Mrs. Bonney had brought a good part of the library along from St. Louis and they almost put their eyes out reading Mrs. Gaskell, Dickens, and E. P. Roe. In some ways, the very worst thing of all was the conversation at mealtime. If the girls had been given half a chance, they might have elevated the tone of it by discussing the books they were reading, but there was never any opportunity. They *could* not take an interest in the talk of cattle and hogs after the cultured life they had led with their own father! And that was all Mr. Kenyon talked about; their mother talked right along with him, seeming to be really keen on hearing how many steers were being shipped to Chicago and how many bulls were being sold off the Texas ranch and how much feed would have to be bought for the Colorado place over and above the timothy that would be put up in the harvest. Table talk in St. Louis had been quite a different matter. Grandfather Bonney, who had owned a button factory, never brought his business home; he would say that he wanted to "forget the cares that infest the day" and besides that he had great respect for conversation as an art and once a year, on New Year's Day, he read selections from Boswell's *Journal of a Tour to the Hebrides*. He directed the talk at his table as adroitly and interestingly as a professional forum leader. He would start the ball rolling by saying something like this: "Today I was just wondering how much you girls know about Apollo. Do you realize how often he figures in poems, pictures, and statues?" And that would lead to a very enlightening discussion from which the girls derived far more facts than they ever would have done in a cut-and-dried schoolroom class. They talked of everything under the sun, often examining such concepts as "justice," "charity," and "truth." Some of Mrs. Fawcett's most cherished values had been developed at that table.

In the late spring of Rose Bonney's last year in boarding school, two years after her father's death and a year after her mother's unseemly second marriage, her mother bore Mr. Kenyon a son. She was then past forty—she had been much younger than her first husband—and to her daughters there seemed something shameful in this middle-aged childbed. Shameful and obscurely disloyal to their dead father. Five months later, she died a lingering death. Mr. Kenyon, so unimaginative in his innocence, thought that he was honoring Rose in asking her, her mother's eldest survivor, to keep house for him and rear the baby, Claude. It was not, of course, that he was the least bit stingy and did not want to hire a nurse and a housekeeper, for of course he did that anyway. Poor soul, he really thought Rose would like to do it. Can you imagine anyone understanding girls so little? But how could she refuse? Well, she just couldn't. Thus for ten years she buried herself alive, ten years of stupefaction enlivened only by the weddings of her two sisters on which

Mr. Kenyon had spent nearly a fortune. (Grandfather Bonney would have done it for half as much and with twice as much dash.) In all that time, she felt so little intimacy with him that she never called him anything but "Mr. Kenyon" and she never called the child by any name at all, just "you" and "he."

And then at last, when she was twenty-nine and nearly hopeless, she had been released from her prison by Mr. Bruce Fawcett, who had taken her to California to a house very much like the one she had known in St. Louis and all the niceties were restored to her that her father had taught her constituted reality. Mr. Fawcett, the children gathered, had been similar to Grandfather Bonney, although he had been a fainter and imperfect copy, lacking the vitality of the original. (For example, his jokes were never quoted and the children doubted if he had ever made any.) She had brought all the treasures that had been in the storage house these many years and those she had kept in Mr. Kenyon's house: the portrait of her father, his books, and the man himself, a heap of dust in a graceful urn whose handles were shaped like flat-headed snakes and whose top ended in a little knob shaped like a water lily.

Both Mr. Kenyon and his stepdaughter dreaded his annual visit, but they looked upon it as a duty which they would not have dreamed of shirking. He set forth from home on the first day of August, visiting first his Oklahoma place, then his Longhorn ranch in the Panhandle, and after a short trip to Mexico to buy presents for the children, he came on to Covina. Once the courteous preliminaries were over, Grandpa seemed to enjoy his stay, for he was fond of the children, especially of Ralph and Molly whose coloring was that of their grandmother and their half-uncle and, curiously enough, of himself. But Mrs. Fawcett enjoyed none of it, and for the whole two weeks was so flustered that when he left she always went to bed for three or four days with a prolonged sick headache.

To the children, this visit was a season as special and separate as Christmas or Easter, and days before he came they conjectured what surprises he would bring them this time in his big shabby grip, crammed with stiff socks and dirty shirts and scraps of useless paper with the writing worn off. All other visitors wrapped up their presents in tissue paper and tied them with ribbon, but Grandpa just handed them out the way he had got them, sometimes loosely wrapped in a crumpled piece of cheese paper. These gifts were not the sort of souvenirs the children saw in the boardwalk shops at Redondo Beach nor were they like the presents their aunts brought: toys for Ralph and Molly, hair ribbons and round combs for Leah and Rachel. Grandpa brought them heavy, hand-made objects, rings and knives and boxes, and Ralph, ever since he could remember, had loved to hold something small but solid in the palm of his hand. Once Grandpa had given him a miniature contour-globe made of Mexican silver. It was his favorite belonging.

Mrs. Fawcett, while she did not conceal her regret that he was coming, made as extensive preparations for him as if he were someone like Aunt Rowena or Aunt Kathleen whom she really welcomed, and for a week beforehand she threw the house into a turmoil of cleaning and arranging and putting away and getting out, not failing to remind the household from time to time that it was singularly obtuse in Mr. Kenyon to come at the very busiest time of year

24

when there was canning to do and when the nuts were being gathered. But there was no help for it: one of the precepts she had learned at her father's table was: "Never be near with your hospitality." Conventions, as a result, had grown up around these visits, so that just as they associated turkey with Thanksgiving and ham with Easter, the Fawcetts thought of duck and wild rice, of Sally Lunn and fig preserves as the only possible fare on the night of Mr. Kenyon's arrival. And on the last Sunday of the visit, Mr. and Mrs. Follansbee came to a buffet supper served on the front porch at which they had chicken pie and hot biscuits with salmon-berry jam. This supper was invariably a fiasco, but Mrs. Fawcett, an incorrigible ritualist, repeated it year after year. Mr. Follansbee was a voluble man, given to telling anecdotes which usually involved a passage from Scripture or from Shakespeare, and he embarrassed Mr. Kenyon, reducing him to a glassy-eyed stupor which Mrs. Fawcett earnestly strove to end by asking him questions about people in Missouri of whom she had no desire to hear nor he to speak. More often than not, he had a seizure of yawning, almost like a spell of some kind, and he yawned exactly like a dog, making a noise at the end that sounded like a thwarted howl.

Except for this one evening, Mr. Kenyon's visit was not interrupted by any social occasions, and he was only that one time required to dress in what he called his "store clothes." Mr. Follansbee, who had known her father, was the only man Mrs. Fawcett met, so to say, in the drawing room, and it would have been quite unthinkable for all concerned to invite any of the ladies of her various circles to be introduced to her stepfather. There existed between the two a cool formality as if they actually had been estranged in some way and did not simply dislike one another; Ralph knew instinctively that it had always been like that and this was one of the reasons his mother perplexed him. She was quite smiling and flirtatious with Mr. Follansbee, almost as silly as Leah and Rachel, but with Mr. Kenyon in whose very own house she had lived for years and years she acted like an impatient schoolteacher. And Mr. Kenyon, for his part, seemed shy and gawky. But there was no such aloofness between him and the younger children. He was amiably talkative with them and treated them as if they were men of about his age. They spent the hours with him after school, rambling till suppertime through the orderly avenues between the lines of English walnut trees. He had been everywhere in the world and had hunted every animal indigenous to the North American continent: deer, antelope, moose, caribou, big-horn, and every game bird you could name. He had caught wild horses in Nevada and had tamed them "into the gentlest little benches a man ever saw." He had killed rattlers as long as a man is tall; he had eaten alligator and said it tasted like chicken. Two things he never had been partial to were possum and beaver tails, though some people counted them great delicacies. The old colored cook at Claude's place would as lief eat beaver tails three times a day.

It was natural, Ralph supposed, for girls not to be so interested in hunting as he was, but that did not give Leah and Rachel any right to say, as they had been doing all this year, that Grandpa made his stories up. They were obviously all true and Molly, who was very smart, believed them. He thought he had never really liked his older sisters, that he had always suspected they were not what Mrs. Fawcett called "true blue," and that this turning against Grandpa proved that he had been right.

Now, in the garden behind him and Molly, they were talking in low voices. They had many secrets and were in love with two brothers named George and Kenneth Taliafero whom Ralph and Molly detested because they put bay rum on their hair and they called Ralph "hot water Fawcett" and Molly "cold water Fawcett." Now and again the girls' golden hair appeared over the tops of the tall flowers, as bright as the petals. They wore plaid hair ribbons to match their dresses. Leah's was blue and Rachel's was red. Their hair was as soft as down, and when it was washed and Mrs. Fawcett was brushing it, it crackled with electricity. She was ever so proud of it and said crossly, "*Oh,* this pesky stuff!" They were very pretty girls. Their mother carefully protected their fair skin from sunburn and freckles and it was uniformly the color of milk. There was a blue vein in Leah's high forehead which made her look delicate. Their faces were oval and narrow and somehow old-fashioned like the tintypes and sepia photographs of their mother and aunts when they were young ladies. Their bones were small and in time they would be prettily padded as Mrs. Fawcett's were. In addition to their winning faces, they had what the members of the Sorosis called "the poise of ladies of thirty," so completely at ease were they when they passed the cakes at tea or played duets, never having to be coaxed. Mr. and Mrs. Follansbee, who were childless, were devoted to them in a way Mrs. Fawcett found quite touching and sad. After church, when he shook hands with her, the minister often said, "Rose, if you ever get tired of these two little ladies of quality, you know where you can bring them." Leah and Rachel kept this love alive by calling on them frequently and drinking cambric tea and by making presents for them at Christmas and Easter, sending them Valentines and making them May baskets. In return, the Follansbees gave them tokens of piety, small New Testaments, packets of Bible scenes, and books of a moral flavor. Ralph and Molly, for their part, wouldn't have been seen at a dog fight with either of the Follansbees.

It was hard to believe that the two girls had had the same father and mother as Ralph and Molly, who were shy and sometimes impudent out of embarrassment. Since their illness, moreover, they had been thin, pallid, and runny-nosed. From some obscure ancestor they had inherited bad, uneven teeth and nearsighted eyes so that they had to wear braces and spectacles. Their skin and hair and eyes were dark and the truth of it was they always looked a little dirty. They were small for their age but they had large bones, and it was predicted with pity that they would shoot up suddenly in that dreadful ungainly way so many children do, going then through several years of coltishness, painful to behold. They were so self-conscious that they could not sit on a chair without looking as if they perched on a precarious cliff, and if they were suddenly addressed by a strange elder, they swallowed in the middle of their words and tears came to their eyes, steaming their glasses. They were always getting cut and bruised and bumped, and this seemed so inconsiderate (of course it wasn't at all, the poor youngsters couldn't help it, but it *was* peculiar) when Mrs. Fawcett felt the way she did about injuries which could so easily turn into lockjaw. Last year Molly had run a sewing-machine needle straight through her index finger and Mrs. Fawcett had fainted clean away. This had seemed to all Mrs. Fawcett's friends not only a deliberate accident but one brought on by the most reprehensible circumstances, for Molly was making a quilt on the machine, not to be outdone by Leah and Rachel who were sewing their pieces together by hand in the regular way.

At home Ralph and Molly were hot-tempered and rebellious, but elsewhere were so easily intimidated that the enemies among their contemporaries called them cowards. And while Leah and Rachel had dozens of fast friends and were invited to innumerable slumber parties and donkey parties every year, Ralph and Molly had none but one another and at Valentine's they had to stuff the boxes in each other's room at school or they would not have got any at all. In some ways the most disturbing thing about them was their precocity. Mrs. Follansbee, who was discomforted by intellect in anyone, said that their reading excesses were very likely the result (not the cause) of their having to put on eyeglasses at such an early age: first they *looked* studious and then they *were* studious. Their tastes, in point of fact, were not in advance of their years, and they really preferred Howard Pyle to Dickens though they did make rather a show of themselves by memorizing the scene in which David Copperfield gets drunk and entangles himself in Steerforth's curtains. Their reputation really derived from their ability to say off the alphabetical syllables on the backs of the *Encyclopaedia Britannica,* no volume of which they had ever opened except "Ref to Sai" where Ralph, with great disappointment, had read the article on Reproduction.

There was only one thing about Molly he did not like,

Ralph decided, and that was the way she copied him. It was natural for her to want to be a boy (who *wouldn't!*) but he knew for a fact she couldn't be. Last week, he had had to speak sharply to her about wearing one of his outgrown Boy Scout shirts: he was glad enough for her to have it, but she had not taken the "Be Prepared" thing off the pocket and he had to come out and say brutally, "Having that on a girl is like dragging the American flag in the dirt." He wished she would not tag along with him and Grandpa. How splendid it would be, he thought, if only the two of them went walking together! How fine if he could tell the cow joke by himself! He lay back on the lawn, crushing the little lippia blossoms, feeling her eyes follow every movement he made. And then, as he had known she would do, she lay back too.

The day seemed strange to him, the very air unusual. It did not possess quite the quality of a dream, but it lay beyond him as the days had done when he had scarlet fever and all the noises on the first floor had been thin and ephemeral. He remembered that late one night he had seen the sky glow suddenly with heat lightning and he called to Molly through the door that connected their rooms, "Heat lightning for the sky is the same thing as scarlet fever for us." Sick as she was, she clapped her hands and cried back, "Oh, Ralph, you always think of things!" He would have asked her now if she, too, felt funny, but he was afraid that if he shared it with her the feeling would leave him and so he lay in his selfish speechlessness pursuing the red globules that sped downward behind his closed eyes.

"Hey," said Molly and abruptly sat up again.

"Straw's cheaper," said Ralph automatically. He wished she wouldn't talk.

"No, listen. I've made another poem."

He opened his eyes in astonishment and looked at her. She was twisting her head around with excitement and he realized that she had not been thinking the same thoughts he had at all and that perhaps she had not even been looking at him when he lay back. Once Grandpa had said that Molly was "a deep one" and Ralph almost thought this was true. He had said it because she insisted that she had learned Braille in kindergarten, and though people would explain to her that what she was thinking of was the beads on a frame which you moved about to learn to count, she replied, "I said I learned Braille and I mean it."

"Will you listen to my poem?" she said pleadingly.

"How long is it?" Ralph did not care for poetry.

"It's real little." And then, without waiting for him to say "All right" she went on. "It's called 'Gravel,'" she said, "and this is it:

> Gravel, gravel on the ground
> Lying there so safe and sound,
> Why is it you look so dead?
> Is it because you have no head?"

"Say it again," said Ralph, puzzled now. And when she had repeated it, he said, "It doesn't make any sense. Gravel doesn't have a head."

"That's what I said. 'Is it because you have no *head?*'"

"Well, I don't know what you're talking about."

"You're merely jealous because you can't write poems yourself," said Molly, close to tears. She took her handker-

31

chief out of the pocket of her middy and snuffled into it and beginning to cry, she said, "Now you've gone and made me have another nosebleed."

He did not even open his eyes. He knew that she didn't have a nosebleed and he was so tired of her poems that he was just not going to make any effort to understand this one or to praise it. But neither did he want her to have a mad on him because that would spoil Grandpa's arrival and so he said, "Why don't you go write it down on a piece of paper and then maybe I can get the drift of it?" It was true that he never could hear things as well as he could see them and until just this year he had always thought that the song was "O Beautiful for Spacious Guys."

"I will! I will!" cried Molly and she ran to the house, chanting her poem.

Now, with her gone, he was completely at peace. The unusual feeling came over him again and he held on to it. It was almost as if he were clutching his broad mold-colored geography book to his chest. Later, Ralph felt he had had, on that long afternoon, some prescience of what would happen when Grandpa Kenyon finally came, but probably he had not and it was only desire that made him remember those hours as peculiar and significant, though they were without event.

CHAPTER TWO

A<small>T FIVE, THE CHILDREN WERE SITTING IN A STRAIGHT ROW ON</small> the railing of the porch like cats on a fence. There was a temporary truce between the two older and the two younger, but they were not friendly enough to talk. Although Leah and Rachel for a week had groaned to think of the arrival of "that old hobo," they were as greedy as ever for the presents which he would take out of the rank gray bundles in his grip. When finally they heard the car slow down at the opening of the driveway, all four of them began to giggle aimlessly and to pound their heels against the uprights of the railing. They did not move until he was actually on the porch, watching his descent from the car spellbound.

He was a big old man, stoop-shouldered and bowlegged. He looked like a massive, slow-footed bear as he heaved himself out of the car which seemed dwarfed just as Miguel, that long, lithe man, seemed small and somehow womanly. Grandpa stood for a moment with his legs wide apart, looking around the yard, glancing at the house and the garden as if to make sure that he had come to the right place, and then he took his grip from Miguel and came stomping up the path, peering at the children over his spectacles. As he passed a clump of turquoise berry, he tapped a sprig lightly with his shillelagh and Ralph, tense with excitement, wondered why and then wondered why he had wondered: why had he suddenly begun to notice all these pointless little things? Then, when Grandpa was actually on the porch and was setting down his bag, the boy observed nothing more and abandoned himself to the joy of shaking the strong, toughened hand—it was inconceivable that Mr. Kenyon had ever kissed anyone. Ralph was always the last to greet him and Grandpa always said, "Well, sir, I'm here again." It was true that if one of the girls had been the last to shake his hand, he still would have said "sir," but Ralph, in establishing this rite, felt personally, privately addressed, man to man.

He pushed his black hat back on his forehead and they could see the sweat running down to his whiskery eyebrows. He sat down in a wicker basket chair and took off his boots and then opened his grip and got out the soft-soled moccasins which had been made for him by a Cherokee named Daniel Standing-Deer. He would wear these all the rest of his visit, even on the night the Follansbees came. As he tugged at his boots, he said genially, "By the Lord Harry, it's as hot as Tophet."

Ralph was always surprised at Grandpa's clothes even though they did not vary from year to year. It was that no other man he had ever known dressed with such unconcern, with such a deliberate second-hand look. His store clothes were a suit of scratchy gray material, cut without relationship to his measurements. The trousers were too short and the cuffs were three inches wide, and beneath them stuck out his tremendous black boots with rawhide laces and his

34

cattle brand, a bar and a K, burned into the leg of the left one. The coat was long and the pockets were so misshapen from the things he carried that they looked like panniers on a donkey. He carried a watch which he called a "turnip," and a jackknife with four blades, a collapsible tin cup, two pipes, a fly-book, a compass, a good-luck scarab, a collection of bolts and nuts and screws and the coins of foreign countries, and a plump brown leather notebook in which he kept his accounts and in which Ralph had one time seen an old entry, headed "Dodge City," which read:

> Mo. steers sold $6,000
> Purchase 1 pr. shoes $1.75
> Purchase 1 rum for Borchard $.10
> Purchase 1 rum for self $.10

Grandpa's vests were his only fancy in the matter of clothes. He had a great many of them and while they were all cut alike, coming almost to his beard, they were a variety of colors and patterns. His finest was made of black velveteen with silver buttons, in the center of each of which was a small turquoise. This vanity had taken root in him many years before when Jesse James and his boys rode into his yard in Missouri one night and asked for quarters. "I can't go any farther," said Jesse. "If you haven't got a bed, you can hang me on a nail." Jesse James had worn a waistcoat of dark green velveteen with large mother-of-pearl buttons which matched the handles of his side arms. Today Grandpa wore a vest of gray doeskin faced with printed challis, as delicate and feminine as the most stylish dress goods.

He tugged and mumbled, preoccupied and at last got one boot off and then the other, then deeply sighed as though the job had been a hard one. He winked at Ralph and said, "Those are damned fine boots, son, but on a hot day like this they try a man's feet." Leah went into the house to call their mother and to take Grandpa's boots to his room and Rachel sat down on the top step, humming "A Capital Ship for an Ocean Trip," hoping that she would be asked to sing out loud for she had a gifted voice. But Grandpa ignored her and turning to Ralph and Molly, scrutinized them fixedly, seeing for the first time the change in them since last autumn. "By Jupiter, you two are poor," he said. "What in the world has laid aholt of you?"

Rachel explained as if the younger children were mutes. "Oh, they had scarlet fever last March. Leah and I didn't though because Mother sent us to Aunt Kathleen's. Don't you love Aunt Kathleen's house, Grandpa? The way it's right on Lake Michigan?"

Grandpa looked at her politely: "I never was to that house that I recall," he said and then turning to Ralph and Molly, "Well, I declare that's a hell of a note. I reckon I'll have to take you back to Claude's place with me and let that coon of his fatten you up. You ain't any use this way."

"We don't *hurt* anywhere," said Ralph anxiously and Mr. Kenyon laughed, showing the glossy coral gums of his false teeth.

Mrs. Fawcett came out, chattering like a bird. "It's so good to see you, Mr. Kenyon! My, you must be hot and tired after that pesky train! Won't you rest here on the porch where it's cool before you go up, and I'll bring you a glass of nice cold punch. Molly, dear, do you think you can run in and ask Fuschia to get the punch out of the icebox? And tell her to put in a nice big piece of ice? And tell her to be *sure* to wash it first? And then bring out some glasses and we'll all have a good cool drink."

Molly started to the door but Grandpa stopped her. "Just bring your grandpa a small tumbler. I have in my valise here a quart bottle of Bourbon drinking whisky which I had the good fortune to purchase in El Paso at a king's ransom. I think that'll do more for what ails me than your punch, Rose, no offense intended."

Ralph trembled all over with delight and dread. Once he had seen a bottle of dark red wine on a shelf in Miguel's house, but he had never seen whisky nor had he ever seen anyone drink. Mrs. Fawcett bit her lip and flushed. Grandfather Bonney had never used spirits but took a glass of claret or port now and again on special occasions and if he had lived to see the Volstead Act passed, he would have forgone even that.

"Just as you like, Mr. Kenyon," she said, her cheeks still bright and her eyes blinking with indignation. "I only thought you would like something *cool*. In that case perhaps we'd better go inside."

"Why?" demanded Ralph.

"Because I say so," she replied tightly.

Leah giggled. "Goody-goody Mother! She means Miss Runyon might go past and see Grandpa's bottle of you-know-what and tell the policeman on him. But if she did see it, Mother, we could say Grandpa sprained his ankle and was putting Sloan's liniment on it." She and Rachel laughed and lovingly ran their fingers through their fine hair.

"Dammit, Rose," said Grandpa, "I'm tired, and if it don't make a world of difference to you, I'll take the liberty of drinking my whisky right here."

Mrs. Fawcett took her defeat in silence, but it was clear that she thought this beginning indicated an even more trying visit than usual. She rolled down the bamboo screen on the south side of the house so that the Freudenburgs (who went right on making beer in spite of the new law) would not see Mr. Kenyon's bottle and wrongly think she had given her approval or, even worse, that she was sharing it with him. She said brightly, "Now tell me all your news, Mr. Kenyon. I'm on pins and needles to hear about everyone back home. I was just saying to Fuschia that good as her duck smelled what I was really hungry for was news."

Grandpa reported that a Dr. Taylor had been operated on for kidney stones and was not expected to live; indeed, since he had been away for five weeks and had had little word from Missouri, it was possible that the old gentleman was already dead. Mrs. Fawcett said, "You remember Dr. Taylor, don't you, girls? He and Mrs. Taylor gave us those nice little salt spoons you like so much. Isn't it too bad he's not well?" Leah and Rachel were moved and Rachel said, "Poor Mrs. Taylor. When you write her, Mother, will you give her my love and tell her I keep my best hankies in the darling case she sent me?"

Ralph, sitting on the arm of Grandpa Kenyon's chair, hesitated a moment and then plunged, "Ain't Dr. Taylor the one you told me was crooked as a dog's hind leg?"

"Ralph!" cried Leah. "You awful little Hun! And you said 'ain't' too!"

An unhappy, beating silence fell, ended finally by Molly's return, and the conversation set forth again, a plodding drudge. Grandpa, never interested in these chronicles of deaths and marriages and illnesses which he dutifully recited for his stepdaughter, seemed even more bored than usual, more inaccurate with names and more uncertain of his facts. He said that someone called Geneva Whatyoumay-callit had had erysipelas and it had disfigured her almost beyond recognition, but as he could neither remember her last name nor where she lived, the news was not thrilling but only tantalizing. He said that on second thoughts she might as easily have been named Mildred and he was not at all sure she didn't live in Oklahoma. One Maude Pease had asked him to tell Rose how much she had appreciated the metal casserole of candy she had sent as an anniversary present. (Leah said: "Mother, is that the one that had the alfresco wedding?" She brought this up whenever she could and it always made Ralph and Molly furious because they never could remember what "alfresco" meant.) The family on the place next to his had had a run of bad luck with their wheat—had rust—and had had to sell their auto-mobile. He said then, "I can't make out what you want to keep that bus of yours for, Rose. Why don't you get a new one? By George, a man of any size feels like a galoot in that tom-fool outfit of yours."

Mrs. Fawcett winced; she could not bear the word "bus" and did not any better like "flivver." She herself always spoke with dignity of "the machine." The Willys Knight had been extremely expensive and, although rumors had come to her that it was out of style, she had great affection for it. She replied exuberantly to Mr. Kenyon that she did not know what she would do without his advice, that it was one of the things she had wanted to talk over with him, and that she also hoped he would take a look at the shaft in the pumphouse in the morning for she felt that it needed to be replaced, even though Miguel said it was sound.

Ralph stared listlessly at a small tear in the knee of Grandpa's trousers and wanted to ask him what countries he had gone to last winter. But it was a convention that he never spoke of his travels in Mrs. Fawcett's presence. He had been to Siam, to Borneo, India, Spain, Sweden, and even to such out-of-the-way places as Lithuania and the Shetland Islands. A trip to Sydney or to southern Mexico was no more to him than a trip to Riverside to the Fawcetts. Once he had written a picture postal card to Ralph from Melbourne saying that he was bringing him a monkey, but Mrs. Fawcett had replied for her son, requiring him not to. The boy never forgave her and sulked whenever he recalled it. Mrs. Fawcett had remarked acidly that it was typical of Mr. Kenyon to select the one sort of pet that could not be housebroken. He had gone by steamer to Alaska and there had seen the northern lights and had gone out in a sealing vessel in the Bering Strait: before they even spotted the seals there had been a thundering great storm and the whole crew had nearly lost their lives; the waves were as high as the Fawcetts' pumphouse and the downside of them was as steep as Mt. Baldy. The noise of the gale had had the tongue of Hades in it.

Now and again Mr. Kenyon looked at Ralph and smiled and patted his knee with a thick, out-of-shape hand. He looked rather like an Indian with his strong cheekbones, his lank black hair and his sun-stained skin and his humped nose, but of course no Indian ever had a beard like Grandpa's: it was as thick as the top of the umbrella tree. He finished his second tumbler of whisky and put the glass on the table. Spreading his hands out on his knees, he looked at his stepdaughter and said, "Rose, you had ought to be ashamed of the looks of these two. You hadn't ought to hold out on them the way you do: you had ought to send them to Claude of a summer."

"But, Mr. Kenyon! What do you mean! Why, they're much too delicate to be away from me and Dr. Haskell!"

This was a controversy that was repeated annually. Mr. Kenyon, whose scorn for Mrs. Fawcett's picayune walnut grove was boundless, saw no reason at all why the children should not summer in the Colorado mountains and each year he offered to pay their train fare; he felt it particularly unjust that she did not at least send the boy who ought to be learning the ways of a man.

"This Dr. Haskell," said Mr. Kenyon contemptuously, "is he the only sawbones in the world?"

"Oh, I didn't mean it that way, Mr. Kenyon, I surely didn't. I daresay Claude has a very fine physician up there in the mountains. I only meant that they're such babies . . . they need a mother's care. I just don't know . . . with all those horses and cows there, just danger everywhere."

Ralph, knowing beforehand that nothing would come of this argument, wondered if he might not now tell the joke about the cow since his mother had mentioned cows, but she hastened on. "You know how I have always felt about horses, Mr. Kenyon."

He replied, "Rose, there's not a damned thing on God's green earth I know any better than that. But it don't make sense that you should want to turn in and spook this boy as well."

Mrs. Fawcett blushed and vigorously fanned herself with

41

a palm leaf, though the breeze was cool. "I want only one thing, Mr. Kenyon: I want him to be a gentleman."

The flame died in Grandpa and he said wearily, "I don't aim to judge in the matter of gentlemen but my son Claude is a fine man."

Mrs. Fawcett put her fan down suddenly and sat up straight. "Mr. Kenyon, I think perhaps we had better discuss this some other time. You were going to tell me about Roberta Wagner's fire. How did it start?"

"Oh, a kerosene lamp or some damned thing or other in the barn."

Reluctantly he allowed himself to be steered back into tame channels, but presently there came a long pause. He could think of no more facts and Mrs. Fawcett was out of questions. They were all so bored! The children waited impatiently for their mother to go in to speak to Fuschia, for this was the signal for Grandpa to give them their presents. But because she revered custom, she would not move until it was really necessary; she did not want the dirty, tippling old roughneck to think he was not welcome, not even when she was so angry with him that she could cry.

Grandpa filled his glass for the third time. Ralph got off the arm of his chair and moved to the railing of the porch where he sat with his hands under him. "Grandpa," he said, "have you got any dogs?" The old man put his glass down on the round wicker table while he corked the bottle. Then, without warning, his head fell forward on his chest, his hat slid off and lay, crown upward, on the floor, and the bottle rolled unbroken to the railing, directly under Ralph's feet. His hands relaxed and lay over the arms of the chair; his breath came unevenly and deeply like wind through his loosely opened lips, and his eyes appeared quite blind though they were open. There was a moment of quiet so long and so pure that it seemed like an hour of dreamless sleep, and Ralph was again reminded of the scarlet fever days when the neat, still hours had been in a row like boxes. He stared intently at the long unkempt hairs in Grandpa's eyebrows and at the coppery gloss of his beard. The old feet, swollen, lay turned on the ankles and the boy saw that the moccasins were not completely on and that the heels, in white cotton socks, stuck out. In one there was a careful darn. He realized that he did not know the name of Grandpa's housekeeper, though he did know that Uncle Claude's was named Mrs. Brotherman.

Then Mrs. Fawcett cried, "José! Fuschia! Quick!" José, still holding his banana knife, came silently across the lippia lawn, the grin now gone from his face. Ralph was sent to telephone for Dr. Haskell and Molly went with him into their father's den. Leah and Rachel had run sobbing in terror to the garden.

Ralph and Molly stayed in the study until they heard José and Fuschia help Grandpa up the steps. There were gasps and moans and curses and the sound of those old helpless feet pad-padding up in the soft slippers. Then they heard the door to the guest room close, and still, for some time, they did not stir.

Unable to understand this unmanly collapse, this strange dissolving of a rock, Ralph fled the thought of it and viewed his father's study, wishing he were alive. This room was kept as he had always kept it, but there was no clue to what sort of man he had been. Its simple and business-like furnishings had no idiosyncrasies and there was little to distinguish it from Dr. Haskell's waiting room. There were no pictures on the walls and the only books in the shelves were government tracts on the growing of walnuts and a set of dusty, yellow-leaved volumes called "Letters and Messages of the Presidents." On the desk there was a surveyor's telescope in a black box and an arrowhead in an abalone shell. The only article that had, so far as he knew, any history at all was the serape on the black leather lounge: his mother had smuggled it in from Tia Juana on her bustle. This had been the only act of daring in her life and Ralph admired her for it, but today he realized that he was tired of the story and he wondered what his father had been doing all the time she was having her perilous adventure with the customs inspector. The man had faded away like smoke. Even Leah, who had been six when he died, recalled almost nothing of him, and the few impressions she did have grew paler and paler until she could no longer give definite answers to any of the other children's questions but would say vaguely, "I *think* he used to say 'jiminy crickets' but I'm not sure." What was truly amazing was that the old woman he had saved in the flood was still alive!

"Oh, I'm lonesome," Ralph said to himself, and then, against his will, he saw Grandpa again, slumping in the wicker chair, and again he wondered why he had tapped the turquoise berry with his stick. And now, clear-headed, he turned on Molly in a cold, exhilarated anger and said, "Why do you always have to follow me?" He went out to the porch and sat motionless in the swing, hearing his sister sobbing and heaving about on the lounge. José had left his

44

cruel curved knife on the round table beside Grandpa's little glass of whisky which he had not got to drink.

It was the last time they saw Grandpa Kenyon until, five days later, he was brought down to the parlor, dead, where he waited two more days until Uncle Claude came to bury him.

The children did not go to school for the three days between Grandpa's death and the funeral. Mrs. Fawcett felt that this was a necessary gesture of respect to the dead man, but it was an unhappy time for the children. Leah and Rachel sorted and arranged their free samples and quarreled with one another saying. "Move *over,* what do you think I am anyway?" and Ralph and Molly roamed silently from room to room trying to think of something to do. "Why don't you settle down with a book?" said their mother. They talked, dispiritedly, in Pig Latin about Molly's poem which Ralph still could not understand. The house was quiet and dark and the Mexicans in the grove were afraid to raise their voices above a whisper. All that time, Fuschia was canning and making piccalilli and the whole house smelled deliciously of mace and dill, and yet it could not obscure the fragrance of all the flowers that lay in the parlor with Grandpa. Ralph was acutely conscious of all the smells, and he was able at last to name what it was that had been so distinct in the odor that clung to the old man: he had smelled like a raisin.

Mr. Follansbee came twice in the evening to call. The second time he left a leather-bound book of solemn aphorisms called "some Starbeams of Solace," which Mrs. Fawcett read frequently with moist eyes. In his sermon at the funeral, the pastor spoke of Grandpa as a man whose "many interests and travels destined him for an active rather than a contemplative life," but since it took all kinds to make the world, there was no reason to suppose that the Lord would look on him with disfavor. "Among men, too," he said, "there are the Marthas as well as the Marys." By way of gratitude, Mrs. Fawcett, enriched by her stepfather's will, subscribed a thousand dollars toward a central heating unit for the church. She would have liked to have a stained-glass window put in in his memory, but she was by no means certain that Mr. Kenyon had believed in God.

The night after Grandpa died, Miss Runyon brought some roses, and because Fuschia was busy with the dishes and Leah and Rachel wanted to listen to the ladies talk and Molly was in bed with hiccups after getting too much sun, Ralph was sent to the parlor with them. Only one lamp was burning, the smallest one of all. It stood on a round marble-topped table at the foot of the coffin and it scarcely illuminated Grandpa's face at all. Although there seemed to be no opening in the room, the flame was unsteady and shifted behind the thin china shade with its design of tulips against a pale green ground. There were flowers everywhere, brought by all the neighbors, not in tribute to Mr. Kenyon since none of them had known him, but in sympathy with Mrs. Fawcett in whose house this had unreasonably happened. It had been one of his orders, repeated throughout his lifetime, that he be buried wherever he died, for he had no use for pomp and thought that the transportation of a corpse from one part of the world to another was wasteful of money and of time. Mrs. Fawcett would gladly have accompanied the casket back to Missouri or even to England,

and in her first telegram to Claude had said so, but he wired back: "Must bury him like he said."

Ralph tried not to look at the body which, even though it had shrunk in death, made everything else look small as if the importance of its metamorphosis had taken on a physical dimension. He put the vase of roses down on the library table where the Bible lay open and as he did so, a petal fell off onto the finely printed page. Simultaneously the tip of a spray of fern in a tall vase of carnations brushed against his cheek, startling him with its subtle touch. He turned quickly as if he had been spoken to and looked full into the dead man's face. He now could see the big hooked nose jutting up and casting a shadow of itself on the satin pillow, and could see the dead white wrinkled eyelids under the ragged brows. Someone had brushed his beard and his square, corrugated fingernails had been cleaned. Ralph put the palm of his hand on Grandpa's cold cheek, feeling the formation of the bones. He was neither afraid nor disgusted: the skin under his fingers was as smooth and meaningless as the fallen rose petal. But then, when he had taken away his hand and had stepped back, he was frightened exactly as he had been frightened last summer when he went onto a submarine in San Diego with Uncle Ernest and he had looked through a periscope; it was so far, what you looked at, and so watery and so strange.

In the days just past, when Grandpa had been dying, the mystery had been withheld from all the children. Rather, it had been obscured by the bustling, the quiet coming and going of Dr. Haskell and of well-wishing neighbors with napkin-covered offerings of custards and broths (the Freudenburgs had sent, of all things, some spiced dumplings!)

47

and the ringing of the telephone, and Miguel's innumerable trips to town to fetch medicine and to send telegrams. The guest room was at the back, in an ell, a part of the house Ralph rarely went into since besides this room there were only his mother's sewing room, the linen closet and a storage cubby; yet in these past days he had been drawn to it, bewitched by the silence, and sometimes for an hour had stood in the sewing room, tossing a bobbin of blue silk thread up in the air and catching it again, trying to hear something through the wall, hearing nothing but the night-like silence, the silence that muted the hurried commotion of the errands and the calls.

Now that everything had ceased, it was possible to look back and to realize that the soft sounds and the agitation had been only trifles superimposed upon a great, unviolent force. Grandpa was like a big river, he thought, but one that had dried up and was gone forever into the ocean. He could take in the finality of this, but he could not understand how the drying up had happened: it had been too quick. He had just been sitting there corking the whisky bottle; Ralph had just asked him if he had any dogs.

Ralph understood that Grandfather Bonney had been dying for some time, in excruciating pain, and he knew that he should be glad—as his mother had said a dozen times—that Grandpa had not suffered at all. No matter how hard he tried, though, and no matter how often he heard the story of Grandfather Bonney's tragic ending, he could not feel really sad as Leah and Rachel did, nor did he wish as they did that he had known the gentleman whose portrait he now looked at in the fluttering light. Beneath the gold-framed picture, on the mantel which was black marble and had been taken from the house in St. Louis, stood Grand-father Bonney's christening cup and the Florentine urn which held his ashes. Between his Alpha and Omega stood a multitude of small mementoes of the intervening years: a silver snuff box embossed with a salamander; a miniature Venus de Milo made of brass which he had used as a paper weight; a gold stamp box with his name engraved on it in German script; a red leather jewel case which held the studs and the cuff links, the tie pins and the Masonic ring which Ralph, who was named for him, would get when he was grown.

Everything in the face and bearing of Grandfather Bonney showed that he was truly the character in his daughter's legend, that is, that he had been a scholar and a gentleman. He was plump and bald, but fat had not obscured the vigor of his face. His gray eyes intelligently searched those of his beholder and in them resided a great self-possession which appeared also in his luxuriously full lips shining as though he had licked them, which were closed and unsmiling above the faintly grizzled and elegantly kempt Imperial. He wore a pink carnation in the lapel of his morning coat; a silk hat and a gold-headed stick, a black Chesterfield and a pair of white gloves lay on the hassock beside his chair. He was so spruced up that the children could never get over the idea that he had not just come from a funeral at which he had been a pallbearer, but Mrs. Fawcett assured them that this was the way he had dressed on the most ordinary occasions. He sat at a large round table laden with gold-clasped books, the same books which were now on the same table in the bay window, opposite the fireplace. The one that was open under his hand—a finger pointed to the middle of the right page—was Tennyson's *Collected Works*. The chances were strong, said Mrs. Fawcett, that the poem he pointed to was "Break, Break, Break" which he had liked especially. Still, it was hard to believe that he had been reading and had suddenly been moved so much by a passage that he had stopped to meditate upon it, for there was no softening of reflection about the lines of his mouth and eyes: they were tense as if he had just come to a decision and intended to abide by it sternly. The picture had been painted when he was in his prime, in his middle fifties. It was very soon after that that he had died.

Leah and Rachel and Ralph and Molly could not remember a time when they had not known that Grandfather Bonney had personally met Grover Cleveland at the Democratic Convention in 1888. He had himself been a Republican and had always voted a straight ticket, but all the same, he never had anything harsh to say of Mr. Cleveland although he was naturally glad that Mr. Harrison had won the election. This connection of her grandfather with the history of the United States had led the eldest child, Leah, to several confusions which she had passed on to each of the others in turn. Chief of these was that President Cleveland, wrongheaded as he might have been, was second in importance only to George Washington. They believed that during his administration the capital had been Cleveland, Ohio. They could not place Abraham Lincoln in time but they could easily do so in space, for Uncle Ernest, their Aunt Kathleen's husband, had gone to the University of Nebraska where, but for a fluke, he would have graduated *summa cum laude*.

Furthermore, because in the delirium of his last illness, Grandfather Bonney had several times spoken of his meeting with Cleveland, they associated the President with blood poisoning and with profuse perspiration and Molly could never hear his name without immediately seeing in her mind's eye a brown custard cup in which her mother had burned sugar to dispel the fetor of the sickroom. Similarly they linked Tennyson with their grandfather, for his last articulate words, spoken to Aunt Kathleen as she was arranging his pillows, were, "It's no use, Kate. I am at the crossing of the bar." Each of the children envisaged this trinity, the poet, the President, and the grandfather, in a different way: Ralph saw them fat, hatless, wearing morning coats, walking abreast along an endless beach, eternally nearing a sand bar. Leah saw them sitting at a round table drinking coffee out of mustache cups while in the distance a band played "When You and I Were Young, Maggie." Through Rachel's mind, they marched in single file down the central aisle of the First Presbyterian Church with such calm and ceremony that they made Mr. Follansbee seem remarkably rustic. Molly, who was often ill, saw them lying all three in one enormous bed with a moon like a jack-o'-lantern shining in on their big rosy faces through a dormer window.

Ralph, glancing from Grandpa Kenyon's dead face to Grandfather Bonney's living one, felt lonely and beset, knowing with unwilling shame that he should mourn them equally because, in a sense, he really knew Grandfather Bonney better than he had ever known his successor. For example, he knew all about his grandfather's fox terrier who had been named Liliolukilani and had been as sharp as a tack: she could pray and she could jump through a hoop and she knew commands both in English and in German.

Ralph could see the man as clearly as he could call up the image of Mr. Follansbee. What a sport he had been! How full of jokes and pranks! He had always been the merriest one of all at skating parties (to tease the girls he once wore a fascinator to a skating party!) and at wiener roasts, at formal balls and informal Sunday evening chafing-dish suppers. He had had gallant manners with ladies, preserving such customs as kissing their hands and paying them compliments which always contained a word or two of French. What young lady did not delight in having him say to her, "Mademoiselle's frock is truly *distingue*"? Besides being chivalrous, he could play tricks that were a scream and afterward he would say, "Forgive me, ladies and gentlemen, but I felt an uncontrollable desire to tickle my risibles." Once he had put burnt cork all over his face and had pretended to be a darky and his imitation was so good that everyone had been taken in for at least five minutes. Another time, he had sneaked up under an open window one dark summer night and when there was a pause in the conversation, he suddenly said, in a spooky voice, "Boo!" and Mrs. Bonney and the girls had nearly jumped out of their skins. At breakfast he would ask a visitor if she wanted onions in her cocoa and he would say it with such a straight face, she wouldn't know what to answer. Once, though, he had been beaten at this game, for a perky friend of Rowena's had answered back quick as a wink, "Not on your tintype, Mr. Smarty," and Grandfather had laughed until the tears came to his eyes. He had always been up to some frolic like that. Now it would be a joke on one of the colored servants (he loved to tease the old colored cook who was *just* as superstitious), now a lark down the river on a steamer to Memphis, now an outlandish slide mixed up with the scenes of Venice in the stereoptican: suddenly you would see a pair of flannel underdrawers flying from the middle dome of St. Marks! He used to say that "one is only as old as one feels" and he never felt old, not even at the last of his life.

The boy felt neither fear nor sorrow for either man. He felt only this unkind solitude that waited for him like a surly dog. In a brief foreknowledge of maturity, he thought how curious it was that it had been possible for them all to eat three times a day the same as ever: they had actually eaten the duck and Sally Lunn the night Grandpa was, as they said, "taken," and Leah had not bothered to take away his place so that it was still there, opposite Mother, the emptiest space Ralph had ever seen. Even now, after dark, alone in a room with a dead person, he was not afraid, and he was able to notice little, useless things like the dust rag Fuschia had left behind on the bookcase beside the vase of cattails. He remembered that his mother had said that just before Grandfather Bonney died she had been in her bedroom looking out the window at a bright red kite that had got stuck in the topmost branches of a eucalyptus tree, and when Kathleen came in to say, "He is going, Rose," she had, even as she hurried along the passage, said to herself, "I wonder if that kite belongs to one of the Van Buskirk children."

The ladies were in the dining room talking. He could not hear what they said, but he could imagine the shape of their mouths and the kind of thing they would be repeating over and over again in that strange belief all grown-ups seemed to have that no one heard the first time. His mother would explain, with pressing urgency, why Mr. Kenyon was to be buried in the Covina cemetery although he had only come here for short visits; Miss Runyon, boisterous and inquisitive, would be inquiring about Uncle Claude who was coming tomorrow; his mother would be apologizing for her half-brother just as she had always apologized for her stepfather. At some point she would say, "First my father, then my husband, and now Mr. Kenyon. But I have my son."

Someone was at the door and he trembled violently; if one of those women came in, he thought, he would throw himself on Grandpa's dead white face and die. But it was only Molly, slinking in like a little ailing cat, snuffling and coming toward him with her hands outstretched as if she were blind. There was a sour smell about her and he knew she must have been sick as she generally was when she had hiccups. "I'm scared," she said, taking his hand. "I don't want him to be dead, Ralph. I don't *want* him to be!" They lay down on the floor beside the coffin, sobbing in each other's arms, but making scarcely any noise lest the ladies and their sisters hear them.

CHAPTER THREE

JUST AS FIVE DAYS BEFORE WHEN THEY HAD WAITED FOR
Grandpa Kenyon, Ralph and Molly lay on the lippia
lawn, waiting for their uncle. An airplane flew across the
sky. Its pilot was stunting and as they watched, breathlessly,
he took a nose dive. "The big fool!" cried Ralph. "He's
going to hit the pumphouse!" And then he smiled as he
saw the plane cleverly climb up again. It occurred to him
with pain that Grandpa Kenyon, who loved all unusual experience, had died before he had ever gone up in an airplane. Nor had he ever got to see the racing fellow, Barney
Oldfield, of whom he had often spoken with admiration.

What would next September be like without him? Associated as he had been with the renewal of crowded days
after the tranquil ennui of the summer, he had seemed to
the children, after he had gone, half legendary like a figure
known only in his identification with a particular place or
a particular day of the year. He was a sort of god of September, surrounded by the gold, autumnal light. What Ralph
missed most already was the early-morning ceremony in
which he alone participated with Grandpa. The old man
kept his usual hours when he visited in Covina and always

55

got up before daylight to make his own breakfast. The fragrance of the coffee he made was so manly and stimulating that Ralph could reproduce the sensation of it at will throughout the day and could therefore daydream under the most adverse schoolroom conditions. Ralph, creeping downstairs in his stocking feet lest he awaken his mother and sisters, would find Grandpa Kenyon sitting by the stove in the half-light, his black hat pushed back from his forehead and his glasses midway down his nose. He would be waiting for the griddle to heat up for his flapjacks, but the coffee would be made already and the kitchen would be full of its strong, rather rancid smell. They did not speak to one another until the meal was over and Grandpa had lighted his pipe; at this point, he always took off his hat, Ralph could never guess why. At these times he told no stories but instead talked with homesickness of the chores that were now proceeding on his ranches: just about now in Texas the whole outfit would be fixing to go up to the range and cut out the beeves to be shipped to Panama; in Colorado, where they kept lazier hours, the old colored woman, Magdalene, would be calling the men to breakfast. As he stated these facts, he kept his eye on his watch. When the second hand had completed its circuit, he would say, "She's settin' the coffee pot down by Claude." Ralph discerned contempt in Grandpa's glance through the window at the tidy grove with its toy-like trees where the Mexicans would not come for two hours yet, and when he heard the milkman come, he sometimes grew angry, thumping his fist on the table and shouting at the boy, "Lord God Almighty, she could keep *one* cow anyway. She had ought to be ashamed." She was not ashamed but Ralph was, and once he declared that he would not touch milk again until she got a cow. Her reply was a familiar and irrefutable one: "Our sort of people don't have cows."

Ralph wondered if, after all, Grandpa would have liked the joke about the cow. He wondered, too, if he dared tell it to Uncle Claude or if this would seem unbecoming on the day of the funeral. Uncle Claude. Uncle Claude. Uncle Claude. He said the name over and over to himself but it brought no picture to his mind. He could not imagine what Grandpa's son would be like and because he could not, the thought of meeting him made him shy.

At the same time that he became aware that Molly was crying and had been for some time, he saw the car coming round the bend in the lane where the blue cedars grew and with no plan at all in his mind he jumped to his feet and ran at top speed across the lawn and past the solar tank. As he ran, he thought: Now I pass the garden and Leah and Rachel haven't seen me. Now I am passing the solar tank. Now I am passing the den and in the den I am passing the deer-head and the deer-head hasn't seen me. Now the pantry and Mother isn't there and Fuschia isn't there. And now I am safe. He ran to the pumphouse and climbed the ladder as quickly as a mouse. Once on top, he squatted on his heels on the round roof. His heart pounded as deeply as the pump pulsed below him. He had no idea why he had not wanted to see his uncle. It was as if he had got to control himself by a complete physical escape, by exposing himself to the perfectly empty sky and by enclosing himself in this perfectly round small area where shapes and colors were of the simplest: the sanctuary was round, its floor was black, the sky was blue, and he was alone.

He would not look down but he could hear voices. His mother said, "Dear Claude. It is a sorrowful time for all of us."

If the air had not been so still, Ralph would not have heard the man's reply for his voice was so soft. It was so soft and sad that Ralph thought he must be sitting on the steps with his head between his hands in anguish. He said, "Can I see Mr. Kenyon, ma'am?"

The boy saw his uncle all by himself, casting his shadow on a white desert, on the terribly unearthly stretch of land he had seen from the train the summer they had gone to St. Louis. There had been miles and miles of nothing but sand until finally the train passed a giant pear cactus and Mrs. Fawcett, in an explanatory voice, had said, "You know, that little bit of shade would mean a great deal to someone who got stranded here."

Mr. Follansbee and his wife came to luncheon after the funeral. Mr. Follansbee sat at Mrs. Fawcett's right and told jokes which the children and Uncle Claude did not understand, although Leah and Rachel pretended to. He was an unpleasant-looking man with a small upturned chin and a large, down-turned nose and his whole face was thin and malign. Mrs. Fawcett said he had a "typical Yankee face," but Ralph could never reconcile this with the song "Yankee Doodle" which was, he thought, about a man something like Santa Claus. Molly had decided, though, that if Uncle Sam were clean-shaven, he would probably look a good deal like the minister. He wore a morning coat; Mrs. Follansbee, like Mrs. Fawcett, was dressed in black. Each child wore a sign of mourning: Ralph wore black knickerbockers and black stockings and the three little girls wore black Windsor ties at the necks of their middy blouses. In this decent gathering, Uncle Claude was a gaudy incongruity. His suit was chocolate brown, his shirt was a rich deep blue, and his tie was scarlet; there was no black about him save for his black hair and his black eyes. His whole color scheme was like that of a rooster. He was a younger and slighter version of Grandpa. His jawbones were broad and his cheekbones high, but his chin was rather small and Ralph realized with a shock that probably Grandpa's had been too and that was why he wore a beard. Uncle Claude's shoulders were massive, bullish, and his arms hung forward from them in an animal heaviness, terminating in the biggest hands the boy had ever seen. These hands, whose fingers had been enlarged and discolored as his father's had been, were long but were so wide that on the damask tablecloth and handling the coin-silver spoons, they looked scarcely like hands at all but slabs of meat with the rind still on. Leah and Rachel, scornful of his cheap ugly suit (it looked like the one the Watkins man wore), had said that he looked simple-minded and they hoped they would not have to sit next to him at the funeral. It was that his face was so innocent; he did not seem to know what had happened to him, and this house, these little girls, the appointments of this table were not in his line. You could tell he wished he had not come; but he was not simple-minded.

He had hardly spoken at all since his arrival. After he had seen his father, he had gone to the guest room and had remained there until it was time to leave for the service. Molly, hugging the trunk of the umbrella tree, had seen him standing at the oriel in the upstairs hall, looking down

59

when the men came to fetch away the coffin to take it to the church. His silence had infected the others, and even Mrs. Fawcett's tongue had been stilled on the drive to the cemetery and home again. But now that all was over, she believed a lighter tone should prevail to efface, if possible, the sorrowful reason for their gathering together. The talk, therefore, at the luncheon table was jovial and irrelevant. Mr. Follansbee started it by telling a story about an earnest young lady, the daughter of a remote cousin of Mrs. Follansbee's, who had been sent to them with a letter of introduction for a short visit before she entered a boarding school in Pasadena.

"Oh, Rose, you will like this, I know," he said. "I can just imagine your good father in a similar position." To Uncle Claude, he explained, "I, an immigrant to California like everyone else—these four little Fawcetts are the only California natives of my acquaintance, ha, ha—and in the dim dark past I had the honor of hearing Mrs. Fawcett's father hold forth on cultural subjects far into many a night. I must confess that sometimes, for me, the midnight oil gave off soporific fumes but—ha, ha—as that most learned gentleman would have said himself, *aliquando bonus dormitat Homerus,* that is, 'even good Homer sometimes nods.'" Claude Kenyon, flanked by Ralph and Molly, looked bashfully at his plate of jellied soup and did not even pretend to smile. The preacher, with a hint of exasperation in his face, but none in his deep oratorical voice, continued, "This good lass came with loads of luggage, all of it as heavy as lead. Full of books, do you see. As pretty as a picture she was, and no earthly reason for her to be smart as well—look there at Leah and Rachel pricking up their ears! Yet she *was* smart, but the pity of it was that she wasn't really bright. You call that a paradox? Well, I have a funny sort of little old mind and I maintain a person can be intellectual and not be intelligent. But don't let me make a sermon right here! On to the story! Well, sir, the first night the pretty little slip of a thing was with us, we were taking our coffee in the library, a custom I have not been able to outgrow even after many years in this new-fangled nation of California, and lo and behold and *mirabile dictu,* milady says to me, very seriously, very soberly, 'Mr. Follansbee, have you ever read Shakespeare?' "

Mrs. Fawcett, who had been ready from the beginning of the anecdote, now laughed until she had to wipe her eyes. Mrs. Follansbee, who had been present and could not be expected to react quite as she had done at the time, was milder. Leah and Rachel covered their mouths with their napkins, through which came peals of laughter. But the minister had expected this applause and did not so much as glance at any of them but fixed his eyes on Uncle Claude with a look of malicious amusement. When Uncle Claude blushed, his skin took on an apoplectic blue and Ralph, who had not been able even to grin, shuddered when he looked at him.

When there had been enough laughter, Mr. Follansbee, still looking at Claude, said, "Sir, I envy you your snowy winters. I miss them here in California. Back in Missouri, on snowy nights, I used to go through the historical plays. Read them and reread them to my great edification. I imagine you do much the same thing. I expect when you're snowbound the time may hang heavy on your hands. Literature is a great medicine: it takes us out of ourselves."

Claude put his spoon down clumsily and it made a loud

clatter on the plate under his soup cup. His ashamed eyes lifted waveringly to the minister's as he sighed. And then he said, "I couldn't rightly say I find the time hanging heavy. I have a sight of cows to feed."

"All the same," cried Mrs. Fawcett, frantically embarrassed, "I expect you manage to find the time to read! Mr. Follansbee, Claude was the most precocious youngster you ever saw, and who should be a better judge of that than I? Why, he was reading *Lorna Doone* when he was just a little bit of a thing!" This profession fell flat, but she barely paused. "Don't you remember the many many times we used to go out to the summer-house and read Tennyson aloud? How you loved *The Idylls of the King!*"

For several minutes she talked rapidly and distractedly about Tennyson, Claude's early love for him, her own love for him, her father's love for him. She did not relinquish the conversation until it was at a safe distance from the question of how Uncle Claude passed the time on a winter evening. Later on she confided in her children that she had been on tenterhooks for fear Claude would tell them what he did read. For she assumed that his tastes would be like those of his father who had never been seen reading a book and who had never mentioned any but the novels of Gaboriau which certainly could not be called "classics." As far as the ancient languages went, these might have been the Dark Ages for all Mr. Kenyon had known of them, and Mrs. Fawcett suspected that his son had not known what *mirabile dictu* meant.

Mr. Follansbee experimented with another gambit. His hobby was taxidermy and his house, which smelled of mud, was full of stuffed skunks, raccoons, woodpeckers, bluebirds and cottontails, the corpses being brought to him by his obedient flock, some of whom felt that for a minister the pastime was unduly skittish. He asked Uncle Claude if he had any interest in the subject and when Uncle Claude replied that he had never thought about it one way or the other, Mr. Follansbee said, "I'm just like a boy about it, as my long-suffering better half will testify. Why, yesterday I got a new batch of supplies and I stopped work right in the middle of my sermon to open the parcel. They had made a rather comical mistake. I had written for eyes of a vulture and they sent instead the eyes of the extinct auk."

Molly spoke for the first time. She closed her eyes and chanted, "A is for auk who lives in the wet, B is for blackbird with wings of jet." And Uncle Claude turned to her and smiled.

But Mrs. Fawcett, to whom actually the minister's handling of dead animals was extremely repugnant, told her not to interrupt and she asked what on earth he had done since obviously one could not substitute an auk's eyes for a vulture's eyes. He answered that he had sent them back and would, until the "genuine article" arrived, work on a gopher which Kenneth Taliafero had brought him. At this mention of her lover's name, Rachel giggled. Mr. Follansbee reached across the table and delicately pulled her hair. *Oh, stop it!* thought Ralph.

The meal progressed as if the silent outlander were not there. Leah and Rachel, interrogated by the minister, showed their wares boldly. Yes, indeed, they surely *were* glad they were going to boarding school next year in New Haven where they would have an opportunity to study French and music, but most of all to study elocution under someone of

63

more gumption than the rather ungifted and certainly homely Mrs. Sawhill to whom they went on Saturday afternoon after their dancing lesson with the equally uninspired but less plain Miss Lanier. Both the minister and his wife laughed happily when Rachel, speaking of Mrs. Sawhill, said, "And I never can keep my mind on the piece I'm speaking because she mouths the words and I'm afraid her false teeth are going to fall right out because they do wobble so." Leah, not to be outdone, said of Miss Lanier, "Yes, but that's not half as bad as in ballet when she takes off her slipper and rubs her *bunion*." It was said that Mrs. Fawcett was brave to let her little girls go all the way across the country even though Aunt Rowena would be near them to keep an eye on them. It was observed by the girls that they were already homesick.

Molly bubbled her water and said, "A child in my grade has the itch."

"Molly," said her mother, vigorously shaking her head. "Shame on you." Everyone ignored the impossible child.

A hideous accident attended the serving of the dessert. Uncle Claude had failed to remove his finger bowl from his plate and when Fuschia brought around the raspberry ice, he put his portion into the water, splashing it on the table. Leah and Rachel could not contain themselves any longer and burst into laughter. To double his humiliation the others chose pointedly to pay no attention to the calamity and Mrs. Fawcett, in a flash of venomous discourtesy, said, "I declare I do not understand why these girls can suddenly laugh their heads off at nothing at all."

Ralph felt physically sick and was afraid that if the meal did not end quickly he might disgrace himself right there at the table. Never had he so passionately despised Mr. Follansbee's cruel, smug face, his pince-nez on a black ribbon, the effeminate white piping of his vest. Grandpa Kenyon had, next to merchants, disliked clergymen more than any other people, and Ralph agreed with him, for he was sure they were all like Mr. Follansbee. Grandpa's shillelagh had been sent to him from Cork by his brother who was a clergyman and who "had undertaken to preach the Gospel English style to those poor backward natives." By the way he said it, the children knew that he did not think the Irish were poor and backward at all and that he was really making fun of his brother. He had another brother who was also a clergyman, a missionary in China, and his sister Nan was an Anglican nun. Mrs. Fawcett always told him, before the Follansbees came to the buffet supper, that it would perhaps be just as well for him not to mention his brothers and sisters as Mr. Follansbee had very decided opinions on anything the least bit Romish. She was afraid he was secretly displeased that her land adjoined that of the Freudenburgs who were Romans and went in for all kinds of superstitions like fish on Friday and statues of the virgin on top of the piano. Ralph wondered if Schöneshund had to eat fish on Friday too. Probably they gave him potatoes instead.

The horrible pastor looked at Ralph and for some reason winked his light green, reptilian eye. The boy trembled and looked away and this time glanced with ardent loathing at Mrs. Follansbee's round puffy face whose vulgar snub nose complemented her husband's downward curving one. He particularly hated her nose because she had chronic catarrh and tried, because of it, to identify herself with him and Molly who were similarly afflicted. While she was therefore ostensibly becoming their contemporary, she spoke of their kinship in baby talk and in the loud voice ladies used in addressing servants and foreigners. The only thing that could be said in her favor was that she did not talk as much as her husband. Otherwise, she was just as bad, and Ralph wished both of them would get bubonic plague.

"Who has the itch?" he suddenly asked Molly.

"Ralph!" cried Mrs. Fawcett. "This is not to be discussed at the table."

But Molly said, "Beulah. The one that stole my nickel."

"That will be enough, Molly," said Mrs. Fawcett. She dipped her fingers into the crystal bowl of water and dried them on her napkin and everyone did the same except Uncle Claude who could not wash in his dessert. Ralph's nausea and resentment ebbed. In a moment it would be over. There would only be two more meals and the Follansbees wouldn't be at those. While he wanted Uncle Claude to like him, he was glad that he was leaving the next day so that Leah and Rachel would stop giggling at his wrong clothes and his table manners and his language. He was determined not to let him go, though, without explaining to him that he and Molly were different from the rest of the family. And there was another thing: there were the presents Grandpa had not given them, so now they would really be Uncle Claude's presents. But how could he ask for them? Again he wondered if he could tell the joke about the cow, but it did not seem quite right; Uncle Claude seemed too serious even though he had smiled at Molly when she recited the alphabet thing.

After lunch it was suggested that Uncle Claude would like to take a nap for he had really had no rest at all since he left home. The fact that he had unaccountably come all the way from Denver by day coach was not alluded to before the Follansbees. The minister, who was the host in any house he entered, thought a game of Twenty Questions would be as decorous an amusement as any; Mrs. Fawcett, agreeing, said that afterward Leah and Rachel could recite their new Scottish dialogue. They sauntered slowly to the parlor, Molly and Ralph and Uncle Claude at the rear. As Uncle Claude turned toward the stairs he said, "If that Beulah stole your nickel, it serves her right to have the itch."

Most of the flowers had been taken out of the parlor and laid on Grandpa's grave, but the air was still heavy with fragrance. The room was altered. Although nothing had been moved or added, it was not the same place it had been before, and Ralph could not imagine the ladies of the Sorosis sitting here eating ice cream in tiny bites off the tip end of their spoons and talking, giving prices, of the January white sales in Los Angeles. But no one else appeared aware of the transformation. They all picked their chairs and settled down and looked around as if nothing at all had happened, as if the long old dead man had not been here just a few hours before. For a little while no one spoke: it was as if they were all consciously digesting their lunch. They heard Uncle Claude move down the ell, quietly like a dog. It was warm so Mrs. Fawcett took off her black broadcloth jacket. She wore a pink crepe-de-Chine guimpe through which showed the deep lace yoke of her camisole, and at her throat she wore a cameo brooch which Grandpa Kenyon had given her as an engagement present. She did not especially like it, finding it too large to be really refined, but she had often worn it during his visits.

"Well," said Mr. Follansbee at last. Ralph, closing his eyes, could believe that they were in church and that Mr. Follansbee was standing before the pulpit while the deacons, Mr. Brewster and Mr. Prater, sat behind him, monumental, bald, inexorably dull, looking very much like Grandfather Bonney. The sermon presently would begin; his voice always trailed dramatically down at the end of every sentence during the last twenty minutes so that you were deceived a hundred times, thinking he was nearly through. He was not quite ready for his flock to play Twenty Questions. Instead, looking up at the portrait, he made an astonishing statement. He said, "Well, Ralph, my boy, it wouldn't be hard to imagine *him* as the President of the United States, would it?"

Ralph was too dumfounded to reply and Leah said, "It certainly wouldn't, Mr. Follansbee. Why do you suppose he never was?"

Mrs. Fawcett touched her point-lace handkerchief to her eyes. There promised to be a scene of sadness and memory but Rachel, who had been seized all day with the giggles, prevented it by giggling, burying her head in Leah's shoulder, and saying in a stage whisper, "Imagine Grandpa Kenyon as the President, though!" Leah said, laughing, "Now you just stop it, you horrid girl." But Rachel could not stop and she went on conjecturing how the Senate would like it when Mr. Kenyon said, "By the Lord Harry," and how funny he would look in a top hat like Mr. Harding's. The grown-ups pretended not to hear, but they were smiling all the same at the wicked, witty little girl. Ralph and Molly, side by side on a hassock, kept a glum silence until at last Ralph said bitterly, "Nobody but a boob would want to be the President."

It was the first time in his life that he had ever shown temper in the presence of anyone but his immediate family, and it gave him a feeling of lunatic power. Rachel looked slapped. His mother, most likely deep in a dream of boating parties on the Potomac and picnics on the White House lawn, looked at him reproachfully. The minister, unaccustomed to having his speculations rejected, arranged his cunning, vulpine face to give him his comeuppance, but Ralph got ahead of him. He said: "Did you know that Grandpa Kenyon killed a man once, Mr. Follansbee?"

Mrs. Fawcett said, "You poor silly it! You should never take any of Mr. Kenyon's stories seriously. He was only telling you a western yarn, Ralphie boy."

Mr. Follansbee could scarcely conceal his curiosity, but he said, "They are the salt of the earth, those tale-tellers. The farther they get from the truth, the better the tale."

"Oh, no, this wasn't a made-up one," insisted Ralph. "Grandpa really did kill a man. Probably more than one, I guess, but I only know just about this one."

The man folded his hands and slightly teetered on his chair and said indulgently, "Let's hear this true confession, laddie."

"Oh! Do you think it's right?" asked Mrs. Follansbee and her pop eyes strayed to the place where the coffin had so recently been. "Don't you think it seems a little disrespectful?" But her husband, quoting in his brief homily from "Some Starbeams of Solace," assured them all that the deceased would have enjoyed this himself.

Ralph began with self-assurance, but it waned as he went on. He could not tell the tale as Grandpa told it: he himself was shocked and disbelieving and could not recapture the feeling of wonder he had known that day the year before when he and Molly and Grandpa had sat together under a tree in the grove. He had been telling them that when he had been in Texas the week before he had had to take measures about some sheep that had got into his pastures and that he had not a bit liked to blow those little lambs to glory, one in particular that he would have liked to bring to Molly. Ralph immediately saw the lamb that Jesus carried in the Bible picture, one awkward leg hanging over His arm. Molly said, "Then why *did* you blow the lamb to glory, Grandpa?" And the old man answered, "Well, I'll tell you, Molly. I'd rather kill the sheep than kill the shepherd."

He stopped to light his pipe. They were far from the nut gatherers now, at the north end of the grove where the trees had been stripped and the ground gleaned. There was an acrid smell everywhere of the splitting hulls and the bleaching acids.

Ralph said, "Did you ever kill a shepherd?"

"Yes, sir," said Grandpa. "I own I did."

As he told his story, Ralph could see him, a young man, riding like the wind through the dark Texas night, his money belt full of silver and gold, his twin revolvers ready to be drawn. Months before he and his outfit had driven a shipment of steers to Dodge City and he was coming back home again. He had left the train at Amarillo and had come horseback the remaining fourteen miles. "My horse was called Pearl," he said, "and she was a dandy piece of jewelry." He had been in sight of his place and had seen a light in the bunkhouse, down in the hollow, some way off yet, when a couple of men had charged him suddenly, riding at a lope out from the shadows of a thicket of screw-bean. There was no moon but the night was clear and he was able to tell who they were by the starlight. They were brothers by the name of MacNeill, not good Scotch, as the name sounded, but half-breed Creeks, murderous and thieving. There had been ill will between them and Kenyon for a long time, for they had used his land to pasture their flocks and if he or any of his men caught a MacNeill sheep there, they disposed of it after giving the boys good warning. In retaliation, the skalawags rustled his cattle. The pattern was an endless circle. As they came on him tonight—they must have heard somehow that he would be riding in alone and with tolerable money on his person—they fired into the air to frighten Pearl, for they were that underhanded: they wanted to unseat him and have him on the ground at their mercy. Grandpa did not wait to find out what their business was and he stuck to his saddle as if he were nailed to it, though his mare leaped in terror. He shot the taller of the two cleanly through the heart and the other turned yellow and rode off the way he had come, not even dismounting to pay his respects to his dead brother. Ralph remembered that, when he had finished, Molly had asked if in the morning the two ravens of the ballad Grandpa sometimes sang had come to pluck out the man's bonny blue eyes.

The way Grandpa had told it, it had taken a long while, fifteen minutes or more, but Ralph, half crying, took only two or three, and at the end he realized that he did not believe a word of it. Leah pursed her lips. "I don't think it's nice to make up stories about killing people. I think it's awful."

Ralph turned on her and with the maniac laugh he and Molly had invented, shouted, "You mean because Mother killed Grandfather Bonney?"

But suddenly a mocking bird, in this broad daylight, began to sing. Mrs. Fawcett clasped her hands together and said "Oh!" as if the sound hurt her. Her large diamond ring, in the gesture, came into a ray of sunlight and two green needles shot out from the stone. Then Mr. Follansbee was across the room in one stride, shaking Ralph's shoulder. "You little cad," he said between his teeth, "you get down on your knees and beg your mother's pardon. On your *knees*."

For a moment he defied the minister by remaining motionless, but the long bony hand on his shoulder propelled him off the hassock and at last he knelt, not feeling sorry, feeling nothing but rage, as painful as a deep cut. He could not utter a word, though this delay was agonizing, and they were all watching him and they were all waiting. He could hear Mr. Follansbee breathing heavily. Then Molly, half under her breath, said "I wish you were a fairy, Mr. Follansbee." Rachel giggled, but Mr. Follansbee did not think this was funny and he snarled, "What's this? Why do you wish I were a fairy, young lady?" And Molly whispered with deadly hatred, "So you'd vanish."

And now he could speak. Now, with this ally beside him, kneeling and clutching his hand, he could tell the lie: "I'm sorry, Mother. Please forgive me, Mother." Molly said it after him in that queer, hoarse whisper in which she had insulted Mr. Follansbee.

Mrs. Fawcett patted his head, but she said firmly, "You may leave the room, Ralph." Molly did not get off so lightly. Mrs. Fawcett slapped her face, not hard, but so that it made a sound. "Mr. Follansbee will never want to come to our house again after this terrible thing you have said. You may go ask Fuschia to lock you in the closet."

Ralph did not go to his room which was directly over the parlor but to Molly's. On the little white desk under the window she had laid out the presents from Grandpa Kenyon in the order in which he had given them to her: a doll made of straw with a sombero that could be taken off; a suède bookmark with a burned-in design of yucca; a pair of bearskin slippers which were now too small; a totem pole, three inches high which listed like the leaning tower of Pisa; a jewel box made of fragrant lemon wood and carved all over with squash blossoms; a beaded belt. Ralph touched them, one by one, and thought of his sister standing in the dark in the coat closet which smelled of naphtha and of buttons. His anger had given way to fear, to the fear of the sermon Mr. Follansbee would preach next Sunday, two days away. They always sat in the very front so that there was no escaping his darting eyes and you had to pay attention every minute, even when you had a hangnail or something like that to play with.

There was a copy of "Gravel" on Molly's desk and he read it again and *still* it didn't make any sense to him. There was also a letter which she had written to their cousin Mildred whom she did not like at all but to whom she wrote once a week because Mildred had sent her some stationery for her

73

birthday. Ralph read it even though he knew it was against the law to read other people's mail.

Dear Mildred.

How are you? I am fine and hope you are the same. How are you getting along in school? Do you think long devision is hard? I do.

The Snake and the File

A snake one day crept into a blake-smiths shop and chaunced to knock against a steel file. This hurt the snake slightly, and, flying into a rage, he at once bit the file as hard as he could. The hard steel file cut the snake mouth, but when he saw the blood he though it was the file that bled, and so he bit it again and again until he had damage his own mouth very badly.

When we try to hurt other people we are much more likely to get hurt ourself.

Isn't that a funny story?

I guess that is all I can say so I will close your cousin.

Molly F.

He put the letter down, baffled. Molly was going crazy, he decided, and the thought made him nervous. If it were true, that was all the more reason he should get to be Uncle Claude's best friend, because if they had to take her to an asylum, he certainly wouldn't stay around here with those women; he would have to go to Colorado. He wanted to go into Uncle Claude's room, but he might be asleep and if Ralph woke him up, he might be angry; on the other hand if he were just sitting there, thinking of Grandpa, perhaps he would be glad to have company. He debated, looking at Molly's presents. Soon he heard them all go out to the front porch and almost immediately Leah and Rachel began their recitation. Now and again the grown-ups laughed and then, when they had quieted down, the girls went on.

It was about a girl and a boy named Jock and Jean and at the end of it, they would sing "Comin' Through the Rye." He felt suddenly that he could not bear to hear the song which always reminded him of the time Miss Runyon had come over to play Snap with them and at the end of the evening sang that song in a trembly voice and to make it all the more terrible, there was a piece of fudge on her front tooth. Hearing more laughter from the porch, he got up and went down the corridor to the ell.

Ralph was surprised to see that the door of the guest room was open and Uncle Claude was lying in the middle of the double bed flat on his back with his arms straight at his sides. He had taken off his bright orange oxfords and his coat so that Ralph could see the black and green horsehair belt; it had a design like a snake's back. The shades were drawn. Grandpa's grip was still on the luggage stand and Uncle Claude's small Boston bag, unopened, stood in the middle of the floor. A cigarette was burning in the pin tray on the dresser.

As he stepped across the threshold, Ralph was uneasy and he would have gone back to Molly's room if his uncle had not heard him and jerked up on his elbow.

"Your door was open," he said.

"You can close it now," said Uncle Claude.

Ralph hesitated, his hand wetly grasping the doorknob. "With me outside or in?" he asked.

"Suit yourself."

He went into the room and closed the door. Something inside him twitched like a cat's tail and he was afraid he might have a nosebleed. Fuschia and Miguel were having their lunch in the kitchen directly below the guest room and he heard a soft and urgent conversation. It was possible here only to hear the voices on the front porch as an uneven murmur; he was sure Uncle Claude had not heard what had happened in the parlor. Desperately he looked around the room: "Oh! Can I bring you your cigarette, Uncle Claude?"

His uncle got up and went over to the bureau and brushed his hair with two military brushes that had belonged to Ralph's father. He wore his hair parted in the middle and slicked down on either side. He ground out the cigarette and lighted a fresh one and then he sat down in the white rocking chair by the window and said, "Is this the room where he died?"

"Oh, yes," said Ralph. "Don't you see his grip still here?"

"I know," said Uncle Claude. "I thought maybe your mother just put it here to make me feel at home."

He was scrutinizing Ralph now and Ralph knew what he saw: a thin, sallow creature with his knickers hanging down to the middle of his spindling legs, hideous braces on hideous teeth, glasses that made him look ninety-nine years old. He felt that he must quickly speak before his uncle passed judgment on him and denied him permanently, but he could think of nothing to say. It would be unkind to tell him what it had been like when Grandpa had had his attack; it would be useless to apologize for his sisters and his mother and Mr. and Mrs. Follansbee; what was there to say? Finally, in a thin, singsong voice he told Uncle Claude the joke about the cow, realizing with each word that it was not a bit funny, just as he had known a little while ago that Grandpa's story about the MacNeills was not true. He did not even finish telling it, and when his voice trailed off, Uncle Claude did not even pay any attention so that Ralph knew he had not been listening.

After a long while, Uncle Claude said, "My father thought a lot of you. He was always saying he wished you'd come to visit me on my place." Then, with a smile which disarmed Ralph so that he nearly cried, he added, "But I guess you wasn't of the same mind."

"My mother . . ." Ralph began.

"Oh, well, hell," said Uncle Claude. He had a funny way of smoking. He drew so deeply that the ember took great bites in the paper. Ralph remembered evenings when Grandpa had sat on the porch smoking and the glow in the bowl of his pipe went on and off like a firefly. Uncle Claude said, "She never got over that about horses, did she? She would of kept me off 'em if she'd of had her way. But Mr. Kenyon was stronger minded than her."

"Well, I guess she worried, you know, about riding a horse and Grandfather getting the infection while he was watching her." He made his voice tentative. He did not really wish to be disloyal and so he said, "I don't really think she killed him, though, do you?"

"Jesus," said Uncle Claude. He sounded tired. In a minute he said, "What do you do around here to keep busy?"

There was very little they did that would interest Uncle Claude. They were not allowed to climb trees because splinters had been known to get into the bloodstream and travel to the heart. They did not have bicycles and they were not allowed to build things (the very thought of a nail brought tears to their mother's splendid blue eyes) nor to have roller skates or wagons. The girls played jacks and had all sorts

77

of silly different kinds of games called "Dropsies" and "Allsies" and "Cart before the horse." He did not think that Uncle Claude would be interested in knowing that the most exciting thing he and Molly did was to watch Miguel harness the team; if Star and Swanee offered any resistance and tossed their heads, the Mexican slapped them on the nose with his gloves or gave them a wallop on the rump. He was not in the least afraid, even when they neighed at him angrily and their velvety lips rolled up, showing green teeth and a line of grass-stained foam on the underjaw.

And Ralph was sure that Uncle Claude did not want to hear about their indoor pastimes. They had sets of water colors and boxes of plasticine and Mrs. Fawcett guided their fingers so expertly and so patiently that the results made everyone believe the children were unusually gifted. In the evenings and on rainy afternoons she played games with them. They played "Lotto" and "Authors" and "Parchesi" and "I Spy," all of which Grandfather Bonney had enjoyed. Sometimes she read aloud to them from *The Little Shepherd of Kingdom Come, Sevenoaks,* and *The Old Curiosity Shop.* When it was cool enough for a fire in the fireplace, they popped corn over the flames while the Edison played records of Grandfather Bonney's favorite songs: "The Green Hills of Home," "All Through the Night," "Old Black Joe," and "I Dreamt That I Dwelt in Marble Halls." All of them, by the time they were six, could recite "The Brook" and "The Chambered Nautilus," and often they said them in unison, standing in a row in front of the bay window, their mother smiling proudly at them when she looked up from her crocheting. Leah and Rachel embroidered dresser scarves and tops for pincushions and talked in a grown-up way with their mother about clothes, to his and Molly's embarrassment. Once Mrs. Fawcett had said, "I am making some curtains for Molly's sitting room," and held up a pair of bloomers, right in front of Ralph.

Ralph could not possibly tell Uncle Claude what a sissy life he had to lead. But he had to say something and so, doubtfully, he began, "Well, Molly and I got sick last year—that's why we're so funny looking but Dr. Haskell says we'll outgrow it. I didn't used to look like this. . . ."

Uncle Claude said nothing, and there was no possible way to tell what he was thinking for he did not smile or frown or have any kind of look on his face at all.

"Anyway, we are too skinny or something to do anything much. We play mumbly-peg a lot . . . we do a lot of things. I'm in the Yosemite Patrol. I'm going to tie knots at the Jamboree next spring."

Why had Uncle Claude asked if he wasn't going to listen? He went back to the bed and lay down in the same position Ralph had found him in.

"Don't you feel well, Uncle Claude?"

"I don't know."

"Did you ever hunt savage animals, Uncle Claude?"

"You mean like tigers?" he said. "Or do you mean like deer?"

"Either kind," said Ralph.

Uncle Claude narrowed his eyes reflectively. "I get me a deer now and again, but a man couldn't call a deer a savage animal. I never seen a bear or a mountain lion. The chances are they might put up a fight if you didn't hunt them just according to Hoyle."

"Is a mountain lion really savage?" said Ralph.

"Why, son, if you was a setting hen, he'd tear you limb from limb," said Uncle Claude and laughed.

A fat autumn fly thumped and fretted against the screen.

"Uncle Claude?" He put his hand out and touched the handle of Grandpa's grip. "Uncle Claude, I think that maybe there's something that belongs to me in here."

Uncle Claude did not open his eyes but he smiled and said, "Sure, help yourself."

The catches sprung back easily and the mouth of the grip gaped wide, showing the familiar gray wads of clothing, a suit of winter underwear, nearly black around the neck, a few blue work shirts, a pair of denim overalls. Ralph took out everything and shook it and looked in the pockets and in the toes of the socks, but there were no presents. He came finally to the bottom where Grandpa's big blue-black revolver lay, and though he again shook each garment as he put it back in, he found nothing but Grandpa's own belongings. So what had happened? Had he felt bad in Texas, too bad to go to Mexico? You would think that in that case he would at least have brought some rattles off a rattlesnake. It was incredible and it gave him a creepy feeling, knowing that this autumn they had been far from Grandpa's thoughts. And now he could not make Uncle Claude include him in *his* thoughts: he wondered suddenly if anyone in the world were thinking about him, Ralph Fawcett, at this moment. If anyone was, it was Molly sitting on top of the galoshes in the closet. For some reason he thought of the crazy pilot banking his plane like a hawk and he said to himself, "Pilot, whoever you are, I am thinking about you."

"Do you want to hear something funny, Uncle Claude?"
Uncle Claude shrugged his shoulders. "I'd just as soon."

"Well, the other day, I went to get some brown sugar and
I put a whole lot of it in my mouth and it wasn't brown
sugar at all. I'll give you three guesses what it was."

"Corn meal," said Uncle Claude.

"No, no. I mean it looked like brown sugar all right."

Uncle Claude next guessed dried milk and oatmeal even
though Ralph had explained that it had *looked* like brown
sugar.

"It was nitrate fertilizer that Miguel had got to put on
the four-o'clocks!"

Uncle Claude chuckled. At last Ralph had won. Pleased
as he was, he was a little disquieted because this had happened to Molly, not to himself, so he quickly said, "But don't
tell anybody because it would make Mother mad."

"I won't breathe it to a living soul," said Uncle Claude.
"You know it's a funny thing. At lunch I was just thinking
about the time Mr. Kenyon got this here impetigo and then
your sister said Beulah had the itch."

Why, he was wonderful! He didn't talk like the usual
kind of grown-up at all. Ralph thought he was probably
sincerely glad that Beulah got what she deserved for steal-
ing Molly's nickel. He said, "I like you, Uncle Claude."

Uncle Claude stretched out his hand, beckoning to him.
"I like you, too, Ralph." Then he lay down beside his uncle,
careful not to touch him. They lay there for a long time,
dozing and waking. In all that time, Uncle Claude did not
say a word, but twice he put his hand on the boy's thin
shoulder. For the first time in days Ralph was free of the

smell of flowers. Uncle Claude had a smell something like Grandpa's but it was younger and had less raisin in it, perhaps because he smoked cigarettes and his father had smoked a pipe.

Soon after they heard Mr. Follansbee cranking his car and driving off, Uncle Claude sat up and yawned and said, "You come on out next summer to my place and bring What'shername along."

"Well, I don't know if Molly can come. I think maybe something is going to happen to her."

"Like what? Is she going to have her adenoids out?"

"No. They're already out. I mean . . . well, Uncle Claude, strictly speaking, I think Molly's going crazy." Then he recited "Gravel" which he had read so many times that he knew it by heart.

Uncle Claude laughed but he was puzzled too and he said, "I wouldn't worry if I was you. I always did think that the folks that wrote poems were bughouse but harmless. No, you bring her along."

Ralph sucked at a wart on the heel of his hand, at first refusing the daydream, but he could not hold out against it and he allowed it to overtake him and to crowd from his mind all else: Grandpa's neverness, the sermon next Sunday, the darkness of the coat closet, the embarrassment of the meal they soon would eat.

When his mother called to him from the foot of the stairs, he left his shoes where he had put them, right beside the orange oxfords. But once again, when he had closed the door, the smell of flowers greeted him like an ocean wave. He moved toward his mother, toward Leah and Rachel, toward the portrait in the parlor. She called again sharply, "Ralph! How many times must I ask you to come downstairs."

"Hush," he whispered, leaning over the banister. "Don't you know Grandpa's dead?"

CHAPTER FOUR

THE BIG DINING ROOM WAS DIM BECAUSE A HOP VINE GREW over the windows. The foreman, the six hands, Mrs. Brotherman and her daughter, Winifred, Uncle Claude, and the Fawcett children all sat at one long narrow table which was covered with mottled red linoleum. In one corner of the room stood a gun cabinet which looked like an upended coffin and showed, in this half-light, the blue glint of a dozen barrels. On the long wall behind Uncle Claude, casting an enormous shadow of itself, was the head of a big-horn. The horns, like white half-moons, curled rakishly away from the stupid and dignified face; it did not look dead but only despondent, unlike the head of the doe in Mr. Fawcett's den which Mr. Follansbee had once said looked more embalmed than stuffed. Ralph realized that this was the first dining room he had ever seen in which there was not a still life of fruits or fish or a rare roast of beef. From this eccentric omission, he proceeded to observe other peculiarities: the knives and forks did not match and the dishes did not all have the same design; the spoons were in a tumbler in the middle of the table.

The men ate quickly and efficiently, bending their heads

low over their plates and not straightening up even when they spoke. The girl, Winifred, who sat nearest the kitchen door, kept a close vigil on the dishes and took them away the moment she saw they were empty and brought them back refilled. The food was strange and Ralph and Molly ate with mistrust. There was strong, tough meat which Uncle Claude told them was "buckskin." Too tongue-tied to ask what he meant by that, they listened for a clue and finally got it when Mrs. Brotherman made the chance remark that this was the last of the deer. There were string beans cooked until they were almost brown and there was fried mush with gravy. At either end of the table stood a quart can of strawberry jam and the men took out tablespoonfuls of it and ate it with their forks. Globules of cream floated on the top of Ralph's glass of milk and he could not drink it. Before each plate was a smaller plate with the dessert, a fried pie which was shaped like a rubber heel.

No one took any heed of the newcomers; perhaps they were as shy of the children as the children were of them, and Ralph and Molly endeavored to be as silent and small as possible and did not look around save when the talk was general and the speakers were off their guard. Ralph's first impression was that all these men were the same size and shape and color, that they were all large, spare, and red-brown, and this, in general, was true, but as the meal progressed, he saw that one of them was very blond, that another was handsome and had auburn hair, that a third had a flattened nose like a prize fighter's. Similarly, their voices had at first seemed indistinguishable from one another but in time he heard variations in the timbre and even, slightly, in the accents.

The talk was endless but it seemed to be made up almost altogether of non sequiturs. The men did not interrupt one another, but they did not listen. Questions were answered, but were usually reshaped to fit a statement that was uppermost in the speaker's mind. At the very beginning of the meal, Uncle Claude asked Homer Armitage, the foreman, if he thought it might not be a good idea to put in a strip of electric fence along the pasture where he kept one of his prize bulls, and Homer replied, "I never was a man for electric fence. If the current goes off, where are you? Old man Terry put some in once but I don't know if it was ever worth the money or not. Don't remember ever hearing anything more about it, only just that he put it in. I seen old man Terry today and he said he seen elk sign half a mile this side Wolf Forks. He said it was as clean as a whistle, and I aim to go up there this coming Sunday if the weather's good."

Uncle Claude and Homer retired into silence, the one to think of electric fence, the other of his hunting trip. Then one of the hands, who was named Dump, said, in the direction of Homer who was now bowed over his plate, "Bernard Tobey's got his still up there to Wolf Forks."

The man next to him said, "I knew Bernard Tobey in Glenwood. He was a barber there. I guess he got tired of drinking bay rum."

"Some people like Tobey and some don't," said Dump. "One that don't is Agnew Prescott. Those two hate each other like poison and have for a dog's age."

"Kenyon," said another man, "did you hear that Prescott took his bulls out to Denver last night?"

"No, I never heard that," said Uncle Claude. "I ain't tak-

86

ing any of mine till fall. I'm studying on whether I ought to sell Advance Anxiety."

Homer exclaimed with surprise and alarm, "Why, you must be touched! Why, my God, he's the best bull you ever had on this place."

Uncle Claude said, "You may be right. I reckon I won't sell him. I wonder if it wouldn't be kind of a good idea to put up a strip of electric fence around that pasture where I got him."

They had all been to a horse sale that afternoon, but each man made a different report. None of them had seen the same people or the same horses and none had heard the same bids, so that it sounded as if there had been eight different auctions in eight different places. And yet each knew what the others were talking about. Homer, who had not known that the blue-eyed stallion had been sold to a dude for seven thousand dollars—though, from Uncle Claude's account, this must have been the high note of the afternoon —said, "You mean that ugly old paint that Bill Prescott sold to Roger Campbell here awhile back? You mean that colt that was that little wild mare's, that one B. F. Ward got in Idaho?" They all knew the names and the lineage of all the horses in the country and they spoke of them as if they were people in the way, Ralph thought, fishermen would speak of boats. They talked of Ruth, the cow pony whose master had once hitched her up with a team horse when his other team horse had lost a shoe; of Poncho, a dandy little chestnut who had thrown Prescott once when he was three sheets to the wind; of Meadowlark who was herself an ugly piece of business but had foaled two good colts.

The children were tired from the long, halting journey

over the mountains from Denver where they had parted from their tearful mother. The train had not been like any they had ever been on before. Instead of little rooms with white towels on the backs of the seats and a little shelf by the window where the porter put the glasses of lemonade, there were just rows of bronze-green seats which were straight up and down and so hard you felt after a while your bones were going to come right through. The windows were dirty and the car was full of smoke. All the towns they passed through, pausing for a long time while freight was unloaded, were exactly the same. The buildings along the wooden walks had high square façades and on them, in faded letters, were printed "Livery," "Odd Fellows' Hall," "Assayor's Office." Undernourished dogs meandered about the streets looking for food in the ruts they already knew by heart. There seemed to be no trees in any of the towns, though the great shaggy mountains beyond were densely forested. The train had labored up and up, going right through the mountains, through tunnels too many to count. They spoke very little but each was conscious of the other's misgivings, and they did not eat any of the Martha Washington candy their mother had bought for them. Once Molly almost cried when they had stopped at a town called Blackriver and a man with a bandanna around his neck looked right in the window at them and then turned and spit tobacco juice at a cat. She felt the same surprise and anxiety as she had one morning when she woke up and saw a grasshopper on her pillow, looking at her.

They were bedazzled by the mountains and the ranch. They had not bargained for anything on so large a scale; it seemed beyond their compassing and they had already begun to withdraw. Ralph looked at the guns in the cabinet, so much bigger than he had imagined them to be from the catalogues, and now, while the whole point of coming had been to learn how to ride horseback, he was afraid. For months he and Molly had planned how they would defy their mother's injunctions ("If there is a Shetland pony there, you may ride that if someone is with you," she had said. A Shetland pony, indeed!) and how they would disobey Mrs. Brotherman who, through frequent letters, had promised that she would exercise the most stringent discipline to keep the children away from guns and horses. The moment they had met the sad, mild-mannered housekeeper, they had known that she could easily be shaken from her resolution and this, in itself, was enough to cloud their passion. Yet, though they no longer felt daring but on the contrary were afraid, there was no waning of their determination. They knew, both of them, that they would try to escape, would invent headaches, would have nosebleeds, would hide behind books, but they would not, in the end, successfully evade Uncle Claude; they were bound to learn.

It was the presence of the genteel Mrs. Brotherman that had finally persuaded Mrs. Fawcett to allow Ralph and Molly to come to the ranch. They had given her no peace after Claude had left and had had tantrums whenever she suggested the alternatives of Puget Sound or Lake Tahoe, and then, when Dr. Haskell said he thought the mountain air might be good for their catarrh, she finally wrote to her half-brother, inquiring whether he had any trustworthy womenfolk in his house who could watch out for the children's baths and clean underwear and health. She put faith in Mrs. Brotherman because she was from Salem, Massachusetts, and Grandfather Bonney had been born in Boston. Besides this, Mrs. Brotherman was herself a mother and a widow and could be expected, therefore, to be more responsible than a spinster or a woman with a husband.

Ralph and Molly had been prepared to dislike and mutiny against the housekeeper. They saw her as a stout, ill-natured and red-faced woman with all the power and habits of a school principal, so that this afternoon they had been astonished and almost disappointed to find her a fragile, dispirited gentlewoman who appeared to find everything in the world immeasurably sad and who spoke mostly in the past tense. She did not say, "I think you will want to wash before supper," but "I thought you would want to wash." She was the widow of a Swedenborgian minister who had come West to die in the sun of tuberculosis. After his death, she had not gone East again because her daughter was said to have a "tendency." Winifred was fourteen, a tall and lovely girl who did not look in the least delicate. She was very brown and clear-eyed; she had thick dark hair which she wore short and which lay in tight little curls all over her head. She had her own horse, a sorrel gelding named Noel since he had been Grandpa Kenyon's Christmas present to her the year she was twelve. Grandpa Kenyon had given her silver mountings for the bridle and a crop made of snakeskin.

Winifred was the first of the household they had met. They had stood, begrimed with train smoke, miserable, already homesick, in the shadow of a cottonwood tree while Uncle Claude got their suitcases out of the back of the car. The ride from the station to the Bar K had been difficult; Uncle Claude had three times inquired after the health of their mother and sisters, twice had said he was glad to see them, and this, together with the children's monosyllabic replies, had constituted their conversation. Now, in the shade of the summery tree, they felt doomed to failure. Unable to take in the huge, snaggle-toothed mountain ranges that completely encircled the valley where the ranch lay, alarmed by the rapid rushing sound of the river which they could not see, frightened by the steady commotion of animal noises—cows bellowing, horses neighing, dogs barking, birds screaming—they had been glad to fix their attention on one single thing, the girl who came riding her horse across the bridge which spanned a slough to the west of the house. She dismounted quickly and looped the reins around the hitching post across the lane from where they stood and when she started forward Uncle Claude told them about Noel, as if this would establish a bond between her and Ralph and Molly. But the gleaming horse, stamping his delicate foot and flicking his handsome tail, made the presents Grandpa had given them seem paltry and perfunctory. However, Ralph remembered that Grandpa had wanted to bring him a monkey from Australia. So, in a moment, he shook hands with Winifred, noticing as he did so, with a shock of pleasure, that her blue jeans were stained with dung, and he thought with contempt of Leah and Rachel who had never got their clothes dirty in their lives.

"I'm mighty pleased to meet you," she said and smiled showing small, even teeth. Ralph and Molly were taken aback by her words and her slow, uninflected speech. They had been taught that the expression she had used was vulgar. You were supposed to say "How do you do."

Molly said loudly, "Who are you?"

The girl looked startled but she smiled again and said, "I'm Winifred Brotherman. I know who you are."

"I don't suppose you write poetry, do you?" said Molly. Ralph wished she would stop that kind of talk. She had recited "Gravel" to the conductor just as the train pulled out of Los Angeles and although he had smiled and said the poem was fine and dandy, it had been perfectly clear that he had not thought much of it.

"Why, no," said Winifred. "I reckon I don't. I've got to go now and get the cows."

She mounted and rode off, over the river this time. Ralph hoped that Molly and Winifred would be friends so that he could spend all his time with Uncle Claude, and when he had finished his unpacking he went into her room and said, "I think Winifred's peachy, don't you?" Molly replied, "She has Nell Brinkley hair," and said no more.

Now, watching Winifred as she moved from the kitchen to the dining room on silent moccasins, Ralph admired her and glancing sidelong, he saw that Molly, too, followed her with fascinated eyes. Suddenly a wave of pity for his sister came over him and he impulsively touched her hand which rested in her lap. His pity was focused on her clothes: she wore a flowered batiste dress with a full skirt, smocked at the waist and at the neck and the prettiness of it made even more ridiculous her thin, freckled arms, her ugly little face framed by black hair with which, Mrs. Fawcett often remarked, nothing could be done. Molly, at the touch of his hand, turned and looked him full in the face and smiled wistfully. Ralph met her eyes only for a moment and then looked away, looked at Uncle Claude and saw that he was watching them inquisitively; he read the look as a question

92

of his worth or of his manliness, and abruptly, despite all these lean, red-faced strangers who, now that the meal was over were thoroughly picking their teeth, he said, "Uncle Claude, when are you going to teach me how to ride horseback?"

Mrs. Brotherman, putting her napkin in a bamboo napkin ring, gazed vaguely at the hop vines. His uncle smiled. It was again that winning, bone-enfeebling smile whose memory he had kept since last September; he was as friendly as a child and he said, "Is first thing tomorrow morning soon enough?" Then he got up and led the way into the living room, patting Ralph's shoulder as he went by. The others followed him in single file, all with a slouching gait as if they would otherwise be unsteady on their high-heeled boots. Ralph longed to join them but Mrs. Brotherman, in her unhappy way, said she was sure he and Molly were tired and should go to bed at once and Ralph realized that he was, indeed, so tired that he could hardly bear to think of going up the stairs and getting undressed.

Before he went to bed, he had a conference with Molly who came into his room and sat on a bench, hugging her knees. She had taken off her glasses and she looked like a black-eyed rabbit.

"Whoever heard of calling an animal Advance Anxiety?" she said.

"I thought of that, too," said Ralph. "But what would you do if you were a man and your name was Dump?"

"I would dump it."

"No, you would have to lump it."

They laughed, delighted with one another. Ralph had decided that Molly was not going crazy after all, although

93

there had been a period of a month during the winter when she thought she was going to be kidnapped and had worn a Hallowe'en mask in the school bus every day. She was just different from other people, he supposed. He liked her when they were alone, but she embarrassed him in public because she said such peculiar things. For instance, she said to Mrs. Brotherman this afternoon, "Do you have any opinion on the false Armistice?" and when Mrs. Brotherman said no, she really had not, Molly had said, "Oh, of course you don't live in California so you wouldn't have seen the Los Angeles *Gazette*." What she was talking about was the old newspaper they had with the one word PEACE printed in letters four inches high on the front page, but how was Mrs. Brotherman to know?

"Do you like it here?" said Ralph.

"I don't know. I'll tell you later. I don't like the food, I must say. String beans are the bane of my existence."

"I liked the buckskin."

Molly frowned and said nothing for a moment and then she said, "You know, I don't think I'll learn to ride horseback tomorrow. I think I'll wait for a few days as I have an idea for a short story about an amateur kidnapper."

How he regretted his headlong contract with Uncle Claude! He heard a horse snorting in the pasture right under his windows and his hands turned as cold as ice.

"Darn you," he said angrily to Molly, "darn you to heck. You *always* make up an excuse." He knew he was quite unreasonable; Molly had said nothing about learning to ride, but it seemed so unfair that she could always get out of anything by saying she wanted to write something. "All right for you," he said, "if you don't come tomorrow, you can't ever come anywhere with me again."

"My literature is more important to me than you are, Ralph Fawcett," she said coldly and left the room, pausing in the doorway to make donkeys' ears and say "Hee haw."

For the first weeks of this first visit to Uncle Claude, Ralph and Molly were not happy and most of the time they were afraid. The landscape itself was frightening. Above timberline the snow was thick in the deep gashes; to the north were two long glaciers which sometimes shone pink through the haze; this pinkness came from bacteria which inhabited the glacier snow, and when he learned this Ralph was curiously disgusted, he did not know why. Below timberline and above the dry sagebrush of the foothills, the forests of conifers were dense, their dark blue-green here and there interrupted by a small grove of golden aspens or a bright upland meadow where Winifred often went to gather columbines. The mountains were at once remote—their summits were often enshrouded by clouds—and oppressively confining. The children had been used to summers at the seashore and the sea, even in a storm, was something that could be taken in at one glance; its evils, however, were quite hidden, so that sharks and sting-rays, hurricanes and calms seemed only legendary and needed not be reckoned in their impressions; and even when they went out in a glass-bottomed boat and saw the fish all golden and green and huge, looking up at the passengers, they did not feel any of this was real but was only like a movie.

But the mountains wore peril conspicuously on their horny faces. Through Uncle Claude's field glasses they could look directly at the ledge from which a packhorse had slipped and fallen to her dreadful, screaming death. They knew the place where a bold dude had frozen in midsummer, having lost his way in a cloud when he was scaling an arête. The foothills were alive with rattlesnakes. At dawn the coyotes wakened them and through their windows they could see the small, shadowy sneak-thieves on the rim of the hill to the south of the house; the howling had a cold and beggarly sound, sometimes intolerably like an outraged human voice.

The house, spacious and rambling, made of white brick, faced north upon the fast stream called the Caribou River which cut the pasture land in half. On its banks grew cotton-woods and weeping willow trees, and dense amongst them, chokecherry and sarvis berry bushes. Here beavers made their clever dams and here hoot owls warned at night: there was no place that was not alive with something. A bridge led to the pasture on the other side of the river where the milk cows grazed and where there were cattails five feet high and where often the children saw blue herons. To the west was a broad, treeless field of timothy, bound on one side by the slough that ran along the red road; its west fence was parallel to the railroad track where the slow mixed train went past in the early evening, ringing its lone-some bell. The foothills leading to the summer range were to the south and the view of them was cut off through the lower windows of the house by a line of eight Lombardy poplars. Between the house and the road was the pasture, and the barn and the many sheds lay to the east.

Everything and all the people, with the exception of Mrs. Brotherman, made Ralph think of Grandpa, and he had the feeling that the old man's other ranches (which now

Uncle Claude would visit once a year in September) were similar, save that this was the only one in the mountains. The men were skillful, good-humored, hard, living within the present time and on a large scale. When they got drunk on a Saturday night, they did so with abandon, behaving exactly as drunk people in the movies did. Their lawlessness seemed natural. It seemed altogether reasonable that they hunted at all times except during the open season when, as Uncle Claude said, "there was too much danger of getting shot at by them dudes from Denver." The revenue officers and the game wardens intimidated no one; strangers to the country, they could not police all the hundreds of hiding places for stills in the mountains, nor could they catch the poachers who wanted wild meat and proposed to have it.

Ralph thought of the house in Covina with all its flurry of little objects, little vases and boxes on little gilt tables and whatnots hanging in the corners; and then thought of the big, bare rooms of the ranch where the furniture was heavy and solid as if it were nailed to the floor and the only small things were catalogues from L. L. Bean and Montgomery Ward, boxes of buckshot, fly-books, odd bits of leather and metal which had no use but which remained undisturbed, week after week, on the mantelpiece and the tables. He thought of the delicate food they had at home and then of the sage hen and puffballs and head cheese they had here, and Ralph felt that when Grandpa left them he must always have gone away hungry.

But the most amazing contrast of all was between Fuschia and Magdalene. Fuschia was young and pretty and good-natured but full of respect so that she called them "Miss Molly" and "Mr. Ralph." But Magdalene! She was the first

Negro besides Pullman porters they had ever seen up close. Molly was so frightened when the old woman took her hand in her skinny black one with its pink palm like a monkey's that she wanted to go home at once. Magdalene seemed hundreds of years old, so old that if she lived another century or two, she would not look any different. Her skin was not yellowish to show that she had white blood; it was rather as if it had faded to a bluish gray. Her lips were purple and they had so many lines that they looked like narrow grosgrain ribbons; her brown eyes were as mean and watchful as a chipmunk's, and the scraggly fuzz on her little head looked like dirty snow. She was not in the least kind; she was always smoldering with an inward rage or a vile amusement over something sexual or something unfortunate, and she spoke chiefly in obscene or blasphemous expletives. But she was wonderfully wise. She knew when it was going to rain and when someone was going to get sick and when a cow was going to get through a fence. Her wisdom was something antediluvian and cosmic and the almanac she went by dated back a million years before the fall of man. She was, Molly thought, the wife of the Skalawag at the Wash. She had her own little cabin between the barn and the bunkhouse and she raised white rabbits in a hutch beside it. No one ever saw the interior of it, but the children imagined that it must smell frightful, for not only were the rabbits so near, but she cooked strange things on her stove, things like beaver tails and the lungs and testicles of freshly butchered calves.

Up on a hillside, a mile behind the barn, Magdalene kept some goats of her own, milking them every morning before sunrise and again in the evening while the others were finishing their supper. One afternoon Ralph met her coming around the corner of the corral, carrying a dead and bleeding goat slung over her shoulder. In her free hand, she carried a small hatchet, bright with thick neck blood. Ralph asked her why she had killed her goat and she replied, "I was hongry, that's why, you lil ole June bug, so I went out and botched 'im on the haid." Uncle Claude could not remember where Grandpa Kenyon had found her, and she would never tell the children where she had lived before. When once they asked her where she had been raised, she said, "I wa'n't *raised*. A cow-bird laid me in the sagebrush and the sun hatched me out." They did know that she had two sons, named Salem and Jordan and a daughter named Psalmetta. Once Jordan sent her a bottle of Ben Hur perfume and while she laughed like a lunatic with contempt, she poured it all over herself and the kitchen reeked. It smelled like the cheap chocolates with pink fillings they got in Covina, four for a penny.

Magdalene's territory was the kitchen and she never went into the other part of the house, for besides bringing the food to the table, Winifred made the beds and did the cleaning. Magdalene did not like to have anyone fussing in her kitchen. She did not mind the men hanging up their chaps there or even having a cup of coffee in the middle of the morning if they were working around near the house; and she suffered Ralph and Molly to poke into the cupboards and watch her make pies so long as they did not ask for anything to eat, although occasionally she would give them bits of raw potato, always with the remark, "Knew a horse died of 'em." But she would not stand for Mrs. Brotherman, whom she called "Miz Bo-Bo" or "Miz Budmanny," or

Winifred to hover over her, and if, in the morning, she discovered that after she had gone to her cabin for the night someone had made fudge with her sugar in her pan on her stove, she swore a blue streak half the day through.

Molly got the idea that she looked like Magdalene and for some time thought that she was probably her daughter. She had never been at all certain about the circumstances of her infancy for Leah had told her that for the first years of her life she had been only the size of a talcum powder can and they had kept her on the mantel beside Grandfather Bonney's ashes. This was, of course, a big fat lie, but all the same there were some peculiar things about those early years. For example, she clearly remembered riding an elephant and the more she looked at her, the more certain she became that Magdalene had been the driver. But she did not ask her about it because Negroes were essentially the same as Mexicans and if you did not keep your distance from them there would be the dickens to pay. But she watched her and listened to her and in her diary she referred to her as "Mrs. Skalawag."

The one part of the ranch that was anything like home was Mrs. Brotherman's sitting room directly above the parlor. Mrs. Brotherman and her room always smelled of apples, giving the children a feeling of perennial Hallowe'en. Everywhere there were small baskets and bowls on the tables and hanging shelves, full of McIntoshes and winesaps and of Golden Grimes. As vivid as the smell, almost, was the sense of oldness in the room, coming from the furniture and the oddments and coming, as well, from Mrs. Brotherman's Boston accent and her strange syntax. Close as they lived to the Brothermans—the Fawcetts' rooms were across the hall

—they were invited so seldom into the sitting room that it always held an air of foreignness for them, and because they never got so used to it that they could take it for granted, the fruity fragrance always surprised them. So also did the coolness and the furniture which sat upon a dim cabbage-rose carpet, between walls on whose yellow paper were tidy rows of dark green laurel wreathes which cast oblique and questionable shadows. In the center of the room there was a large round table with a single stout leg. It was covered with a blue velours and the four corners hung straight to the floor, weighted and decorated with wiry gold tassels. On the table was an armadillo sewing basket which Ralph found so revolting that if Mrs. Brotherman asked him to fetch her scissors from it, he shuddered. There was a music box on the table which played first "O Mistress Mine" and then "Why Does Azure Deck the Sky?" There was a bust of Socrates on a shelf and a picture of George Washington over the fireplace. There were two wing chairs covered in chintz with tatted antimacassars on the arms and the backs, and there was a terrarium with a peaked roof in which grew brake fern, partridge berry, and wintergreen. She had a silver candle snuffer and a glazed bowl holding aromatic pine cones, a Van Briggle vase of everlastings, and a souvenir sofa pillow from the Garden of the Gods. There was nothing chipped or marred or stained or dusty; only time had altered the looks of things by draining away the colors as it had drained them away from Mrs. Brotherman's cheeks and hair and eyes. She was as secretive almost as Magdalene about her past life, but once, in a thin burst of expansiveness, she told them that before Winifred was born, she and Mr. Brotherman had gone to Manitou Springs for two weeks, and she showed them a photograph of herself and her husband, sitting on a rock, holding up two folding cups of mineral water. In the background was a cement pop bottle ten feet high. They both looked bleakly into the eyes of the camera. The children could tell by the looks of the narrow-faced and wasted man that he had been as sad as his wife; they concluded that she had been born that way and it was not her widowhood alone that had cast her into eternal twilight. They often spent hours with her helping her weed in her flower garden which was famous for its roses; she dried the petals for potpourri and gave them to the ladies who sometimes came to call in the hot afternoons to visit with her in her sitting room and drink iced tea and eat gingersnaps.

They liked Winifred more and more, although at the very beginning they had been in doubt about her because she had taken them swimming in the pool behind the barn and had said she was going in without her suit. But she didn't, of course, and after a while they realized she had only been teasing. They started a detective agency and found clues all through the foothills; they believed that Dump was running a gambling den in a gulch and they collected a great deal of evidence against him, but he outsmarted them all summer long.

Ralph could not make up his mind about Uncle Claude. One thing was certain, he was not as nice as Grandpa. He laughed unkindly at their blunders and told about them at the table. Once poor Molly asked who milked all the cows up on the range and he laughed so hard he made her cry. Mrs. Brotherman explained to her that this was a breeding ranch, not a dairy farm, but she was unconsoled and hated Uncle Claude for three days.

And still, he would occasionally give Ralph a friendly push or invite him to ride along with him in the pick-up to town, and when he did this he smiled with the same sort of generosity in his mobile face as Grandpa used to. The trips to town, though, were never a success. The sun was always so glaring on the asphalt that Uncle Claude was too preoccupied with his driving to talk, so Ralph stared at the fields where the whitefaced Herefords grazed and at the dreary, unpainted farmhouses that stood here and there along the road, unprotected by any tree, bleak and dusty in a grassless field. Then, on the way back, Uncle Claude was wrapped up in remembering what news he had heard in town and the purchases he had made, and while he was talkative enough then, Ralph was really not interested in learning that Bernard Tobey's horse had the sweeny or that Shorty Peterson had hired a Mormon kid who had been baptized a hundred and twenty-five times or that Roger Campbell, always as independent as a hog on ice, had refused to give back Claude's hackamore, maintaining that possession was nine-tenths of the law.

There were times when it seemed to Ralph that Uncle Claude was somehow trying to get even with his mother. Every time he took them riding, he would say, laughing as he got into his saddle, "I reckon your mother would have a set of dishes if she could see you now." It both thrilled and frightened them to think what she really would do, probably send them to the penitentiary. He and Molly rode only the oldest and safest horses, but something always went wrong. Uncle Claude told them that a horse had a sixth sense which could judge whether his rider was afraid and would, out of pure orneriness and show-off, play tricks on him if he were. So that the old white horse Eye-Opener whom Molly rode would pretend that he was half blind and would deliberately stumble into gopher holes so that she pitched forward, clinging desperately to the pommel with a flushed face and wide, staring eyes. And Studebaker, the black Ralph rode, refused to wade the streams. "Give him your spurs!" Uncle Claude would cry and Ralph would tentatively push his heels into the horse's flanks. "Harder! Give him something to think about!" So that Ralph would dig harder, driven by shame, mortally afraid of being thrown into the water. Then Studebaker, snorting, would fling back his head and rear so that Ralph had to rivet himself to the saddle to keep from falling; but he did not, like Molly, grasp the horn, for Winifred had told him that this was something only dudes did.

Although, more and more often, he enjoyed the rides through the ripe meadows and along the red roads, beside the river where the sarvis berry brushed its cinnamon-smelling flowers against his face, into the cow pasture as the sun was setting, Ralph did not outgrow his uneasiness at being so high off the ground and being dependent on so capricious an intelligence as that which lay in the long black head. And when he began to saddle his horse himself, it was hard to keep back the tears when he put the bit in Studebaker's enormous mouth with its enormous square teeth and yellow-green tongue. Uncle Claude occasionally praised him and his confidence grew, but he was so mean to Molly ("You set on that bench like a sack of potatoes," he would say to her) that she seldom went with them but stayed at home to help in the garden or to write. She was now writing an article for *Good Housekeeping* called "My Summer at the Bar K."

In the latter days of June a series of tragic accidents took place, following one another as if by a spiteful plan. A horse, frightened by the backfiring of a car, stumbled and fell on the rain-slick highway, breaking his leg and crushing the foot of his rider, Homer Armitage. Nauseated with pain, Armitage roused himself enough to shoot the horse and then lay half an hour in the road until a passing motorist found him. The men at the Bar K carried the dead horse in a truck up to the place where the coyotes gathered most often after they had robbed the henhouse, and they poisoned the meat with cyanide. Later, a magpie brought a chunk of the meat down into the yard where Uncle Claude's favorite dog, a beagle, found it, ate it, and died in convulsions. Ralph never forgot his uncle's rage when Magdalene brought him the news at dinner. He got up and went at once to the gun cabinet and then strode through the kitchen. Dump said, "I reckon he'll pick off a magpie. A man cain't blame him." Everyone was silent, waiting for the shot.

There was only one report from the .22, but Uncle Claude did not come back to his dinner, and someone said he had probably gone to bury the dog. When the meal was over, Ralph went out into the yard and there, beside the milk house, he saw nine magpies standing in a circle round a tenth which was dead. They were scolding in unison, their harsh, hawk-like voices clawing at the noontime quiet. Their impeccable feathers, coal-black and snow-white, gave them the look of professional mourners, formally attired. Ralph approached, but they did not fly away; instead, two turned and faced him, shrieking abuse and hopping with anger. Their racket continued until one of the men came out of the house and tramped through their circle to pick up the dead bird and fling it with disgust into the slough, crying back to the others, "Shut up, ya goddam buzzards." They left the ground then, but for a long while afterward sat in a neat row on the fence, remembering from time to time to mourn raucously.

Uncle Claude was mending fence today, Ralph knew, and after a decent time had elapsed, he got on Studebaker and set out for the farthest pasture, up behind the barn. He had hesitated as he mounted, partly because he had never ridden so far alone before, partly because he was not sure that he should intrude upon his uncle's sorrow, just as he had not been sure after Grandpa's funeral. But he thought that since the circumstances were so similar, they might again reach the same kind of amiable understanding they had done the other time.

It was hot in the sun and he had forgotten to bring his hat; the glare on the meadows was as blinding as if it shone on tin. There was a violet heat haze hiding the tops of the mountains toward which he rode. He was stupefied by the silence and by his solitude and by the even trotting of his horse who, today, behaved himself and even forded the river at the shallows with hardly any persuasion though Ralph, for an unseen audience, gave him his spurs and felt the rowels spin lightly against the tough flesh. Only once was he afraid, for it occurred to him that Uncle Claude might have finished the fence this morning and was mending somewhere else; the possibility of not fulfilling his mission made him uneasily self-conscious; he would feel like a sap when people asked him at supper where he'd been and he would have to say, "Oh, I just went for a ride," for no one here did anything without an end in view.

He ascended a ridge and then, across a wide field of alfalfa, he saw Falcon, his uncle's horse, cropping peaceably near the fence. Falcon, a young palomino and the handsomest horse on the place, was sought after by all the other horses, but he had singled out Studebaker as his particular friend and in the early evening, as soon as they were unsaddled, they trotted up the lane together and then went running up the road to disappear in the foothills. When they were pastured with other horses, they were stand-offish and if one of them came too near, Studebaker would rear up and kick the air with his hind legs.

Studebaker, catching sight of Falcon, neighed, his whole body shuddering with vibrations and then, though Ralph tightened the lines, he broke into a lope and then into a run. Ralph was claimed by the wildest terror he had ever known. The hot wind stung his cheeks and ears and his feet, flexing in the stirrups, his knees, hugging the horse, ached so intolerably he could have screamed with pain. Blinded by the speed and by the sun he could not see his uncle but he did see Falcon, huge, blond, his creamy mane waving, come running toward them, whinnying passionately. In his quick agony Ralph scanned the field in vain and screamed his uncle's name. Instantly from some place he could not determine, his uncle shouted "Falcon!" and the palomino slowed down with a final, disappointed whinny. But Studebaker paid no heed and raced on. Then Uncle Claude, appearing suddenly from nowhere, came running bare-headed across the field, hollering words Ralph

107

could not understand, and when he was fifty feet from them, Studebaker changed his gait to a gallop, but swerved suddenly to avoid the man and in doing so, reared, not high but so abruptly and surprisingly that Ralph's feet flew out of the stirrups, his sweaty hands turned loose the lines and he went crashing down into the sweet, gentle clover, his glasses falling off to lie unharmed beside his nose. He closed his eyes and listened to the hooves retreating and the lunatic neighs saluting and responding, listened to his uncle approaching him on running feet: "You damned little numskull, are you hurt?"

He did not know whether he was hurt and he did not care now that he was safe on the ground, but the annoyance in Uncle Claude's voice wounded him. Uncle Claude knelt down beside him and Ralph opened his eyes. The sunburned, sharp-boned face was, when Ralph first looked at it, so stern that he thought, "Now he will send me back to Covina." But then the look gave way to that rare smile and Uncle Claude said, "You better see if you're hurt. You can't trust that fool bench when he's around my horse."

Ralph sat up cautiously and pulled up his Levis. His legs were not hurt except for a big bruise on his left knee. His elbow was skinned and there was a bump on his left temple, but these were his only injuries. He was giddy, though, and the meadow swam like fishes under the high sun; then he realized that his glasses had fallen off and he groped for them with both hands as if he could not see at all.

Uncle Claude found them for him and handing them over, said, "What's the matter with your eyes that you have to wear those things?"

"I don't know. I've always worn them ever since I had scarlet fever. The nosebleeds come from that, too."

"Will you always have to wear them?" There was a curious eagerness in his voice. This was the first really personal question he had ever asked Ralph.

He replied, "I don't know. Dr. Haskell never said."

Both he and Molly had grown so used to their glasses that they did not even mind particularly being called "Four Eyes" by other children; indeed, there were times when they took pleasure in their weakness which distinguished them from others and which served, as well, as an excuse for not playing baseball or pom-pom-pull-away at which, before scarlet fever, they had been so poor that they were the last to be chosen on a team.

"Well, you look a whole hell of a lot better without them," said Uncle Claude.

"Thank you," said Ralph, although he realized it had been what his mother would have called "a left-handed compliment."

"What did you come up here for anyway?"

"I came to see if I could help you bury Juanita," he said.

"Well, that was nice," said Uncle Claude and Ralph, once more unsure of himself—despite the smile—thought he used the word "nice" contemptuously. "It wasn't much of a job. She was a little dog."

"Ken Burkhardt threw the magpie you shot into the slough."

"Did he now?" said Uncle Claude, but he was preoccupied; Ralph could not get through. He remembered a time when he and Grandpa were in the grove one Sunday morning; for some reason he had not had to go to Sunday school and he was exuberant with a holiday feeling, but he could not make Grandpa talk to him. He asked for a story but the old man refused, not crossly but distractedly. Ralph had felt compelled to force him to talk and so he began to ask questions: Was it true that if you swallowed a lemon seed a lemon tree would grow in your stomach? Did he like Post Toasties? Had he ever seen a buffalo, not in a zoo? Did he not think that monkeys looked a lot like people? Did he have very many dreams? At first Grandpa had answered briefly, but not unkindly, but then suddenly he jabbed the ferrule of his shillelagh into the ground and said sharply, "Dammit, lad, can't you see I've got something on my mind?"

Today he felt that same compulsion, even when he remembered how hot and faint he had been after Grandpa's rebuke, and seeing his uncle light a cigarette and lie down full length in the alfalfa, covering his eyes with his handkerchief, he said, "Where did you bury her?"

"Yonder," said Uncle Claude vaguely motioning toward the river. "By the shallows."

"Oh! I must have passed the place."

There was a silence. Studebaker and Falcon had calmed down now and were cropping side by side in the middle of the meadow. It was not really silent; there was a steady undercurrent of the noises of the land, but they were so closely woven together that only a sudden sound, like the short singing of a meadowlark, made you realize that everywhere there was a humming and a rustling. And then, the separate sound, the song or a splashing in the river, was like a bright daub on a dun fabric.

Ralph said, "Are you going to get a new dog?"

"Sure, I'll get me a new dog. I'll miss that little old hound but I'm not a fellow that goes to the mope-house over a dog."

"What is a mope-house, Uncle Claude?"

"It's a place where the niggers go and mope when somebody dies."

Uncle Claude grew rather talkative after that. He told Ralph that there were towns in Oklahoma where only Negroes lived and at the outskirts there were signs saying "White man, get out of this town before sundown." He said Ralph could come along with him this fall when he went to look at Grandpa's ranches; he'd be glad to have company.

"I haven't finished school yet," said Ralph. "I don't think I'll go on past the seventh grade. How far did you go?"

"Eighth. I wouldn't of gone that far if it hadn't been for your mother. Mr. Kenyon used to tell her and tell her that you couldn't make a silk purse out of a sow's ear but she didn't believe him. I reckon she believes him now, all right, after the way that preacher showed me up that day."

"I'll tell you something funny, Uncle Claude, about that day." And he told what Molly had said to Mr. Follansbee. Uncle Claude laughed so that his belt buckle hopped up and down on his stomach like a jumping bean. "That Molly!" he cried. "She's a caution."

"Do you like her?" said Ralph.

"Sure I like her. Sometimes she's too many for me but she's as funny as a crutch. Sometimes I don't think she is on purpose." He sat up, laughed again, and said, "Come on and help me mend this outfit. Just as quick as I get one stretch mended then she busts out in a new place. Beats me."

All afternoon Ralph worked like a grown man, holding

the posts steady while Uncle Claude nailed on the barbed wire. He was happy at first but gradually he got cross from the heat; the smell of alfalfa became cloying; a dozen times he asked his uncle what time it was. He was depressed at the thought of having to mount that crazy Studebaker again. Uncle Claude had said, when they were working on the first post, "A fall like that one don't amount to anything, but the first time it happens to you, you feel kind of worried." Ralph had replied, "Oh, I wasn't scared!" He wanted the time to pass quickly so that he would be safe at home again, but when he thought of the moment of getting into the saddle, he trembled all over and wished the sun would never set.

But when the time came, he was not afraid. Claude had something of a time catching Falcon who took it into his head to run around in circles like a trick horse, but he was outwitted at last and Uncle Claude led him to where Studebaker stood, for once oblivious of his friend. They were almost like people who were temporarily not on speaking terms. Ralph mounted and realized intuitively that he was in complete control of his horse. He spurred him at the river and Studebaker leaped forward at the pricking and then, when he had crossed the water, resumed a steady gait. Uncle Claude pointed out the place where he had buried Juanita and said, "I don't know why I wasted a bullet on a magpie. A dead magpie ain't going to bring back my dog." He said he would bring Ralph up here at dusk one day and see if they could catch the beaver that was damming up the west slough that ran off from the river at a right angle. He went on then to talk of hunting trips he had made and hunting trips he would like to make. This year he would miss his expedition to the Bear's Ears because he would have to make the rounds of the ranches. At the Bear's Ears, he hunted elk and deer and it was there that he had got the bighorn whose head hung in the dining room.

Two things he had never seen were bears and mountain lions. To be sure, they weren't anything a man would want to eat, but he'd like to see them anyhow. About fifteen years ago, before Uncle Claude came here, there had been a raft of mountain lions in this country, but they seemed to be all gone now. At least no one he knew had ever seen one.

"What do they look like?" said Ralph.

"How should I know? I just got through saying I never seen one."

"Well, I'd like to see one." He wished he would be hiking by himself in the mountains one day and suddenly come on a lion's den. He would shoot the mother and the cubs and then take Uncle Claude up to see. He could just hear Uncle Claude suck in his breath and say, "Well, I'll be a son-of-a-gun."

CHAPTER FIVE

O N A WINTER SUNDAY AFTERNOON WHEN RALPH WAS FOUR-
teen, the Follansbees had come to call and he and
Molly were sitting in their Sunday clothes and Sunday so-
lemnity on the hassock in the bay window. Looking at the
portrait of his Grandfather Bonney, Ralph read into his
face vacuity and self-pride; he saw the plump hands as
indolent and useless and believed that in a handclasp they
would be flaccid. He understood now why Grandpa Kenyon,
when he had used the word "merchant," had uttered it like
a curse. He decided that the world was made up of two
groups of people. The first he called "Kenyon men" and
this included those who, like Uncle Claude, knew the habits
of animals and subjected themselves to the government of
the seasons and who, with age, became neither fat and bald
like Grandfather Bonney nor bony and ragged like Mr.
Follansbee. The other group he called "Bonney merchants"
and this included everyone he had ever known with the
exception of the people at the Bar K, Grandpa, and Molly.
The fundamental distinction between the two groups was,
he thought, their attitude toward horses and, vice versa, the
attitude of horses toward them.

For four years now Ralph and Molly had divided their year between the men and the merchants. Their lives were like those of the children of divorced parents who spend a season of each year with their father and the bulk of it with their mother and who feel themselves thus split in half and sometimes find their memories confused, so that they cannot be sure what books have been read, which ideas acquired, which sounds and shapes perceived in the two separate households. Their own relationship was likewise a double one. At the ranch, they all but ignored one another, but in Covina, alone with their mother now that Leah and Rachel were away at boarding school, they were still close friends.

Their estrangement at the ranch had begun on a day late in August in the very first summer they went to Uncle Claude's, a day on which Ralph's whole life had been changed. Uncle Claude had taken him and Molly and Winifred up to the nearest of the glaciers. They went horseback as far as they could, a little below timberline, then hobbled the horses at an abandoned mine and climbed the rest of the way. Uncle Claude's clowning Newfoundland, Walter, charged into every pool they came to and slunk out, shuddering and coughing. Claude and Winifred were skilled and tireless mountaineers and the two of them went straight up without stopping, leaving Ralph and Molly far behind. When the children finally got to the top, weary, cold, hungry, and exasperated, they almost cried to see that the others had not waited for them there but had gone on and had climbed a cluster of rocks near by. They were sitting on the topmost one, side by side, and they laughed down and waved, turning then to one another to say something the children could not hear. Ralph was too depressed and too tired to take any interest in the vast slide of ice to which he had been looking forward for weeks, nor in the strawberry snow at the head of the glacier. Warm with resentment of Uncle Claude's desertion, he glanced around him casually and then joined Molly who had begun to pluck the waxy yellow orchids growing profusely there, for they had promised to take a bouquet to Mrs. Brotherman. Actually he was less angry than perplexed, for he did not understand why Uncle Claude should prefer the company of a girl to his nor, on the other hand, why Winifred should desert a child for a grown-up. Suddenly it occurred to him, stunning him, that Winifred was really not a child but was as old as Leah. This realization made him feel colder and tireder than ever and he would have lain down amongst the flowers if this would not have appeared an act of weakness to the sitters on the rock. He looked at his weedy sister with dislike as she crouched on her heels, plucking the lilies all around her, and when she looked up at him, her large humble eyes fondling his face with lonely love, he wanted to cry out with despair because hers was really the only love he had and he found it nothing but a burden and a tribulation. She kept a diary in which she recorded everything he said and everything he did and she insisted on reading each entry to him before they went to bed. At first he had been flattered but now he was only embarrassed. She was especially rhetorical on the subject of his shooting at which, if the truth were known, he was quite inferior. Molly would not learn to shoot, and she did not like to touch a gun even when it was unloaded, for their mother had frequently warned them that it was the unloaded ones that always went off. But she went on about Ralph's handling of his .22, under the tutelage

116

of Winifred, as if he were a champion. His first game was only a portly pack rat which had got into the potato cellar on the side of the hill, but later on he shot two jackrabbits and a sage hen. Molly wrote in her diary that he had shot three Rocky Mountain laughing hyenas.

For the most part she did not pester him much but hung around Winifred on whom she had a crush. But he was always conscious of her, always nagged by the suspicion that she felt left out. Half the time, though, it was he who was left out like right now when Winifred had stolen Uncle Claude.

Later, after they had eaten their lunches of salmon sandwiches and Baby Ruths, Uncle Claude offered to let Ralph look through his binoculars to see if he could spot any automobiles on Cuthbert Pass, and when he took off his glasses, Uncle Claude said, "Why don't you leave them things off all the time?"

And Ralph obeyed. He began by not wearing his glasses for an hour at a time and then for two hours and then for whole days except when he went out to shoot. It caused him at first to have hammering headaches and they, in turn, made him eventually vomit and then writhe miserably on the settle in Mrs. Brotherman's sitting room with a damp washcloth over his forehead. But he persisted, and within a few weeks his headaches came infrequently and he was able to see almost as well as he had done with his glasses. Molly tried it too, but in vain: her eyes were much worse than his and without her glasses she was as blind as a mole. After that, everything happened. For example, Uncle Claude took him one day to a deep wet-weather branch where a cow was calving and at the moment he saw the horrible little hoof appear, he felt a painful exultation and he tried to remember what Maisol and Maisako had said that day in the watermelon patch. He was not in the least embarrassed, only filled with wonder at the bewildered wet calf that was finally born and immediately stood up although it was so small and weak it swayed piteously under its mother's big rosy tongue. But when he told Molly about it, she stuck her fingers in her ears and screamed at him, "You're a liar! You're a dirty liar!" and her nose began to bleed.

And Uncle Claude always let him help with the butchering when he was doing it himself. He would shoot the steer through the skull and then would fling his pistol to the ground and run to slit the creature's throat. He stood back after that while the blood gushed out and waited until the reflexes stopped and the dainty legs ceased kicking. Most of the process was sickening, but there was one part he liked and this was the skinning of the carcass after it was strung up. The tight hide came off like an eggshell under his sharp knife and he was always surprised that there was no blood at all and that when the hide was off, nothing showed but another skin of white fat. It looked like someone in winter underwear. He turned his head aside when Uncle Claude commenced to draw it, for the blue guts were hot and steamy and as they slithered out, they stank like a backhouse. Sometimes, by accident, the knife went into the stomach and then green grass came bulging out, fetid and slimy like the stuff around the stems of zinnias that had been too long in water. Ralph carried the tongue and the liver in a pail to the kitchen and the bloodthirsty old Negro woman looked on them as greedily as a scavenger bird.

For four summers now Ralph had been his uncle's constant companion. Occasionally they went into town in the early evening to visit one of Uncle Claude's friends. They would sit around the kitchen table drinking iced tea or sometimes home brew; Ralph had Coca Cola or Orange Crush which Uncle Claude would buy at the drugstore on the way. They talked of murders, of hunting, of horses, of dudes. Some nights, though, Uncle Claude went in alone, not telling anyone what he was going to do, and deeply and secretly Ralph suspected that he was going to a particular street whose nature he would not allow himself to imagine. It was a street one block long and on either side of it were small white one-room houses; at the end of the block there was a larger house made of red brick where lived a woman named Dago Mary who one day had called out to Ralph as he was hurrying by at dusk to meet Uncle Claude at the post office and had asked him to run down to the drug store to get her a package of Luckies and an ammonia coke. He had not even refused; he had run on, his heart pounding. Often, on those nights when Uncle Claude had set forth mysteriously, Ralph thought of how, before he had seen the birth of the calf, he had been like Molly, savagely refusing the knowledge of such things, but now, bad as he knew it all to be, it sometimes gave him a warm feeling like cocoa on a cold night.

Winifred did not like him and he did not know why. In the very first year he had tried to win her by praise, by telling her jokes, by teaching her Boy Scout knots, but she was always aloof with him. And then one day, they had a real falling-out. They had gone hunting and he had shot a prairie dog but she had not hit anything. They sat down to rest on a knoll near the river and Ralph, on an impulse, asked her if she had ever heard about the time Grandpa Kenyon had killed a man. He had assumed, in his possessiveness of Grandpa, that she would not possibly know and his question was rhetorical, holding the expectation of her astonishment and eagerness to hear the story. He even forgot for a moment that Molly knew and that Leah and Rachel and the Follansbees did; he felt that he was offering Winifred a new and precious gift, so that he was completely taken aback when she said she had known it before Ralph was "dry behind the ears." She spoke with such ferocity that he blushed deeply. Molly turned on Winifred, enraged. "He was not your grandfather! He was *ours!*" Winifred jumped up, her eyes blazing, and she said, "He was as much mine as he was yours. He wasn't any *kin* to you, you dirty little snobs!"

Recalling this now as he looked at the portrait, he wondered if there were not some kind of operation you could have to drain off the Bonney blood in you. You could then have a transfusion from Uncle Claude. The terrible danger was that he might get fat like his mother; it was awful that she had named him for Grandfather Bonney and that she kept saying all the time that she wanted him to be exactly like him when he grew up. Sometimes he really hated her just as he had moments of intense hatred for Mr. Follansbee when, listening to the sermon, he knew that he did not believe in God. Especially he hated his mother when he hurt her feelings and she cried. The tears did not move him, nor was he taken in when she blubbered that he was all she had left in the world, but he could not bear the display: her pretty face became dropsical and red and she made piping noises like a fretful kitten. She was a Bonney merchant, through and through.

Ralph handled the symbols of his life delicately like superstitions. Round Grandfather Bonney's portrait and urn he walked with care lest he arouse his ghost, and when, on the anniversary of Grandpa Kenyon's death, he went with his sister and his mother to lay flowers on the gravestone, fixed his attention on the impersonal junipers that hugged the slopes of the low mound and refused himself the memory either of the living man or of the corpse in the parlor. For he believed that if he did not allow even his most hidden mind to prefer one dead man above the other, Grandfather Bonney would not creep forth to haunt and discolor his days at Uncle Claude's where his whole existence betrayed his mother. She knew, to be sure, that he rode and shot and was around dangerous machinery and she cried a good deal over this and there was always a wretched scene in Denver when she saw them off on the train to the Bar K. But she was secretly glad to be rid of her volatile two in the summer and to bask in the sunny dispositions and pretty faces of her two older children.

Today, in the damp twilight, Ralph seemed unable to escape the man in the portrait and he was filled with a terrible physical disgust. Momentarily he closed his eyes and allowed the voices to seep into his mind. His mother was speaking of him and she was saying, "You know, Mr. Follansbee, the single disappointment in my father's life was that he had not studied law at Harvard. It is my dearest wish that Ralph will."

Mr. Follansbee, who had a "digestive condition," belched slightly and perfunctorily sought pardon. He said, "An excellent plan, Rose. And how about it, sonny, how do you feel?" He did not expect an answer; he was a rhetorician and cared little for give and take. He made a speech as if he were in the pulpit, scattering Latin phrases where they fell and bringing in such subsidiary matters as a friend named Dr. Lucius Kennedy who lived in Somerville, a felicitous conversation he had held with a Mr. James Brooks on a bench in the Boston Common, and a Pasadena lawyer of high reputation who had been discovered recently to be the owner of a still in the neighborhood of Carson City. He concluded, addressing Ralph directly, that it would be an ungrateful son who did not grant his mother's dearest wish. He pointed to the portrait and said, "Emulate *him,* my boy. For he was a man among men, a man whose motto was the single word 'Honesty.'" Ever since the scene in this room on the day of Grandpa's funeral, Mr. Follansbee had been spitefully on the look-out for ways to nettle him and Molly. He would refer obliquely to "tall tales," to Paul Bunyan and Baron von Munchausen and pinching Molly's sallow cheek would say, "Hello, hello, my pretty little fairy. Take care you don't fly away."

Now he spoke of the fine blood that ran in Ralph's veins (it was as if he had read his mind!) and went on to speak of the love that bound a son to his mother. Ralph's embarrassment—the preacher ruthlessly kept his eye upon him—was so febrile and agitated that he could not keep his feet and hands still and they danced foolishly. He tried in vain to envisage Uncle Claude, but could see, in his mind's eye, nothing but his mother, bending over him anxiously as he lay sick of scarlet fever, the neck of her gray silk blouse open so that her breasts showed. And then, once, her image was replaced by that of Grandfather Bonney, Tennyson, and President Cleveland plodding arm in arm toward the sand bar.

When Mr. Follansbee had paused, Mrs. Fawcett said, "I know many things may happen in these years before he is ready to go to college, but I do not feel that anyone has ever suffered by taking the longer view of things. Besides it is not much more than two years. When the time comes, I will sell this place and we will go East to live."

"Not me," said Molly.

Mrs. Fawcett smiled. "Molly doesn't want to do anything anyone else does."

"The rugged individualist," said Mr. Follansbee with a chuckle. "Well, Molly, what do you want to do?"

It was, Ralph knew, all she could do to keep from sticking out her tongue. "I want to stay here with Grandpa," she said.

They all were shocked. The depths of this child were unfathomable and Mrs. Fawcett at times was really afraid of her. Somehow time did not soften her, did not make her have thoughts and feelings like other children. Now Ralph, although he was still unusually sensitive and in some ways eccentric, had normal interests—much as she wished the object of his admiration had been someone of more culture and refinement than Claude Kenyon, Mrs. Fawcett was bound to admit that it was right for him to enjoy the company of a grown man—and, moreover, he was beginning to look . . . well, to put it bluntly, to look like a human being. But poor Molly, although she had shot up and was taller than any of her schoolmates, looked just the same as she had done when she was eight. And the things she said!

Mrs. Fawcett faltered, "Molly, dear, you mustn't say things that make us sad." Molly stared at her and curled her lip. Mrs. Follansbee rescued them, asking in her domestic voice, what sort of house Mrs. Fawcett would buy in the East. She said she would settle somewhere in Connecticut, near Aunt Rowena, and that in the winter she would rent a house in Cambridge so that Ralph would not have to lead the irregular life of the dormitories. It was planned, parenthetically, that Molly would go to a boarding school in the vicinity of Boston and would then go either to Radcliffe or to Wellesley. Mrs. Fawcett said, "I should like *one* of my daughters to be a college woman, and the other two give me no hope—they write of nothing but beaux."

It was time for tea and Mrs. Fawcett rose to wheel in the table from the dining room. As she passed her son, she stooped and kissed the top of his head and with a small, sweet-smelling hand, patted his cheek. And then, as a sop to her conscience, she ran her fingers through Molly's hair. The preacher and his wife smiled benignly on the scene, exchanged the sorrowful glances of the childless, and the man belched, the woman sighed. In the few minutes that Mrs. Fawcett was gone from the room, the Follansbees changed their pious, general tone and inquired of Molly and Ralph lightly and condescendingly—Mrs. Follansbee speaking in a very loud voice—whether they did not keenly look forward to going to college.

Molly said, "We're not going to college, neither one of us, and we decided that before you were born."

Mr. Follansbee humorously clucked his tongue. "And what do you Methuselahs intend to do?"

She said, "We will get married and stay right here with

Grandpa." And then she turned to her brother and said, "Won't we?" She would never believe him when he told her that marriage was not what she thought it was. The first summer at the ranch she had wanted to marry Studebaker and a long time ago she had told everyone at school that she was engaged to Schöneshund. The Follansbees looked at her with horror and Ralph whispered in her ear, "Don't say anything more. I'll tell you why later."

There was always a long, uncomfortable pause when the water was coming to a boil over the spirit lamp, and no one seemed to be able to think of anything to say. Today, as always, there was an expectant hush and Mr. Follansbee's stomach made a noise like a querulous voice. Disgust overwhelmed Ralph. Would they never take their awful Bonney bodies away?

He took a drink of his tea and said, "The milk is sour, Mother."

"Nonsense," she replied. "I poured it into the pitcher myself. Mr. Vogelman brought it this morning."

He drank again and repeated, "It's sour, I say."

Sour spit flowed from behind his jaws into his mouth and he swallowed desperately. He tried to think of something else but he could think only of milk and of its smell. Shaking like an old man, he returned his cup to the tea wagon and said, "May I be excused? I am going to be sick."

"The milk is fresh," insisted his mother. "Sit down, son. It is very rude to behave this way."

"My brother will be sick," said Molly dully, stating a fact. He put both hands over his mouth and ran to the door. His illness lay in small pools of froth on the carpet and all the way up the stairs to the bathroom. When he had finished being sick, he went to his room and lay down on the bed with his eyes open, watching the green sky darken and the rosy clouds divide, assume new shapes, then disappear from sight. He did not know what had happened to benumb him in this way, and he knew that the milk had not been sour. But he felt as disabled as he had done when his tonsils were removed and the ether mask had been fitted over his nose. He had never forgotten the blue, spicy smell; now, six years later, he could remember it accurately and he gagged again.

He could take no pleasure in thinking of the Bar K. Next summer would bring him closer to the end of these summers, nearer to New England, a cloudy abstraction no more imaginable than the world of sleep. He knew that his mother would not let him go back, once she settled in Connecticut. He could not bear the thought of not seeing Uncle Claude again and the ranch itself and the mountains which both he and Molly loved as if they owned them. Sometimes he went swimming naked in the cold, amber pool of the Caribou behind the barn. (How long ago it seemed that he and Molly had been horrified when Winifred had said she was going in without her suit!) Alone in this rustling, humming wilderness, he pretended that he was an Indian. Later, coming back to the house, he paused on the ridge to the west of the barn and surveying the buildings and the pastures, he imagined himself as Uncle Claude's partner, saw himself riding in a caboose to Mexico with carloads of stock in front of him, saw their consultations in the office on what to buy and what to sell. In time, growing taller and filling out, people would take him for Kenyon's brother, Grandpa's younger son. Often he went climbing with Molly and Winifred. They hunted for beaver dams, filling their pockets, for no reason at all, with the chips of wood that littered the ground around the fallen trees. They found sweet piñon seeds which covered their hands with pitch that smelled like medicine. Winifred had taught them how to climb without getting winded and to go up the chimneys of the pinnacled red rocks, their hands on either wall, their rubber-soled shoes squealing at their pressure against the narrow footholds. Each time they went into the mountains, something unusual happened: they would come upon a ranger's saddled horse, cropping in a field of columbine, an old man panning for gold in a stream. Once they found an empty whisky bottle covered over with pine needles in a place so far from everything that they could not imagine what sort of person had put it there. From a favorite cliff they looked down into the valley and could see the pretentious dude camp west of Uncle Claude's, set in a barren waste of scrub oak and sage. A cattle train, puffing out a clean-lined cloud of white smoke, burrowed through the red banks like a mole, disappeared, and sent back a faint, protesting valedictory. There was always the possibility that they might see a mountain lion; they never did, but often they saw eagles.

The very life would be crushed out of him if he were deprived of all this! Of late, he had been wild with all sorts of angers and with an anxiety which he could not name but which pestered him continually so that he could not keep his mind on reading and sometimes he could not even pay attention to the movies. Sometimes he loathed his physical being for the alterations that were taking place in it: when his voice cracked, he wanted to die of shame, and when Molly laughed at him, he was abjectly humiliated.

He was filling out now; he had lost his pallor and his eyes, quite strong, were clear. He would have taken pleasure in his appearance if it were not for Molly with her ugly face and her lankiness and the slouching, round-shouldered gait which she had developed and which caused her enemies to call her "the crab." There was something wrong with her and while he still loved her, he wished oftener and oftener that she did not exist.

The sky darkened suddenly and in a few minutes it began to rain. The calm sound of it in the turquoise berries outside his window soothed him. He lay as still as a stone. He thought: there was something preying on Grandpa Kenyon's mind that day—perhaps he knew he was going to die —and that was why he had absent-mindedly tapped the turquoise berry with his shillelagh. That was the sort of meaningless thing you did when you had a great worry.

As soon as Ralph left the room, Molly returned her cup to the tea wagon and said, "If you will pardon me, this is the pause in the day's occupation which is known as the children's hour."

Mrs. Fawcett shook her head and sighed, "She's simply not happy unless she can be with Ralph. If he's asleep, don't wake him."

Mr. and Mrs. Follansbee said, "Good-bye, Molly," and Molly said, "So long," so that she had to come back and curtsy and say it properly. She stepped around Ralph's sickness which the grown-ups had chosen to ignore. It was just spit and it was already sinking into the carpet.

She had no intention of going to Ralph's room. It had been perfectly clear that he was not going to marry her and she suspected that he was going to marry Uncle Claude. She went down the hall to the kitchen. It wore its Sunday-afternoon look of lifeless cleanliness. Fuschia did not prepare their supper on Sunday night but left a pot of soup to bubble slowly on the back of the stove. This was all they had except toast and peanut butter and a chocolate drop a piece. The funny papers were on top of the refrigerator and she read "Out Our Way." It was very funny today. The two kids and their father were out cleaning the backyard and getting terribly dirty. They had to pass the living room door to get upstairs to the bathroom to wash and the mother was having company. So they took a sheet off the line and the father said they would all get under it and it would just look like a white flash going past the door, but it didn't work because they got mixed up and went *in* the door instead of *past* it. She laughed for a moment and then, looking in the mirror over the sink, she said, scarcely moving her lips, "Ha. Ha. Tee. Hee."

Molly let herself out the back door without a sound. Budge, who was old now and insensate, lay on the top step, unmindful of the rain, but she did no more than look at her and murmur, "Hi, purr-cat."

She went to the shed where the bleaching vats stood ready for the next year's harvest. There was a chemical smell here and this, together with the murkiness and the drizzle against the window panes, made her think of *Dr. Jekyll and Mr. Hyde* and she proceeded as if she were walking in her sleep. She went directly to the beakers of acid on their racks which Miguel had warned her and Ralph against since they were tiny children, pulling out their stoppers to show the sour blue vapor emerging from the hidden heat.

One drop of it, he said, on the bare skin would hurt like a red-hot poker and he put an eye dropper of it on an old piece of canvas to show them how quickly it would eat through any substance. Miguel had taken a correspondence course in chemistry and the shed looked almost like a laboratory with test tubes everywhere stained purple and green and bile color; there was a Bunsen burner and a collection of beakers of bizarre and attractive shapes. He experimented with all kinds of things; once he had let Molly and Ralph watch when he combined his spit with something and it turned bright green. Ralph asked him if the acid would burn off warts, but Miguel said no.

There was a test tube marked H_2SO_4 which Molly knew was the most dangerous of them all. That was what was used to make the walnuts pale. She took the small flat cork out and smelled the nasty smell. Then she held her left hand over a basin and poured the contents on it. At first it did not hurt at all; it stung a little like the liquid soap in the basement at school, but that same blue smoke came up from her hand and almost at once big puffy blisters came out, as white and opaque as mushrooms, and there was a new and terrible smell. The smell, not the blisters, alarmed her and sent her plunging to the sink where there was a cold water tap. But the more water she allowed to flow over her hand, the bigger the blisters got and when she took her hand away and sniffed at it, the smell was worse than ever. Then she began to cry, not with pain but with terror at this odor of her destruction and she stood in despair in the shadowy room, full of the sound of rain.

She ran out of the shed as if she were being chased and

back through the kitchen sobbing, "Mother Mother! I have hurt myself!"

Ralph was in the kitchen cutting himself a piece of raisin bread so she knew he had not been very sick, and when he heard her, he stumbled out, dropping the knife on the floor.

"Look," she moaned, "look what happened to me."

The pain was not severe; it was the knowledge that the acid was *eating* her, the way the Follansbees were eating cake, the way Ralph had been about to eat the raisin bread, and in this revulsion she paid no attention to her brother who was saying, "What *is* it, Molly? What did you *do?*"

She sat down at the table and put her head on her right arm and stretched out her left arm in front of her so that Ralph could look at the burn and she wept with pity. Ralph stared and impatiently repeated, "What *is* it?" until finally she was able to say, "Miguel's acid," and then he went crying along the corridor to the parlor as she lifted up her head and screamed, "Help! Help!"

Molly lay on the lounge in her father's den and refused to answer any of their questions. Through her half-open eyes she saw them standing in a row beside her: her mother was wearing a pink dress with an accordion-pleated skirt and her cheeks were as pink as the cloth with passion as she insisted, "Tell Mother, my baby. Mother is not cross with her little girl," but Molly knew that this was a lie for she heard the anger in her voice as clearly as she saw it in Mr. Follansbee's eyes which were green like the cases of fish in the aquarium. He stood at the foot of the lounge, looking from time to time at his watch. He had promised Mrs. Fawcett that he would stay until the doctor came, but he was nervous for fear he would not have proper time for his supper before Epworth League. Mrs. Follansbee, who had declared herself to be "chilled to the marrow," sniffed into her handkerchief and often repeated that the best thing in the world for burns was butter. Molly thought slyly: then the acid would eat the butter; the acid would have a buttered hand sandwich. Ralph stood at the head of the lounge and she could not see him but every so often he stroked her forehead and said, "It won't hurt in a little while."

At last they heard Dr. Haskell's car in the drive and Molly said, "I don't want you to stay in here."

"Young lady," began Mr. Follansbee, but Mrs. Fawcett checked him with a wave of the hand and said, "Yes, sweetheart, if you are sure you won't be afraid."

"Ralph can stay," she said and Mrs. Fawcett looked at Mr. Follansbee and said, "You see?" and then they left the room.

Both Molly and Ralph had always been fond of Dr. Haskell who did not take their mother seriously and who had a nice angular face and curly red hair. When they had scarlet fever, he brought Molly a brown candy reindeer and Ralph a bear. He drew up a chair and glancing at Molly's hand said, "Molly, you give me a pain in the neck. I was just sitting down to my supper and I was going to have waffles."

"I can't stand waffles," said Molly, and Dr. Haskell laughed.

"Now tell me what you did this time," he said, picking up her hand and touching the blisters lightly with his finger.

She could have told the truth without embarrassment, that she had done it on purpose to punish Ralph, but while she liked Dr. Haskell, she did not entirely trust him. Once he had told Mrs. Fawcett that she and Ralph were "nervous" and their mother was stricter than ever after that, saying, "I think you need a little rest. We don't want to get tired out and then be nervous, do we?" The word "nervous" came to be as disgusting to her as "body." So now, if she told the truth, she had no assurance that Dr. Haskell would not tattle—for that matter she was no longer even sure of Ralph, and she said, "I went out to the shed to see if I could find my art gum."

Ralph said quickly and suspiciously, "Why would it be in the shed?"

"I thought maybe Miguel had borrowed it." Now she was disquieted and her heart beat strongly. "I was looking around there but it was dark as a pocket and all of a sudden I knocked over a little bottle of stuff and it went all over my hand."

Dr. Haskell went to the door and called across the hall, asking for a basin of hot water. Coming back, he said quite matter-of-factly, "And the cork was out of the bottle?"

"Yes," said Molly. "Yes, it was."

The doctor clucked his tongue. "That is very careless of Miguel. We must speak to your mother about it."

"Oh, no!" she cried. "Oh, please don't! Miguel would knock my block off. It wasn't his fault."

The doctor's smiling glance went straight through her and he said, "This time, then, I won't. But if it should happen again, Molly . . ." And his smile went off like a street light.

"What did you do then?" asked Ralph.

Molly, remembering the basin where some of the acid would still be lying, remembering the cork which had just been sitting there beside the rack of test tubes, was afraid now and her hand began to hurt dreadfully. She whimpered, "I put my hand under the water faucet, but it didn't do any good."

"I guess not," said Dr. Haskell.

Mrs. Fawcett, returning with the basin which steamed into her face, asked, "It isn't serious, is it, Doctor? I cannot tell you how often and often I have warned them about the acids."

Dr. Haskell said, "It isn't too serious. There is danger of infection, though, if we are not careful."

"Infection!" cried Mrs. Fawcett, stumbling from the room, her hand pressed to her bosom, and Molly's heart said, "Goody! Goody!"

For some weeks it seemed possible that Molly might lose her hand. She wore upon it a cast of paraffin, for Dr. Haskell was afraid that if air got to the wound and a scab formed, the acid would continue to eat its insidious way through the flesh. In time it began to have so unpleasant a smell that she lay in bed with her arm stretched out, her head turned to the wall and a sachet of lavender pinned to her pillow. The pain was never great, but she was obsessed with the horror of being consumed alive.

She did not go to school for a few days and as this was a time of cold rain, she stayed indoors reading *Bleak House*. It was not like being sick, for she did not have to stay in bed but could go wherever she liked in the house. Sometimes she sat in the parlor and sometimes in the guest room, but usually she sat in her father's den. People rarely came in there except to use the telephone so she would not be bothered in the middle of a paragraph by someone saying, "How do you feel, Molly girl?" or "Would you like some Ovaltine?" People were always looking at her and she knew none of them believed it was an accident. Ralph hadn't, from the beginning, and the night it happened Ralph came into her room and whispered, "If you have to do dumb things, I don't see why you have to be so dumb about it. I went and got the cork."

"I did it to punish you," she said.

"What did I do to you?"

"You said we were not going to get married and stay here."

"Molly!" he said irritably and then, more kindly, "I never said that."

But though she asked him every day if they were going to get married, he always somehow changed the subject. She had almost come to the conclusion that she would marry Dr. Haskell.

One day Mrs. Fawcett came into the den to sew. She had never done this before, but Molly could tell by the way she frowned as she bent over the buttons that she meant to tell her something of importance. Molly glanced at her from time to time over her book.

"Molly," she said at last, "what do you do at Uncle Claude's all the time? Do you play with other children your age?"

"Of course not," said Molly. "What do you think he lives in? A *town*?"

"But what do you *do?*"

"I swim. I hike. I ride Eye-Opener. I talk to Magdalene."

"Magdalene? Oh, the cook. I wouldn't talk too much to a darky if I were you, Molly."

You would, thought Molly, if you were probably a darky yourself and Magdalene's own child.

Molly said, "What do *you* do while we're gone?"

"Why, just what we always do," said Mrs. Fawcett with surprise. "Do you know, Molly, I sometimes think you and Ralph are happier with your uncle than you are at home."

"I do not believe in happiness," said Molly.

Mrs. Fawcett bit her lip. "That is a very foolish thing to say. You are a very foolish girl, Molly." She had something up her sleeve. She said two mysterious things. She said, "Well, I used to think it was wrong to let you go, but now I think it's a very good place for you at your age. There must be lots of cunning little calves and lambs and colts and so forth." Molly did not know what her age had to do with it; the colts and lambs and calves were a lot younger than she was. And the other thing was, "I hope you don't try to tag along with Ralph too much." Molly replied with falsehood, "I am with him every minute every day every week every month."

They did not talk for a while and Molly went on reading about the man who went up in spontaneous combustion from drinking too much gin. Shortly before the school bus came, Mrs. Fawcett let the cat out of the bag. She said, "Molly, I wonder if you and Ralph wouldn't like to spend a whole year with Uncle Claude?"

"Why?" said Molly. She was not at all sure she would

like to spend a whole year at the ranch. The public library was too far away, for one thing.

"I just wondered because, well, Molly, I may as well tell you. Now I don't want you to be disappointed because your turn will come. I am going to take Leah and Rachel around the world."

"When?" said Molly tensely, closing her book.

"As soon as Rachel has finished school. This spring." Leah had finished the year before but she was staying with Aunt Rowena so that she could enjoy the cultural opportunities of New York.

Molly, thinking of the pictures in her geography book of the Taj Mahal and the pyramids and the Rock of Gibraltar which her sappy sisters would get to see, threw *Bleak House* on the floor and stamped both her feet. "See if I care!" she howled. "You just wait till I tell Ralph!"

"There, there," said her mother. "Don't fuss, Molly. Didn't I say your time would come?"

"I'll be too old by then."

"Would you like to go to boarding school instead of to Uncle Claude's?"

"No. I want to stay here if I can't go around the world."

"But you can't, Molly dear," said Mrs. Fawcett nervously, "because the house will be sold."

She had done all this behind their backs. She wasn't content to make the far future look horrible, she had to make it start right away. Molly stared at her bandaged hand in which now and again there was a slow pain. Dr. Haskell said she was out of danger now and she was glad that she was not going to lose her hand but she was also glad that the burn would leave a bad scar. Her mother was going on talking about how necessary it was for her to take the girls around the world because she did not belong to a society to which she could present them; this was a substitute, to be sure, but she felt a very satisfactory one. As for Ralph and Molly, she thought the year in the mountains would be very character-building and she was pleased with Molly's wisdom in not wanting to go to boarding school. In public school one learned a great deal about responsibility and democracy. Fortunately Leah and Rachel had sterling characters and had not become snobs; all the same she realized now that sending them to so fashionable a school had been a dangerous experiment.

"But, Molly dear, before we go, I want to have a long talk with you about a few things."

"About what? Go ahead. Shoot."

"Not now, not yet. Goodness, Ralph is late. The roads must be bad." She put her sewing away and got up. As she left the room, she said, "We're having your favorite dessert for dinner tonight, lemon pie."

When April came and Molly looked at the spring in Covina for the last time, she was homesick as if she were only remembering the sweet orange blossoms in the Freudenburg's grove, the palm trees, the bee-filled lippia lawn, the workmen with their doe-like eyes. She visited both the graves of her father and of Grandpa Kenyon and she sat for hours in the shade of a blooming tulip tree in the cemetery. She was restless when she thought of strange children lying under her umbrella tree and strange women cracking the walnuts.

Now and again her care-worn melancholy made her suddenly self-contemptuous and she brushed it off like a spider. Once to prove to herself that she was not a crybaby, she took a still live wood mouse from a trap and drowned it in a milk bottle half full of water, rejoicing brutishly in the swimming and the squealing which became slower and fainter and at last ceased while the small speckled body swelled and the sharp teeth showed themselves in an angry grin.

Ralph was as sad and jealous as she. They often quarreled. She wondered sometimes if she liked him as well as she used to. Once they were walking home from school together when a girl on a bicycle came riding by. Her name was Ardis Westerlund and she enjoyed the distinction of having fainted several times in school. She was frail and pretty and had long yellow hair which was held in place with a round comb; her mother dressed her to look like Alice. This year she had given Ralph a Valentine and once Molly had seen them earnestly talking together by the parallel bars at recess, and when the bell rang she saw Ralph touch his fingers to his lips and blow Ardis a kiss. Today, as she went whizzing by, she cried, "I name Molly for the prettiest girl in school!"

Both Molly and Ralph halted and Molly snarled, "Why don't you stop breathing?" but Ardis Westerlund was far away, streaking past the Wash.

Ralph made a convulsive gesture to take Molly's hand, but she brushed him off and said in a cold, level voice, "I know I'm ugly. I know everybody hates me. I wish I were dead." Unappealing, unloving, she continued to stand motionless in the bright sunshine. She knew the light made even yellower her yellow skin with its hundreds of shining bronze freckles. She could see herself as clearly as if she looked in a mirror. A blue Indian-head jumper hung on her slackly; her ruffled organdy blouse was mussed and soiled from the long day at school; one knobby knee was covered with a scab from a wound of two weeks before; one of the ear pieces of her glasses was bound with adhesive tape. Molly was not only ugly, she had a homemade look, a look of having been put together by an inexperienced hand.

She closed her eyes and teetered. Ralph shook her, "Come along, Molly, we've got to get home."

"I haven't got a home," she said and she let go her school-bag so that its books and pencils and loose-leaf notepaper scattered in the dust at her feet.

"Listen, Molly . . ."

"Go away. I wish they had had to cut my hand off."

"All right!" he cried and his voice rose to a shout. "All right! Why don't *you* stop breathing?"

Molly smiled a particular smile that always made him crazy-mad. He spat at her feet and yelled, "I hate you. Damn you, I hate you! Stay here all night for all I care!" When he had gone, running down the road, she picked up her books and her papers and wiped the dusty pencils off on her skirt.

CHAPTER SIX

MRS. FAWCETT AND HER ELDER DAUGHTERS, ON THEIR WAY
West from Rachel's commencement, met Ralph and
Molly late in June in Denver. As in former years when
only their mother had been with the children, they stayed
at the Brown Palace hotel. While Leah and Rachel and
Mrs. Fawcett were shopping and Molly was at the Museum
of Natural History, Ralph sat in the lobby where one looked
up past gallery after gallery to a fretted dome, and he
imagined the days of the gold and silver harvest when
towns sprang up in the mountains to exist for a few opu-
lent years and then to be abandoned. The train that took
them to the Bar K passed through several of these ghost
towns: the sagging, rotten, tall Victorian houses, window-
less and with the porches maimed, still wore traces of their
original elegance, and there was something deeply mourn-
ful in the sight of a cupola whose gingerbread remained
intact but which listed like a hat on a drunk man's head.
Patches of gilt still clung to the pillars of the boarded-up
opera houses; the saloons and gambling dens, as haggard
as death itself, still wore their flush names: The Golden
Horn, The Gold Nugget, The Silver Dollar, The Silver

Moon. The mouths of old mines yawned blackly beside the pyramids of ore. Grass grew in the streets, all the houses were tenantless, and even the trees looked dead.

The Brown Palace had been part of those days, and while it was as flamboyant as ever with its profusion of marble, of tall rubber plants, of gilt-framed mirrors and of frescoes, it failed to recall the life of the Eldorado as clearly as did the derelict opera houses. It seemed like any hotel in Los Angeles, and the businessmen who sat in the modern leather lounge chairs, smoking good cigars, were pale-faced and stout, not Westerners. Only occasionally did ranchers, unmistakable by their gait and their hewn faces under tall buff hats, amble through the lobby like restless dogs; uneasy in their city clothes they picked the chairs behind the rubber plants so that they would not be seen. The others, the buyers and the sugar merchants, were often in the company of women who were too young to be their wives and Ralph, against his will, was pleased by this just as he was pleased that his mother and Leah and Rachel were the objects of admiring, libidinous stares when they came into the dining room.

On the eve of their departure, the family gathered in Mrs. Fawcett's bedroom for a farewell visit. Mrs. Fawcett talked of her grief at leaving her two babies behind, but brightly promised that they would have their trip around the world in that most far-off future "some day." She was grateful for her own bravery in being thus able to face a year without them, but said she knew that it was for their own good. "It will be very good for you to be on your own. Grandfather Bonney used to say, 'Solitude is the greatest tonic in the world. Loneliness is the poison put into solitude by weaklings and cads.' And I know you aren't either of *those*. Molly, you must ask Winifred to use the fine-comb on your hair after you wash it. And when we come back—you'll see how quickly the time passes—we will all be together in a lovely new home in Connecticut."

Molly, who had been captious for days, said, "How many times must I explain to you that it is incorrect to use the word 'home' in that way? You mean 'house.'"

Mrs. Fawcett smiled patiently. "Very well, my dear, *house* since you know so much more than your mother. May I continue what I was saying when you interrupted me?"

"Molly, you are becoming an intellectual snob," said Rachel, taking out a gold and white Coty's compact she had got for graduation.

"Becoming?" said Molly. "I have been one ever since I was nothing going on one."

Ralph, while he was in entire agreement with Molly on the distinction between "house" and "home" and had, in fact, suggested it to her in the first place, hated the smirk on her thin ill-natured mouth and hated the unblinking vigil of her nearsighted eyes. This disconcerting stare often caused people to falter nervously in their speech or to flush, and frequently, in front of company, her mother scolded her, "Molly dear, you must *not* stare. It is very much like pointing." And in school these eyes, missing nothing, intimidated her teachers, already intimidated by her intelligence and her talent for writing themes of a savagely satiric nature. Everyone said that she had the brains of the family, but as Mrs. Fawcett was not interested in brains, she thought this a handicap rather than otherwise and often told Molly that there were other things in life besides books. But, thought Ralph, what else could there be for that scrawny, round-shouldered tall thing, misanthropic at the age of twelve? It was curious that she bore so close a resemblance to him. She had the same coarse, straight, black hair, the same heavy eyebrows, and the same prominent nose that looked as solid and unbreakable as a stone. But in a girl such ruggedness was not handsome as it was in him and Uncle Claude, and nothing could be done to improve the features nor, probably, would she have permitted any alterations even if they had been possible, for she took a vindictive pleasure in her plainness. She would stand before the mirror in the hall and when someone passed by would point to her reflection and say, "Admit I'm prettier than Mary Pickford."

Looking at his older sisters with their fine, tender faces, their shining hair, their dresses of flowered pongee, catching their clean, delicious smell of soap and talcum powder, he wished Molly had never been born. He was still contemptuous of the others, but he was so conscious of their beauty that sometimes he desired, to his horror, to put his lips on their smooth white necks or on the long green veins in their arms. They had been completely oblivious of Ralph and Molly and had talked about esoteric things like "the Winter Carnival" and "the Yale-Harvard game," "the sixth-form dance at St. George's" and "Olivia's coming-out."

Mrs. Fawcett's voice went chattering on, joined sometimes by Leah's or Rachel's (once Rachel said, "But, Mummy, I think it will be too *poky* not to stay in Paris for at *least* two months." Ralph and Molly exchanged glances and each formed the word "Mummy" soundlessly.) It was hot.

Ralph's pants stuck to the varnished chair and he drank water slowly out of a sweating hotel pitcher. He gazed greedily at his sisters and the desire to kiss them became almost irresistable so that he had to blind himself from time to time by staring into the blazing ceiling light. Then, suddenly, he thought of Winifred Brotherman and in an instant, he was floundering in his first real love. For a few minutes he sat motionless; then, from somewhere in the hotel, a jazz band began to play "The Sweetheart of Sigma Chi." The woodwinds, grieving their hearts out, the dancers he imagined with their eyes closed, the dimmed lights he saw, the smell of the girls' perfumed hair and of the boys' breath sweet with gin, made him tremble like a tree. He thought of her as he had seen her once last summer, lying on the lawn, a bottle of Coca Cola, half drunk, forgotten in her hand. The sun seemed to darken her skin as he watched and her curls looked molded out of metal. He had been pleased to look at her, and now he understood why he had stood so long at his window looking down at her, keeping Uncle Claude waiting for the knife to skin a beaver.

On the pretext of a headache from the movie they had gone to in the afternoon, he went to his own room across the hall and lay in the darkness with his hands crossed on his chest. The music here was louder than it had been in his mother's room. Each time the tempo changed, the scene in his mind changed. With the fox trots he imagined them dancing, although he did not know how to dance; with the waltzes he saw them sitting in Uncle Claude's car in the darkness, outside the dance hall or driving up Cuthbert Pass until they came to an unfrequented road where they would park the car to kiss for hours. This was nothing like what he had felt for Ardis. That had been a sweet and nebulous romance and its only incidents were that once she had given him a Valentine and had blushed and said that someone else must have signed her name and once he had blown her a kiss. They had loved in their silences and in their sidelong glances exchanged in study hall. It gave him a sense of almost conjugal comfort to know that Winifred was three years older than himself. It did not occur to him that she might already be spoken for; he felt that this was not a sudden miracle but that it had been prepared for since he was a little boy and it must, therefore, have been simultaneously prepared for in her. How curious it was that in all these years he had barely been aware of her! How curious that she had seemed to dislike him!

Toward eleven o'clock there was an intermission, and when the music ceased, his mind wandered perversely to Leah's high, cool forehead, and as if he were already married and already unfaithful to his wife, he exultantly felt her enclosed in his arms while he first put his lips and then the tip of his tongue upon the small blue vein which marked it like an artist's signature. Then, when the music began again and he returned to Winifred, he fashioned out of his sister and out of memories of girls in movies and girls in books the rival to whom he would allude in his first days with her. He wished to miss nothing and when he remembered, at first with pain, that she would be away at college, he rejoiced that there would be love letters and that she would come home for the Christmas holidays and then in the spring. He whirled round and round in his rapid love; it pricked him on the breastbone like a needle.

He wanted to be shut up in a small space to think about it. He wanted to grab it and eat it like an apple so that nobody else could have it.

At the train, Mrs. Fawcett and Leah and Rachel all cried, for departures and railroad stations required sorrow and they honored ceremony. They had brought farewell presents. Mrs. Fawcett's and Rachel's were boxes of candy, but Leah gave them nothing except an envelope which she pressed into Molly's hand, telling her not to open it until the train left. Kissing them all good-bye, Ralph felt a twinge of envy of the boat they would sail on but he did not fail, as Molly stubbornly did, to wish them a bon voyage when his mother said, "Now aren't you going to wish us a bon voyage?" He and Molly waved from the observation platform until they could no longer see three separate figures but only a single clump, and then they went back to the rusty green seat where their presents were. They opened the envelope first. On a sheet of thin Japanese writing paper with a heading of two ladies drinking tea, Leah had written:

Dearest Molly girl and Ralphie boy,
Mother made me *promise* not to tell but she can't do anything now since by the time you read this I will be on my way to China!!!!!! On the third finger of my left hand, I am now the proud wearer of a diamond ring! Mother is quite silly (don't we all know it!!!!) and says I cannot announce my engagement for a whole year and that's why I have to go around the darned old world. Of course she's the limit, but I must say I am looking forward to the Taj Mahal not to mention the Holy Land. Garden of Eden, here I come, right back where I started from. (Apologies to California.) If you are good and don't breathe this to a

soul, I'll bring you back a whole trunkful of presents and will write you every day about what we have seen and the adventures we have had.

I will hang my close on this line,

Loads of love,

Leah

P.S. The Donor of the Famous Engagement Ring is named Robert Appleton and he is a senior at Dartmouth. I'd give anything to see your faces when you read this.

Molly went over the letter, sentence by sentence, devastatingly, and when she came to the parody of "California, here I come," she put her hand over her mouth and said, "Hasten, Jason, bring the basin, ulp! Too late, bring the mop." Recently she had been very much attached to the word "bourgeois," and she used it as if it were the most venomous in the language. She had once said to her mother that she thought the Sorosis was "as bourgeois as all outdoors," and of Ardis Westerland, once she had recovered from the shock of her insult, she said, "Why should I bother about that lousy bourgeois stick-in-the-mud?" So now Leah's letter, Leah herself, and the trip around the world were, she said, the most bourgeois things she had ever heard of in her life. "Bonney Bourgeois," she said with finality.

Ralph was deeply disturbed by the effect of the letter on himself, feeling somehow cheated and, furthermore, he was ashamed that Leah, engaged to be married, was the very figure he had meant to use to rouse Winifred's romantic jealousy. He felt, as well, a terrified guilt as though he had despoiled his own sister, and now, to make everything even more sinful, her letter, a clear confession of a relationship with a boy, tempted him again to think of her high

148

forehead and again to imagine his lips upon it. The wicked-
ness fluttered round him like a moth-miller which he could
not catch.

As a safeguard against betraying himself, he changed the
subject quickly and said, "Will I be glad to see old Studebaker!"

And Molly said, "Will I be glad to see Eye-Opener!"

Now they were really glad to be going to the ranch and
they talked with amiable venom of their mother and sisters
and said that, among other blessings, they would not have
to hear Mr. Follansbee again as long as they lived. They
planned and remembered, and then Ralph, looking in a
pause at Molly's hand which was still puffy and blue,
pointed to it and said, "Why did you do that?" But Molly
said, "I'm through talking now," and opened *Les Misérables*
so that Ralph had to contemplate once more his evil
thoughts.

At the end of ten miles he was already tired and Molly
was deep in her book, leaving it only now and again to
goggle at the open box of candy on the seat beside her
and, with maddening regularity, to select a gum drop. The
journey always made Ralph homesick, not for people or
for a place, but for cleanliness and comfort and orderly
houses. For always on the train were the most pathetic
travelers in the world. Not the ranchers, returning from
Denver or Omaha, rumpled but still well dressed; and not
the rodeo riders on their way from Pendleton to Frontier
Days in Cheyenne; nor the dudes in their mottled silk
shirts and ten gallon Stetsons, but the others who belonged
in no classification. Each year there was always a group
consisting of a gaunt young woman and three or four small

children who ate graham crackers out of an oiled paper parcel and whined nasally. Years of hard work and bad food had given the women a canine look in the mouth and eyes; their skin was brown and old; if their teeth had been replaced, the false ones were gold, but generally there were only spaces where they had rotted and fallen out. The groups varied little, but they could not always have been the same one, for the children were the same size. The mother's hair was always reddish brown and hung about her sunken face like dirty strings, but her children were tow-headed and their eyebrows were too light to see. Sometimes they had skin diseases or birthmarks or Hutchinson's teeth. If another passenger struck up a conversation with the mother, the car usually learned that they had been to Denver to a doctor and the complaint was always something dangerous like mastoid or rheumatic fever. They would get off some hours before Ralph and Molly did at a bleak, treeless town where a mustard-colored depot and a mustard-colored water tower glared in the sun, and where small cottages and outhouses with drooping doors straggled up the dry sides of the foothills. The halts were so long that it was often possible to watch the whole progress of the woman and her children up the dirt road onto the porch of the house itself. They moved so slowly they did not seem to be glad to be at home at all. The scene gave Ralph great thirst, and when the train moved on again, he would go to the back of the car and drink cup after cup of tepid water.

This time the woman wore a tall, tan hat which sat on her head like a pail; it was spotted with mildew. Her dress was a sleeveless evening frock of azure georgette and its scalloped skirt was longer in the back than in the front.

A flower made of orange crinoline with spiny, life-like pistils was pinned to her shoulder, and she wore a choker of pink beads. As the train mounted to the high country and it grew chilly, she put on a black satin coat with a neckpiece that looked like toasted cotton. She smoked cigarettes in a carved bone holder and ground them out on the floor of the car with the heel of her tennis shoe.

There were only two children this time, a little girl of about three and a boy a little older. They stared vacantly with pale blue eyes at their fellow-passengers and ate Cracker-Jack with their mouths open, forgetting what they were doing and allowing the boxes to fall from their laps, spilling their contents everywhere. They were silent for the most part, but now and again, for no visible reason, they wailed loudly as if they were in pain and then stopped as abruptly as they had begun. They absent-mindedly plucked at the tussocks of their mother's collar and she told them, without any feeling, to "lay offn' me."

He tried to read *The Girl of the Limberlost* and could not. He worked at the crossword puzzle in the Denver *Post* but gave up when he came to "the soubriquet of Ferdinand II." He endeavored and in vain to feel the rapture of last night and he even hummed to himself some of the songs they had played: "Glow Worm," "Sleepy-Time Gal," "I'm Looking Over a Four Leaf Clover." He fled from Leah's face but it gained upon him and was before his mind's eye, doll-like and china-white. The train, the slowest on earth, seemed to rocket up the peaks and hurtle down the valleys and through the long tunnels, taking him, at this mad rate, miles away from Leah, miles on the way to Winifred whom now he was bound in conscience to love in order to purge from his heart the unholy image of his sister.

At noon they went into the forward car where there was a small buffet at one end. An amiable Negro sold dry ham sandwiches and coffee of a strange buttery flavor. Opposite Ralph and Molly, sitting with a table between them, were four ranchers, drinking whisky out of Lily cups. Farther up the car was a sandy-haired little man with a small, spiteful mouth and blue pop eyes. He wore a cerise silk neckerchief and a black and yellow braided belt; his Levis were stiff and new and he had turned up the cuffs to show his black boots with curlicues burned into the tops of them. He had a bottle too, but he did not fool with a Lily cup; instead he put the bottle to his mouth and gurgled loudly. Molly continued to read as she ate, having made the statement when they came in that Napoleon was a man she wished she had known platonically. Ralph gazed out the window at the deep gorge of the Wolf River, full and foaming from the big thaws. The train slowed down so much for a steep grade that he saw a fat woodchuck calmly eating something on a rock at the edge of the track-bed. They came then into a brilliant valley, checkered with neat fields, and here the river was deeper and was the color of dark, dim gold.

A large Germanic man who smoked a pipe said, when they stopped at Peacetown and he had scrutinized the landscape, "Don't Luke Fisher live up there? Yonder, I'm talking about, past them cottonwoods? Seems to me like he does."

His companions first agreed, then doubted, then denied, and it was established finally that Fisher lived twenty-seven miles to the east. But this did not dissuade the speaker, as it would not have done a man at Uncle Claude's table, from talking further of Luke Fisher. "He done mighty well with them kids after his wife died, that's one thing you can say for him. All of them but the oldest boy and that one, Milton, turned out ornery as a bobcat. You ever hear about the time he was working for Roger Campbell and turned loose a stallion with the saddle horses? You know the stallion I mean? He was an ugly bastard of a paint with one blue eye. Campbell bought him off Prescott and sold him to some blooded dude here a while back for seven thousand dollars. Well, this here Milton—Milt, they called him—was wrangling Campbell's horses up there one summer. Campbell used to have a whole hell of a lot more dudes than he's got now, don't ask me why because I don't know. Anyway, I guess this Milt got aholt of a bottle of rotgut whisky and drank it one Saturday night because the next Sunday morning when the dudes went out to get on their horses, there wasn't anything in the world in the corral but that ball-face stallion kicking the bejesus out of every goddam bench on the place. Campbell had some good horses too. Bought a colt off him myself once, pretty near the finest horse I ever had. Ken Burkhardt's got her now down to Kenyon's place."

It was not unusual for Ralph to hear his uncle's name in these conversations. Indeed, he could not remember a time when Uncle Claude had not come up in connection with something or other and it gave him a sense of security and pride. His name was as well known here, as much taken for granted, as that of President Hoover. Sometimes he and Molly talked loudly to establish their identity so that the men would speak to them, but they never did, although usually they knew who the children were, and when they got off at White Woman, someone would look out the window and say, "Well, there's Kenyon's pick-up, so the kids won't have to walk home."

Between swallows, the solitary man cut his nails with a jackknife and whistled tunelessly between his teeth. He finished his whisky as they sat there, and when he had tucked the bottle away under the seat, he smiled at the men across the aisle. His smile was only a physical adjustment of his lips; it was like the grin of a panting dog. He spoke with a Texas accent, and he said, "I don't like to horn in on you boys if you're discussing something private, but I was studying on maybe one of you all having an extra bottle of corn whisky that I could buy off you. I aimed to stock up better than I done, but I'm a stranger to Denver and only got just this one pint. Hadn't stocked up on the password was my trouble." There was a pause during which he did not close his mouth. The four men shrewdly sized him up, and although it was clear that they did not approve of him, one of them nevertheless fetched down his valise from the luggage rack and got out an unlabeled pint bottle. The Texan handed him three silver dollars and the man pocketed them wordlessly.

The stranger drank and then, to the men who had not taken their eyes off him, he said, "Well, no offense intended, but that ain't worth three dollars and it ain't worth two. If a man felt right free, he might give six bits for it. By Jesus, they got us coming and going between the goddam government and the goddam bootleggers."

His listeners' faces were expressionless. Presently, the tall Germanic man said, "Where you from?"

"Well, Mister, as of seventy-five hours forty-five minutes ago, I'm from San Fernando Hospital, San Anton'. I laid on a bed for six holy months. Broke my leg bulldogging a steer on Christmas day."

He had recovered now and was on his way to Laramie to put on an exhibition for a millionaire and his pals who had hinted of Madison Square Garden. "Can you feature a rodeo indoors?" he said. "I can't, but, Momma dear! I *can* feature the cash in them New York dudes' jeans." He had never been through this country before, he said, but in Reno once last November he had met a man from here. He had met him at a gambling table and he would swear on a stack of Bibles that he had never seen a man with such luck. "I can't call his name, though I'd remember if I heard it. But anyway, that man had the most gorgeous luck I ever saw in my born days. He won him one hundred twenty-five dollars before he said quit, and if I'd of been in his place, I would of gone on. But then, I always was a sucker."

It was agreed, finally, that the lucky gambler was Homer Armitage and the details of his fortunate career were reported, how, at Spit-in-the-Ocean, he had bluffed his way into a twenty-dollar pot, had never been known to lose a cent at Stud, and was the one man in ten thousand that could make a slot machine pay off. The stranger said, "He cheats, don't he?" and grinned.

The four men sat up straight and the one who had given him the whisky said, "You had ought to watch the way you talk, Mister. Homer Armitage don't cheat and you're among his friends."

Molly looked up from her book and laughing noiselessly, said, "Ride 'em, cowboy." Ralph, who until then had seen nothing amusing in the native's defense of a fellow-citizen against an outlander, scowled, annoyed that, as usual, she was twice as quick-witted as he even though she had appeared to be absorbed in her book.

After that the Texan drank in silence, sucking his bottle like a baby, and the others did not speak to him again, but went on talking of Homer. When his luck at cards had been exhausted, one of them said, "Hear Armitage bought a quarter interest in Kenyon's place. If the man's got money to do that, I don't see why he don't get his own place. It ain't any good working for somebody else."

"Kenyon ain't bad to work for," said another. "He pays his men good."

A yellow-haired and cross-eyed man said, "Hear Kenyon's going to get married."

"You don't say? Who to?"

"I haven't got the foggiest. Just something my wife picked up and told me. She didn't know either. I asked her."

"Well, it's time. It ain't that girl of Kennedy's, is it? The one that has the school up to the Forks?"

"Christ, no. She's Harmon Tucker's girl."

"Well, I'll be damned. I wonder who it is."

Molly closed her book and leaning across the empty plates and cups, whispered, "Did you hear that? Do you know what I think? I think Uncle Claude is going to marry Magdalene."

He did not bother to be irritated with her. The thought

was immediately in his mind that Uncle Claude was going to marry Winifred, and now the blustering passion of last night returned. Imperfectly, as if he looked through waves of heat, he saw his sister's forehead furrow with surprise and then smooth out again as her lips curled in a smile whose intention he could not grasp. He thought: what has given me away? But Molly said nothing and prepared to go back to the other car. For one interminable moment he sat still. The train was picking up speed, for they were coming down off Booth Pass. Between this and Cuthbert there was a ride of three more hours during which they would pass through fourteen tunnels, one of which, the longest, they were rushing toward now. This was the part of the journey he and Molly had always looked forward to. Sometimes they saw a man standing in a niche at the side, the pale light from the lamp on his cap giving his grimy face a corpse-like luminosity. Once a bat had flown against the very window at Molly's elbow.

As Ralph lurched through the buffet car, he heard the train hoot, protracting its note of warning so long that he knew they were almost at the mouth of the tunnel. By the time he had passed through the vestibule, the lamps in the car were turned on. They were not powerful and the blackness of the tunnel, even at its entrance, was so complete that the light was crepuscular. Coal smoke, forced back from the locomotive, seeped through the door of the observation platform. His mouth already tasted foully of sulphur. He made his way toward Molly. The woman with the children leaned out into the aisle as he passed by and she said in a flat voice, "You got a match?" He flushed in the dim-ness as he shook his head, ashamed that he did not smoke. He saw that she wore no wedding ring.

He sat down beside Molly, although the seat in front was pushed back so that they could be opposite one another. Partly he did not wish her to read any further in his face and partly he wanted to feel her near by. He thought of her as if she were the last foothold beneath which the world fell away in a chasm: it would be so easy to lose his footing, relax his fingerholds, and plunge downward to wedge his bones in a socket of rocks. Vile fogs baffled him and vileness was below him. Molly, alone, he thought, did not urge him to corruption.

For the moment he was protected by her elbow and her knee which touched his, and by the sexless odor of her new white shirt which she wore with a pair of black sateen gym bloomers. He saw the tunnel as an apotheosis of his own black, sinful mind which had incestuously coveted Leah (he trembled to think of Mr. Robert Appleton) and the girl who might well be his aunt-by-marriage, the mind that had observed with delight that the mother of the seedy children had no wedding ring. He urged the train to make haste. Once out in the bright green meadows of the valley he thought he would be safe from the thoughts that swarmed about him like a dream of reptiles. As long as Molly was here beside him, though, he could hang on.

And then he knew he had been wrong, that he was not safe; he was weakening and ready to fall, and now he actually slumped down in the seat so that his shoulders were on a level with Molly's and he said, in the lowest voice, "Molly, tell me all the dirty words you know."

He heard himself almost with relief. Before there was

time for Molly to move away or to utter a cry, they had emerged into the light which streamed like glory through the dirty window panes. The sun was high and the fields shimmered. Round them, for miles, as far as the eye could see, were the violet mountains, clean-lined, clear of haze. The eye could not detect a single impurity in all the scene.

Ralph's childhood and his sister's expired at that moment of the train's entrance into the surcharged valley. It was a paradox, for now they should be going into a tunnel with no end, now that they had heard the devil speak.

CHAPTER SEVEN

WHEN THEY CAME INTO THE LONG LIVING ROOM LATE IN the afternoon, Mrs. Brotherman was waiting for them as she had always done in former years. She sat, thinner, sadder, more pearly than ever, beside a table where she had put a bowl of apples and a pitcher of cider. These days of early June were still cool in the mountains when the sun was setting, so there was a fire in the hearth and the housekeeper, whose aging blood was pale, leaned toward it with a wan, inadmissible hunger. Ralph recalled the gritty heat in Denver: it had been as recently as last night that, sweating in the hotel bedroom, he had listened gluttonously to the music of the jazz band which was itself suffused with summer heat and moistness. The room had been cleaned that day and it shone dustlessly in the light from the fire and the light from the setting sun that burned through the windows. All the catalogues and the magazines of western stories were stacked up neatly and there was a feminine order in the arrangement of sacks of Bull Durham, boxes of cartridges, and tins of pipe tobacco on the big varnished table, an order Uncle Claude, seeming almost

driven by necessity, at once demolished by seeking cigarette papers with a planless hand.

Familiar smells came to Ralph faintly after he had been
greeted by Mrs. Brotherman and had sat down for a cere-
monious moment of silence. There were the smell of fat
meat cooking in beans, the smell of the apples and of the
pitch in the spitting pine logs; over them all was the name-
less smell of the house itself whose elements comprised
leather, saddle soap, oily ramrods, dogs and drying hides.
With the well-known smells came the sounds of a cow
bellowing for the calf that had been butchered that morning; the team horses, turned loose, neighing as they ran
foolishly in circles round their pasture; the barking of
dogs on distant farms; the clatter of milk buckets down at
the barn; the obstreperous arrival of the tractor across the
bridge over the big slough.

He could taste the apples in the cider and he wondered
if wine really tasted of grapes. Often in the past summers
Uncle Claude had given him a glass of Dago red, but it had
only tasted thick and faintly sour. He had liked, though,
to sit in this room with him and the other men on special
evenings—Saturdays or when it was storming—and watch
them pass the gallon jug back and forth as they filled their
teacups, bragging that they were getting as tight as ticks,
although Ralph could see no difference in them.

Uncle Claude now stood with one leg flung over the end
of the table, rolling a cigarette. His hat was pushed back
and a lock of black hair lay on his forehead like a leech.
He had not shaved and the small blue spines made his
jaw look sunken. Although he was otherwise unaltered,
this detail made Ralph quickly alert to him, not as his

uncle nor as the man's man, drinking bootleg wine, but as an almost anonymous man, old enough both to have a heavy beard and to marry a girl. Indeed, he had never known how very old Uncle Claude was until today, on the way from the station, Molly had asked him and he had told her that he was thirty-six. "You're the same age as my father," she had said. Further, Ralph observed that if he himself had been looking for the cigarette papers, he would not have messed up the other things and he wondered if there would ever be a time in his life when he could be untidy without being self-conscious about it. At this moment of resentment, as if he had spoken his futile envy aloud, Uncle Claude said, "Where's Winifred?" Ralph was sure he heard a note of possessiveness in his uncle's voice and that when Mrs. Brotherman's reply came, he saw a flush under the stubble. "She went to see *The Scarlet Pimpernel* with one of her beaux." Molly gave Ralph a rapid, spiteful glance and then looked at her feet, smiling with dreadful secrets. It seemed to him that something was going to happen and there came to his mind, quite inexplicably, the idea that an arrow was going to be shot from an unseen bow the length of the room to imbed itself in the neck of the antelope on the south wall. But the charged moment ended when Mrs. Brotherman, refilling Molly's cider glass, said humbly, "How nice for your sisters and your mother to go all the way around the world. I expect they will have wonderful tales to tell when they get home."

"I suppose so," said Molly, "if you happen to like that sort of hogwash and soul-butter. I happen not to be the type."

Uncle Claude laughed. "Hogwash and soul-butter, that's a new one. Where'd you get that one?"

Molly said, "In a book I read when I was a child. A book by Samuel Clemens."

"Listen to Grandma," said Uncle Claude.

Ralph was quite unable, even though he concentrated so hard that his head began to ache, to feel any emotion at all over Mrs. Brotherman's announcement that Winifred was at the movies with a beau. And not just "her *beau*" but "one of her *beaux*." The word had a fusty, old-fashioned sound and made him think of his mother who would say, "When I went to a taffy-pull with a beau," or "a beau of mine gave me the souvenir spoon from the Alamo." All that really took his fancy was the fact that Winifred was seeing *The Scarlet Pimpernel* which had, to his regret, been scheduled in Covina for the week after they left. He wished somehow to convey his indifference to Molly, but she sat, incommunicable, enclosed within herself, staring at the flames as she munched her apple, an enemy to both the fire and the fruit. It was barely possible that he had misread her smile in the buffet car, and in this case, silence was the only possible policy.

Uncle Claude and Mrs. Brotherman asked them questions about who had bought the walnut grove, the name of the ship on which the travelers were sailing, whether Mrs. Fawcett had spoken to the caretaker about Grandpa's grave. Molly replied in pig-like monosyllables, watching Ralph as he politely filled in and then, in his turn, inquired after Homer Armitage who, for some inscrutable reason, was taking a correspondence course in shorthand and who had not, as the man on the train declared, bought an interest in the Bar K; and after Magdalene who had made more than a hundred dollars last winter by trapping skunks; and after the men to whom, it appeared, nothing at all had happened.

"When's the wedding?" said Molly at length, biting an apple seed between her front teeth.

"What wedding?" said Uncle Claude.

"Yours and Magdalene's."

"Molly!" cried Mrs. Brotherman, horrified.

Uncle Claude looked at her as if they were exactly the same age. "If you don't watch out, they're going to put you in the booby hatch. I never seen anybody in my life with such damn crazy ideas."

"Well, if you're not going to marry Magdalene, who are you going to marry? Me?"

"Shut up, Molly," said Ralph, beside himself with embarrassment, and then, to Uncle Claude, he explained what they had heard on the train.

"Well, I'll be," said Uncle Claude, pleased. "It don't happen to be true but I'm obliged to those boys for thinking I'm a ladies' man, which I am as far from being as Molly is from having good sense."

"Then you *aren't* going to get married?" said Ralph with an eagerness he could not suppress.

"You bet I'm not," said Uncle Claude.

Molly said crossly, "Why isn't there any salt for the apples?" and glared balefully at Ralph.

It was only a question of minutes, he thought, before the grown-ups would begin to suspect that some issue had been raised between him and Molly, even though neither was quick to observe such things, Uncle Claude because he wore his own feelings clearly on his face and expected everyone else to do likewise, and Mrs. Brotherman because she had imposed on all the world a smooth, unruffled sadness in which all events were exactly the same. She returned with a melancholy warmth to the world cruise and asked Molly if she were not proud of the travelers.

"Why?" said Molly. "Why in the world would I be proud of them? I could have gone too if I had wanted to, and now I'm sorry I didn't."

"Why, Molly," said Mrs. Brotherman. "Why, Molly, what a thing to say. Your uncle will think you aren't happy here."

"I'm not," said Molly.

Uncle Claude colored and Molly, fearless and level-headed, looked from him to Ralph and back again, disliking them both. It was true, of course, that she had never been close to Uncle Claude and had held a grudge against him for ending her companionship with Ralph; but if a word of criticism were spoken against him in Covina, she was savagely defensive, principally because he was Grandpa Kenyon's son and Grandpa Kenyon continued in her rapt memory as the only hero of her life. Today, in her fault-finding gaze, there was something besides this old resentment, but Ralph could not put his finger on it.

Mrs. Brotherman was distressed and said, "Oh, dearie, you are worn out from the journey. Have another apple, do." Molly took the apple, her third, and slumped down in her chair to eat it in small bites like a squirrel, mumbling once, "I prefer bananas, of course," and then subsiding into a vigilant silence. Everyone but this forthright monster was embarrassed; black-haired, studiously misshapen, noisily nibbling, she tyrannized them into a gawky silence and then suddenly she kicked Ralph sharply on the shin. It made him gulp with pain but he said nothing although he could feel the very skin draw tight over his cheeks.

Uncle Claude looked curiously at them both and said, "Did you two have a scrap somewhere along the line?"

"No," said Molly shortly and returned to her apple. Anyone else would have been fighting back tears, but Molly's tantrum was controlled and dry-eyed.

"Then what's eating on you?" Often Uncle Claude did not, as Mrs. Fawcett would have said, "know when to let well enough alone."

"None of your beeswax, Mr. Kenyon," she said, "and that's that."

Uncle Claude was furious. For a moment Ralph thought he was going to pull her hair or twist her arms behind her back, and he did take a step toward her, but checked himself and pretended he had only moved nearer the fireplace to throw his cigarette away and then, ignoring her entirely, he said to Ralph, "Come on up to the gallery. I want to show you something."

The gallery ran the length of the short wall of the room. Most of the space was taken up by the poker table and the chairs, but at one end there was a sort of alcove, called "the office," with a rolltop desk where Uncle Claude kept the registration papers of his pedigreed bulls and all sorts of other documents of an important historical nature, such things as land grants, dark yellow with age, signed by Buchanan and Lincoln, a trap-shooting certificate belonging to Homer Armitage and Uncle Claude's birth certificate in which his middle name was written down as "None." Over this desk, obscured by the shadows of a lodgepole pine which grew close to the house and thrust its needles against the window screen, was a picture of Ralph's grandmother. It was a journeyman portrait with a background of a blue lake in the distance and nearer at hand an ailanthus tree in flower. She wore a lace cap over her brown hair which hung in ringlets to her shoulders, and in her hand she held a white silk fan. Mrs. Bonney-Kenyon had a firm Scotch face with narrow lips and a small thin nose which ever so slightly tilted up. None of her children or her grandchildren bore any resemblance to her at all, but this, really, was no wonder, since both her husbands had been such powerful characters. Ralph could not tell whether she looked humorless or beaten or whether the unhappy look in her hazel eyes, set close together, came from embarrassment at the anachronistic curls which beset her plain face. As he came up the stairs behind Uncle Claude, he glanced in at her and he was struck with terror, thinking of how she had died giving birth to the man ahead of him.

They went to the window opposite the poker table and Uncle Claude pointed out to a bull in a small pasture by himself. He had a hairball in his jaw the size of a grapefruit. The vet had not been able to come to operate yet and the beast suffered noisily. As they watched, he faunched up the grassy ground around him and then, bellowing with pain and fury, rubbed the great tumor against the trunk of a poplar tree. He seemed to stare directly into their eyes with hatred as if they were responsible for his torment. There was something horrible in the spectacle and Ralph was absorbed by it. His uncle, likewise, seemed half hypnotized, and in this brief time of their brutal preoccupation, their companionship was so complete that it almost frightened Ralph; it was as though he had set forth on an adventure whose terms were so inexorable that he could not possibly change his mind and go back, as if they were on a boat in the middle of a landless sea. He looked at the heavy, small-chinned face in which, as the dark clear eyes studied the sick bull, there was a certain ponderous stupidity, a sort of virile opacity, an undeviating dedication to the sickness and health and the breeding of animals. The bull, by acquiring this infirmity, had temporarily become a nothing since he could not perform his function as a sire. It was almost as if he had made a fool of himself, for surely the smile that came and went in Uncle Claude's face was a mocking one. While this discovery appalled him, he was determined never to be degraded in the man's eyes as the bull had degraded himself, as Molly had done, simply by being the kind of person she was, bookish and unhealthy. Even so, he was mixed in his feeling about Uncle Claude and his resolution was the result not of a refreshed admiration but of the desire to go unnoticed by having no short-comings. Because his own masculinity was, in its articulation, so ugly, and he could therefore take no pleasure in himself, neither could he respect it in anyone else, and he was sorry now that he had heard Uncle Claude use dirty words to Magdalene. Was it possible that even Grandpa had been like that? He quickly thrust away the dishonorable thought.

Mrs. Brotherman, in her sighing monotone, was telling Molly about the bad luck she had had last winter with her house plants. Several times Molly said something in reply, but Ralph could not catch her words which she uttered as softly as a secret. Poor Molly, so unflower-like, should have been interested in something like minerals, but she loved flowers, and at times, when her writing was not going well, thought that she would be a nursery man. Mrs. Fawcett always sent Leah and Rachel for the delphiniums and the roses, but Molly picked the marigold and the calendula. They would come across the lippia lawn, Leah and Rachel in front, carrying dozens of full-faced roses whose gentle petals touched their perfect little chins, and Molly following behind with her sidelong lope, clutching the hairy stems of the harsh, scentless orange flowers. But Mrs. Brotherman, leaving the winter's woe to talk instead of her summer hopes, included Molly in her gardening plans and once Ralph heard his sister say, without a bit of cynicism, "Do you think we can *ever* have a rambler, Mrs. Brotherman?"

Suddenly Uncle Claude put his hand on Ralph's shoulder and said, "I'm mighty glad you've come to stay a while this time," and Ralph, while he did not move, felt himself grow cold with withdrawal and with something like distrust for the enthusiasm in his uncle's voice, so boy-like that it actually cracked. For right now he did not want any attention paid to him at all. But when Uncle Claude went on, he realized to his relief that it was not he that had so inspired the man, but the tale he now commenced to tell him.

"Don't you know how I've always said I wanted to get me a mountain lion?" he said. "Don't you know that? Well, I'm on the trail of one now."

He paused and smiled, waiting to be questioned and Ralph cried, "Where?"

Uncle Claude had seen the lion in the foothills before you got to Garland Peak. He had seen her only once early in April and had gone back time after time to have another glimpse of her or of her mate. He had been so bent on having her hide that he had wasted a lot of hunting time just fooling around looking for her and he hadn't got a piece of game this year, though there had been plenty to be had and the boys had stocked up well. She was about as big as a good-sized dog, he said, and she looked for all the world like an overgrown house cat. He thought about her so much that he had given her a name; he called her Goldilocks because, running the way she had in the sunlight, she had been as blonde as a movie star. He had told the boys, including Homer, that he would fire any one of them that drew a bead on her because if anyone got her, it was going to be him. Old Magdalene had ragged him a God's plenty, saying that *she* was going to catch the lion with fresh kid meat. No one had quite understood why he was so all-fired crazy to get her and he could not quite make it out himself. "But you know, every now and again a man will get a bug like this and there's no more rest for him." Sometimes he would go up and spend the whole day, packing his lunch along with him, and by sundown he would be cursing her, talking to her image as if she were a person.

He had decided that he was going to let Ralph hunt her too. They were never to hunt alone and were, when they separated, to keep within hailing distance of one another. This singular honor made Ralph feel as if he were actually rising in the air and he warmly thanked Uncle Claude while, deceitfully and unsportingly, he resolved that it would be *he,* not the man, who got the lion. For a few minutes his joy was immediate and unspoiled, and then it was smashed and he remembered again what he had said to Molly in the tunnel, for through the quiet—all other noises were suspended for this new sound—came the roaring of a car, tearing along the road with the cut-out open, and he could see it, a scarlet Model A roadster with the top down as it appeared and disappeared in the lacy sarvis berry that grew along the bank. He knew at once that this was Winifred and her beau, and when the car came fully into view and turned in at the lane with a brash squeal and he saw the girl (*his* girl!) sitting beside a boy in a porkpie hat, he was overcome by the most painful sensation he had ever known and thought he was going to become too limp to stand up straight. And yet, in spite of his consuming daze, he had the presence of mind to look quickly at his uncle and to see, with another emotion that he could not name, that nothing had registered in his face at all, that he did not even glance at the car but turned to look at the sick bull again, saying, "Laid up thisaway, that bastard is losing me money right and left."

The car now passed out of sight, drawing up to the front of the house. Its engine was suddenly raced and then it idled like a loud whisper. Molly and Mrs. Brotherman continued their secret conversation about the roses and Uncle Claude muttered to himself about the bull. Only Ralph was conscious of the laughter of the boy and girl which, high, prolonged, gasping, was immodest and exciting and he felt himself to be in extreme danger. At last there was an antiphonal good-bye which, lacking the greed of the laughter, rang out mournfully over the yellow valley and the sudden car went back up the lane like a clowning dog.

He heard her come through the screen door and he turned jerkily, leaning against the railing of the gallery.

Uncle Claude did not stir. Winifred raised her hand in salutation to him, smiled widely, and said, "Hi, chum," and then went to Molly and kissed her after the manner of cousins and grown-up women friends. She was plump now and so mature and feminine that Ralph could not recognize in her the shooting companion of earlier summers, that rather negative and taciturn person who, without playing a role, had seemed like another boy. Now she was a positive creature, self-assured, beautiful and glowing with an interior smile. She threw her polo coat over the back of a chair and sat down on the milking stool before the hearth. She was wearing a white dress, sleeveless and low in the back and low at the neck, and her flesh looked as brown as Fuschia's against it. He could not remember ever having seen her in anything but blue jeans and a faded work shirt; she was shorter than he remembered. There was, somehow, a settled look about her; she had a tender, untroubled, and vacuous gaze, and it would have been impossible for anyone to tell what she was smiling at.

He was uncertain. As soon as he no longer heard the red car, he was no longer jealous. And when he saw her sitting there, as native to the stool as a cat, he felt nothing at all, but the void was not painful; rather it was like a great soothing boredom. He turned to Uncle Claude and said, "What'll we hunt her with? A thirty-thirty?"

But Molly drowned out his uncle's reply with a sudden laugh. Her voice was deep for a girl and her laugh was slow and muffled but, though now she laughed her same laugh, it seemed to Ralph it had in it some of the same immodesty Winifred's had when she lingered with the boy, and in panic he thought, "She has *told!*" He knew this to be untrue, but the pleasure of the hour—scattered as it had been and filled in the interstices with embarrassment and guilt—was gone. Darkness was beginning and he felt friendless, separate, unclean. Again he tasted the sulphur at the back of his jaws and again he saw the woman in the train and her claw-like, ringless hand.

After supper Molly refused to play Continental Rummy because there was too much danger of having to speak to Ralph, and she went directly upstairs to take a bath. She drew the bolt and turned the key in the lock as well and she pulled down the window shade even though there was nothing outside but night. She was very dirty from the train. Dirt had seeped through her basketball shoes and her feet were a sight. Her arms were uniformly gray, beginning at her wrists and going up to her elbows which felt like dried-up biscuits. She had washed her hands before supper so that she appeared to be wearing a pair of pinkish gloves. Molly enjoyed being this dirty; when you were not black or at least gray, bathing seemed wasteful and self-indulgent just as did making your bed if you had not mussed up the covers much. But if you were properly dirty and could take a long, large bath, it was fun.

She had brought to the bathroom with her a Boston bag which she kept locked and hidden away on the topmost shelf of her closet. It contained green bathsalts and violet bathsalts of so inferior a quality that no matter how hot the water was, they did not melt but lay, as sharp and shining as quartz on the bottom of the tub so that it was necessary to sweep a place clean with her hand before she got in. Even so, they gave off a sweet fragrance and she could imagine that she was in a garden. Besides the bathsalts, there were a cake of soap in the form of a yellow rose, a can of Armand's talcum powder, a bottle of Hind's Honey and Almond, a jar of Daggett and Ramsdell vanishing creaming, a bottle of Glostora shampoo, a jar of Dr. Scholl's foot balm, a jar of freckle remover, some scissors, a nail file, a toothbrush, some dental floss, a comb, a brush, a buffer, a chamois skin, and a pearl-handled corn parer. Covering them all was a maroon bathing suit.

She hung a towel over the back of the chair and moved the chair in front of the keyhole to thwart any Peeping Tom. Then she stood on the chair and took off her blouse and her gym pants and threw her wrapper around her shoulders while she took off her undervest and bloomers and got into the bathing suit. She sat on the chair waiting for the tub to fill, thinking of nothing, for there would be plenty of time once she was in the bath. It was unlikely that any of them would come up and try the knob because they were all sitting around the table in the gallery, all but Mrs. Brotherman who spent her evenings, and always had, crocheting a bedspread for Winifred for when she got married. They would be sitting there, those illiterate men, scratching themselves and getting the ends of their cigarettes wet and saying things like "he don't" and "you was" and "those kind" and if the subject came up, pronouncing "apricot" with a short "a." As likely as not, if Winifred had decided not to play, they would drink whisky and wine which, as everyone knew, was nine-tenths fusel oil and the chances of going blind on it were ninety-nine out of a hundred. However, they were quite unimportant to her.

Under the roar of the hot water, she said, "*I* should ish-kibibble if they all commit suicide."

She turned off the water and got into the tub, but she had run in too much cold and had to get out again and run in some more hot, for Molly never sat in the bathtub while the water was running: a slender snake might come right through the faucet. At the thought of snakes, she shivered all over and remembered every single encounter she had had with them, beginning with the very earliest when she was four and was too little to go to school. She was waiting one day under the umbrella tree for the bus to bring home her sisters and her brother. When she heard it coming, she walked across the lippia lawn to the patch of clover and there she stepped on a coiled-up snake which uncoiled under her bare foot and slithered off. She had stood there, unable to move but screaming at the top of her voice until Miguel came running and picked her up. She had never known whether it was the feeling of the snake under her foot or the smell of Miguel's sweaty shirt that made her throw up over his shoulder as he carried her to the house. "Aren't you ashamed," said her mother. "Why, it was nothing but a harmless garter snake." Ralph found it and killed it with a rock and took Molly out to see, but the sight of it, even dead, only made her scream again until he had to carry her piggy-back to the porch so that she would not have to step on the ground. There was another time when she and Ralph, acting out "The Little Swiss Twins," had taken a lunch of cheese and crackers to the Wash and all of a sudden Molly discovered that she was sitting right beside a bright green grass snake. This time Ralph was not kind to her. When she screamed, he slapped her face and said, "Oh, you make me sick, you big fat baby." The worst of all had happened right here, the first summer, although a real snake was not involved. She had been reading *The World Almanac* one day in the leather chair in Uncle Claude's office and had taken a horse hair out of a tear in the arm to play with in her mouth because she had forgotten to bring a match and quite unexpectedly she had swallowed it. She went down to the kitchen to ask Magdalene what to do and Magdalene said she must quickly drink a glass of water or it would turn into a bull snake in her stomach and eat up everything she ate so that she would die of starvation; Magdalene had known at least eleven people that this had happened to. She rushed to the sink and Magdalene said, "That's hard water. That ain't no good for what ails you." So she ran upstairs to Mrs. Brotherman to say that she had better get right back to Covina so that Dr. Haskell could operate on her and Mrs. Brotherman told her that Magdalene had made the whole thing up. She returned to the kitchen and said, "You're a nigger," and Magdalene replied, "You're pore white trash."

Mrs. Fawcett said she would outgrow this fear as soon as she was able to distinguish between the harmless snakes and the poisonous ones, but Molly knew this was not true because she did not even like to look at the pictures of them in the illustrated part at the back of the Unabridged. It enraged her to be told that they were useful because they ate destructive insects, and when Leah and Rachel said that if she had any sense of beauty at all, she would see that their colors and patterns were wonderful, she replied, "Who cares about a sense of beauty? I'd a whole lot rather have a sense of *proportion,* vou conceited Elsie Dinsmores."

Molly lay soaking in her bathing suit so long that her skin became white and ridged. Every now and again, she got out and stood dripping on the rag rug while she ran more hot water in. She washed her hair in the bath water and let it drip down her back, the drops crawling like flies. Lying full length sometimes she let her feet and hands float to the surface and saw that they looked like something drowned; she thought of the flood when her father had brought the old woman into the kitchen. The only other thing Molly knew about the old woman was that it was said that when she was a child she had lived in a goiter belt, so now she had to drink iodine in her water.

She looked at her long feet which she allowed slowly to sink again. But for the most part, she was not conscious of her body (she was never conscious of it as a *body* and had never spoken this word aloud and almost died when one of her sisters would jokingly say, "Don't touch my body"; Molly thought of herself as a long wooden box with a mind inside) but of what had happened that afternoon in the train and she went over the whole scene time after time, each time redeeming the brilliant hatred that had spread over her exactly like bath water. Often she had hated Ralph but she had always got over it. She hated him for a month once because, when she showed him a picture in tempera of a New England kitchen, he had laughed so hard that he spit and made the red and white checked seat on the rocking chair run. Once he had brought her a little horseshoe magnet and told her that the teachers had voted to give it to her as a reward for being so diligent in collateral reading, and when she went to thank Miss Bandy,

Miss Bandy said, "Why, Molly, I think this is just something out of a Cracker-Jack box."

But while she would never forget these injuries, they no longer made her feel as if she were going to have a nosebleed. This new outrage, though, was a horse of quite a different color, and she vowed several times, raising her right arm out of the water, that she would hate Ralph Fawcett for the rest of her life. She was not certain yet how she would show him that she was his permanent enemy, but she was in no hurry to decide. For the time being she could simply lie here in the tub, safe behind a locked door, and contemplate the thing he had done, so terrible, so blackly wicked that it was thrilling. It was sharply pleasant, too, to think that she could now add Ralph's name to her list of unforgivable people, a list that included almost everyone. There were some doubtful cases (she was not completely sure about Winifred and Uncle Claude), but there were only two people who were purely forgivable and these were her father and Grandpa Kenyon. She did not forgive her father simply because she had never known him, or Grandpa just because he was dead; after all, Grandfather Bonney was a foremost unforgivable and even Grandmother Bonney was a doubtful. She often wondered, proudly, why she hated people. Sometimes she could figure back to the moment the feeling began. For example, she had hated Pinky Freudenburg beginning one day when she had stayed in at recess to work on her long division and he had stayed in too; she had gone to the pencil sharpener and he had sneaked up behind her and kissed her on the cheek and at that exact same moment, a front tooth fell out onto her tongue. She had liked Pinky until then because he made up dances to illustrate her poems besides others which he made up on his own. There was a "Pineapple Dance" and a "Ten-Cent-Store Dance" and a "Mashed Potato Dance." They were all rather alike but very exciting to watch, and Molly was sorry that she had to put her handkerchief over her eyes every time he did one of them in the playground. She had known, too, the moment Grandfather Bonney had become unforgivable. It was the day Ralph threw up in the living room and she poured the acid on her hand. She had looked at the portrait just before Ralph said the milk was sour and had thought "I h. that man," and had known that this would be true forever and ever. But she could not remember when she had begun to hate her mother and Leah and Rachel. As for the Follansbees, of course, she had hated them before she was born.

It occurred to her as her fingers grew more swollen and furrowed that she hated them all for the same reason, but she could not decide what the reason was. You could say, Because they were all fat. But this was not true of Mr. Follansbee and it was not true of Ralph and strictly speaking it was not true of Leah and Rachel although they talked in whispers of corselets. But fatness did have something to do with it. There was something fat about the way Mr. Follansbee belched and the question Ralph had asked her had been fat. She remembered, closing her eyes to see precisely the horrible image, the day early in April when the Follansbees had gone with them one Sunday to Redondo Beach, and Mrs. Follansbee had come out of the bathhouse in a bright red swimming suit. Her thin, knock-kneed legs were traced with thickened varicose veins; her stomach was soft and pendulous and made Molly think of a cake that had run over the side of the pan. But Mr. Follansbee was every bit as bad in his emaciated half-nakedness; his spindling legs, covered all over with black hair, came out of long, loose trunks with a white band around the edge and his arms were hairy too, but his neck was as white as a fish. She would not go in swimming with them but sat on the beach, writing her name and grade in school in the sand with a piece of driftwood. Her mother came once, dripping and glistening, to sit beside her and plead with her to "be a good sport," and she looked at the dimples in her mother's pink knees and hoped she would get bitten by a crab. Ralph had been embarrassed that day, too, and when they had their picture taken against a fake background of the ocean with sea gulls painted on the canvas, both children had refused to be in it and Ralph had muttered, "I wouldn't be in a picture with those ginks if you gave me the Statue of Liberty." But it was clear that no one could be trusted, Ralph least of all. He had always hated the right ones before and now he had become one of them. It did seem a shame, really, that he had turned out so badly. He had told her in so many words that the day he got sick over the tea it had happened because he had seen through Grandfather Bonney, and they had been best friends for a month or so after that, marveling that it had come to them at the same time.

After a long while she pulled up the stopper and let the water run out, slipping down her sides, tickling a little, and deep in her throat she imitated the sound it made as it gurgled down the drain. If she ever got fat, she thought, or ever said anything fat, she would lock herself in a bathroom and stay there until she died. Often she thought how comfortably you could live in a bathroom. You could put a piece of beaver board on top of the tub and use it as a bed. In the daytime you could have a cretonne spread on it so that it would look like a divan. You could use the you-know-what as a chair and the lavatory as a table. You wouldn't have to have anything else but some canned corn and marshmallows, and if you got tired of those, you could let a basket out of the window with a slip of paper saying, "Send up some hot tamales" or some hard-boiled eggs or whatever you particularly wanted at the time.

But she doubted if she would ever get fat enough to have to live in a bathroom. She looked at her thin upper arm and gave it a monkey-bite. There were too many simple ways to avoid it as well as the drastic one of getting a tapeworm. She did profoundly hope, though, that Ralph would get fatter than Tweedledum and Tweedledee put together, and she put both her fists in her eyes, thinking with rapture of how tightly his pants would fit over his seat and his shirt would just barely button over his awful stomach. His cheeks would get so fat they would nearly cover up his eyes. All this time she, Molly Fawcett, would be getting thinner and thinner until she was practically famous for it, and when the time came, she was going to drop the fat name of Molly and be called Clara after Aunt Clara, Father's sister, of whom there was a full-length portrait in the album. Aunt Clara had been as straight up and down as a yardstick and she had enormous stick-out teeth. In the picture she wore a straight black skirt and a straight black jacket, black gloves, black shoes, and a black hat with a wide brim so that all you could see of her was her crooked nose and her great big teeth resting on her lower lip. Molly often stood before the mirror holding her teeth out and saying "Clara? Clara?" as if she were calling to her in the grave, calling to tell her that she would try to look just like her. Otherwise, Aunt Clara had not been very admirable as she had died having a tumor removed, and Mrs. Fawcett, in telling this, would say, "Why, girls, it was such a big tumor that everyone thought she was in a certain condition." She would lift her eyes questioningly and Rachel and Leah would wisely nod. Molly would not have dreamed of asking what the condition was, but she supposed it had something to do with all that tommyrot with which people were constantly trying to ruin her life.

Finally the last of the water was gone and she stood up, putting one foot on the rim of the tub and drying it and then standing on the rug while she dried the other. She gently moved the chair and tried the knob in case anyone had picked the lock while the water was making so much racket and then, taking off the bathing suit, she dried herself and bound her stomach with a piece of outing flannel. She wrapped it so hard and pinned it so tight that it gave her a pain and she had to lie down on the floor to get her slippers because she could not bend over. Then she put on her long-sleeved, high-necked pajamas, and the nightcap she had made over her drenched hair. It was her desire to have tuberculosis, and at the ranch, where she was not supervised, she often went to bed with her hair soaking. She had tried for years to find out where Winifred kept her toothbrush.

She packed up the Boston bag again, having used out of it only the soap and the bathsalts, and let herself out. The voices of the card players came twanging up the stairwell and there were no lights showing under any of the doors save Mrs. Brotherman's and she got to her room without being seen. If she had been seen by anyone, she didn't care who, in her wrapper on this particular night, she would simply have dissolved like a slug with salt poured on it. When she got to her room, she pushed the washstand against the door and she didn't care who heard her. If they did, they did not bother; they bothered about very little around this place and this was one of the few good things about it.

When she had hung her bathing suit up in the window, she got into bed and took up her diary which she kept under her mattress. She wrote:

Ralph has gone beyond the pale. I am his permanent enemy and do not know whether I will ever speak to him again as he has literally beat a rivet of hatred into my heart by a remark he passed on the train today. I am not sure about Winifred this year. She is too fat but she told me a good joke and for the first time in a month of Sundays it was funny enough for me to laugh at.

WINIFRED'S JOKE

You call someone up on the telephone and say, "Are you the lady who washes?" and the other person says, "No," so you say, "Why, you dirty thing," and hang up.

I am not sure about Winifred, as beforesaid, because she told me that she had been to the show with her steady and when I asked what she meant by a steady she said the boy you were dippy about and was dippy about you.

But getting back to the subject of my former brother, what he did is so devilish I could like Leah by comparison in spite of the letter she wrote that made her sound non compus mentis. I will not mention the subject of this letter nor will I write down what Ralph said to me in the train, but I can assure you, Molly, that they were plenty bad. I intend to read all of Sir Walter Scott, Dickens, Stevenson, and James Fenimore Cooper while I am here so that I won't have to have anything to do with R.F. He and Uncle Claude were talking about hunting a mountain lion. I can think of nothing more boresome personally. Uncle Claude looks very old. Naturally. He is thirty-six. I am not sure that I tolerate him. He didn't know what I meant when I said "hogwash and soul-butter" and I am perfectly certain he didn't know that Mark Twain's real name was Samuel Clemens. There are only two I am sure about, Mrs. Brotherman and Magdalene. Mrs. Brotherman will let me do the roses with her, but I do not know whether they will be any good because I read on the train in the Denver *Post* that the aphids are going to be very bad this year. I have not as yet conversed with Magdalene, but she said she had a rabbit foot for me which is said to bring good luck.

Resolution: think all the time about Ralph getting fat. Tomorrow I must look at the pictures of the stout men's underwear in the catalogue and decide which one I want him to be.

CHAPTER EIGHT

In former years, ever since he had seen the calf being born, Ralph had been excited to a point of ecstasy by the robust and perpetual birth of the farm creatures. He had trembled all over at the sight of a mare being carried away in a truck to the stud farm and he had been on hand at every calving. He regretted always that the lambing came in the spring before he got there. Molly, of course, had steadfastly held her ground, and once, two years before, when he had tried to explain to her the difference between a stallion and a gelding, they had had a serious quarrel. She would not be shaken from the belief that they were simply two different breeds of horses. He had not, in any conscious way, really connected his knowledge with people, as now he did, to his shame and sorrow, wondering, with especial revulsion, about the Follansbees. He found himself compelled to study the faces of the men at the dinner table and to look with stunned amazement at Mrs. Brotherman.

Now, this summer, he took no pleasure in the colts and in the sucking calves, and he was glad that his horse and his uncle's had a pure masculine friendship and that they ran away from Winifred's mare whenever she came near them. Winifred herself made him shy and uneasy but he was not in love with her; yet he thought, in a cloudy way, that if he had not committed the crime in the tunnel, he would have been.

For a time there was little, indeed, that he took pleasure in. When, now and again, he lost himself in some small enjoyment, his guilt started and the world was spoiled. He was obsessed with the phrase "the bowels of the earth" and imagined blackened intestines spilling forth from the carcass of a gigantic steer strung up on a pulley as high as a mountain, butchered out by a knife as long as a train. Wakeful at night, he lay with his head under the pillow to shut out the brilliant starlight; he was alert to every sound, hearing Molly, who despised him, turning and grumbling in her sleep; the owls cautioning in the cottonwoods; the men coming home late from White Woman. On these cool nights, full of the clean, unripe smells of June, he could not summon any daydream. For now he aspired to be nothing but what he had been before the evening at the Brown Palace, and he could not even pretend to be that person again because Molly knew his secret, nasty nature. Not even his favorite and foolproof image would come, that of himself as Uncle Claude's partner. If he did not become Uncle Claude's partner, what would happen to him? He had no variety of ambitions as had Molly who, in the course of a week, would plan to be a salesman for the *Book of Knowledge,* a grocer, a government walnut inspector, a trolley conductor in Tia Juana; of course her real vocation was writing and these were to be only sidelines.

Ralph was troubled by the loss of his desire to enter Uncle Claude's world completely. He had continued, against his will, to remember how he had looked at the sick bull and he thought, "If anything happened to a *person,* he'd be the same way." How was this possible, though, when Grandpa Kenyon's death had broken him up in pieces like a plate? Perhaps it was not death that annoyed and disgusted him but only the circumstances leading to death, and Ralph remembered that he had not asked a single question about Grandpa's attack or his three-day illness.

He would brood for a while about Uncle Claude and then brood about Molly. In time he invented a reason, abstruse and clever, for his defection in the tunnel. He said that something, some dark creature like the Skalawag, had cast a spell over him and he had been powerless to break from it. The fact that Molly had been the victim was pure chance; he could as easily have abused the anonymous woman in her dispirited party dress. At times he could almost believe that he had said, "*It* told me to ask you to say all the dirty words you know." But this was little consolation, for he could never explain it to Molly; he could never refer to what had happened in the slightest way, even though she herself mercilessly used the words "tunnel" and "dirty" so often and with such contriving that he felt sure someone would one day remark it. She never spoke to him except to say something unkind. Once she clapped her hand over her mouth and through her fingers gasped, "Oh, my gosh, for a minute you looked just like Grandfather Bonney." And another time she said to Winifred, "You know it runs in our family to be fat. It's bad enough for a woman to be fat but don't you think fat men are terrible?" And she had looked at him as if she wanted him to get fat.

There was no escaping his anxieties, and plagued as he was by them, he sought solitude, but Uncle Claude, who could not bear to be alone, frustrated him, insisting that he go mending fence, hiring the hay crew, fishing before daylight. Ralph found himself hiding when he heard his uncle call. He would hide in the barn in a grain bin or behind the skins in the slaughter shed, his heart trying to burst out of his shirt and his mouth as dry as paper. Often, on butchering days, he went off to town right after breakfast, hitching a ride on the highway to spend the whole day lounging with the high school loungers in the doorway of the old livery stable or in the booths of the drug store. Sometimes a tangle of hysterical girls would come sweeping down the main street, shrieking, into the booths with porcelain-topped tables. It was a prolonged giggle there in the drug store, a battle of wits with the boys who sat in separate booths and courted them by tossing over wet straws and wadded-up paper napkins. Occasionally Winifred and John Fulbright, the boy with the scarlet car, sat in the very last booth, silent and bedazzled.

Uncle Claude was puzzled by this desertion and he said, "I can't make out what's got into you. Why, I thought you was going to turn into an A Number One butcher," and Ralph could only reply, lightly, "I don't rightly know why I'm off it myself." He began even to resent the fact that he was obliged to speak like Uncle Claude in order not to sound impolite.

They were leaning one afternoon against the railing of the corral, their hats over their eyes to keep out the sun. Ken Burkhardt and Dump were hog-tying the sick bull, and the vet, a fat, dapper little man in green gabardine

188

trousers and a pink silk shirt, was sorting his instruments beside the gate. Ralph had not wanted to come, but Uncle Claude had insisted. "It's part of your education," he had said. The bull was thrashing and bellowing and Ralph, certain that he was too much for just two men, did not put his foot up on the railing but stood alert, ready to run.

When the operation began and the knife went in, he had to keep his jaws closed tight and he shut his eyes, swaying sickly. There was a smell which hit them in a hot wave, and the bull made a wailing screaming sound that went splintering though his skull. He dared not look but kept his eyes fixed on the green ball and the two red arabesques that floated behind his eyelids. While all this was going on, while the poor beast was being cut up like a piece of food, Uncle Claude said, "We'll go fishing tomorrow up to the Hell Hole."

He felt no anger, but he was determined not to go, and he said, "I am sorry, Uncle Claude, I can't."

But Uncle Claude only said, "You be up by four. It ain't any good if you wait longer than that."

"I can't go," said Ralph. "I'm going to do something else tomorrow."

"My eye," said his uncle.

"I am. I'm going to play pool."

"At four in the morning? Where you going to play it? In the swimming pool?" He poked Ralph in the ribs, laughing at his joke. Ralph moved away irritably. The bull roared and the vet said good-naturedly, "Take it easy, old man, we're comin' right along here."

"I can't go fishing tomorrow, Uncle Claude," said Ralph stubbornly.

189

His uncle said, "Well, I ain't going fishing to the Hell Hole alone and I ain't going to take your sister, so it looks like I'm taking you."

"Looky here," cried Ralph, "looky here, not you and not anybody else is going to tell *me* what to do, goddamit to hell." He left the corral, walking in enormous strides back to the house, immediately remorseful, his pride receding. He knew—and even when he had had his tantrum he had known—that Uncle Claude did not want to impose his will upon him, he just wanted company, and when you came right down to it, a man couldn't deny another man that. So he would go as he had known all along he would go and as Uncle Claude had known.

Never had there been such weather. It was clear and hot in the day and cool at night. Curds of bruised clouds hung motionless in the sky. If rain came, it came as a spectacular storm, beginning with brilliant lightning and thunder which sometimes stuttered far away in the distant ranges and sometimes was so close at hand that it sounded like blasting at the very base of Garland Peak. The rain followed with a push like the heavy wings of an eagle, obscuring the mountains, the timothy fields, and the outbuildings. During the storm, everyone sat moody and damp in the parlor, stubbornly listening to the radio over which came nothing but an outraged cackling and, at great intervals, a thin wisp of song. Uncle Claude paced the floor restlessly. He hated rain just as he hated illness or anything else that kept him indoors.

Very late on one of these days of storm, a man stopped by, riding at the head of a string of twenty blooded horses.

He asked for quarters for the night. Uncle Claude, who never turned anyone away nor asked a stranger what his business was, said he could sleep in the bunkhouse and his horses could shift for themselves in the cow pasture. It was nearly as dark as night when Ralph and Uncle Claude rode out with him to lead the horses, but now and again the sky was split with lightning; the frightened neighing of the horses and behind that sound the thunder seemed unreal, like something in a western movie. Ralph experimented; he spurred Studebaker to a run and standing up in his stirrups he screamed but he could not hear his own voice, he could only feel it in his throat.

The stranger, by his very coming, elevated everyone's spirits. Uncle Claude built up the fire and he said to Ralph, "Go tell that coon to pack up a jug of Dago out of the cellar." But Ralph went himself although Magdalene argued, saying that she didn't want him "amessin' around in my spuds and my engerns and my conserves." He was so excited by the storm and the stranger and the twenty horses that he could not remember, once he was down there, what he had come for. He turned the flashlight over the shelves and a pack rat ran with a glittering eye behind a crock. When the light fell on the jugs of wine, he remembered, and instead of taking just one, he took two.

Warmed by the fire, freed by the wine, the man talked volubly, and all the other men and Ralph and Winifred sat around him listening and laughing as if they were outcasts to whom at last a visitor from the world had come. He told them that he was riding to Vernal, Utah, to take his horses to a gambler (he pronounced it "gambular") to whom he had lost them on a bet. Uncle Claude said, "That's a long ride, Mister. Would you do better to put them in some boxcars?" The man had a long, lopsided chin and rheumy eyes. He laughed and replied, "He took my fare as well as my riding horses."

The lights went off and they had to eat supper by kerosene lamps. They did not come on again that night, but the fire was bright all evening and they crouched around it, some of them sitting on the floor like Indians. Molly was learning to play the ukulele and she sat in the darkness on the gallery, plucking the unresonant strings and singing softly over and over again, "My dog has fleas." The stranger would not tell them what the bet had been for which there had been such high stakes, and all of them passionate with curiosity and with the wine and the howling storm that did not abate for more than a minute all evening, questioned him time and again, sometimes impatiently, sometimes uneasily. Now and again he looked quickly over his shoulder, but this was only meant to tantalize them for afterward he laughed in their faces.

Ralph drank several glasses of the wine and the effect of it was as odd and elusive as the atmosphere which the stranger had imparted to the evening. He was by turns drowsy and keenly awake. Winifred sat crosslegged in front of the fire on a deerskin, saying nothing at all, but looking up with an abstracted smile at the stranger sometimes and at Uncle Claude who was the company's principal spokesman. It was one of the few nights since Ralph and Molly had come that she had stayed at home, and the men had teased her about it at supper, saying they guessed her boy friend was no great shakes if he let a little thing like rain keep him away. Her mother gently remonstrated, "Winifred has better sense than to make herself sick by going out in the rain," and the man who had started the raillery mumbled an apology, recalling her "tendency."

For the space of this long evening, secure in the darkness from questioning eyes, safe from Molly whose meaningless plinking was as steady as the rain, Ralph allowed himself to think of Winifred and a guiltless desire ruffled warmly over him. It was hardly possible, he thought, that she and John Fulbright did not kiss. Often he heard them coming down the lane at midnight, coasting quietly, and then there was an interval of a quarter of an hour or more before the car went away and he heard Winifred coming up the stairs so softly she must have walked in her stocking feet. She was not like the other girls who were boisterous and brash, liking to walk loudly in their high heels across the drug store's tiled floor and, in the booths, suddenly begin to sing. They were loud-mouthed and posturing and could perpetrate their tomfoolery for hours together. But Winifred was demure, soft-spoken and almost pensive, and always upon her lips was that enchanting, mysterious smile. Ralph had heard in the town that she was a very good dancer and he marveled that she had this skill as well as the masculine ones of riding and shooting. When he first heard this, he said to her, "I have a t.l. for you." She said, inadequately, "Homer says you are the best help irrigating he ever had." When he told her what he had heard, she said nothing and was not at all embarrassed, as if this were her simple due. Molly who, according to her custom, had been lurking unseen in the room, sidled forward, *The Pathfinder* folded over her thumb, and said, "What I heard is of far more import than that. I heard you could read Latin at sight." Winifred frowned and cast down her eyes as if her character had somehow been impugned.

Winifred stirred, and looking around at Ralph, she said, "Where are they now?" so that with surprise he realized that she, too, had not been listening to the men.

"Where are who?" he said.

"Your mother and Leah and Rachel."

Everyone listened as he said, "I don't know. The last letter was from Hong Kong."

The stranger peered at him closely. "Well, I'll be. So your folks are in Hong Kong. I was there once and I seen one of them mongooses kill a cobra snake."

The ukulele immediately stopped and Molly, out of the darkness, said, "I doubt that. The mongoose is native to India." Her voice was firm and clear and its effect upon the stranger was so prompt that sweat came out on his forehead, glittering in the firelight, and his hand trembled so that some of the wine spilled on his khaki Army and Navy store pants. He did not dispute that voice, like the voice of conscience there in the pitch blackness, but he replied quickly and nervously, "By golly, that's right. I must of been thinking of Bagdad." Molly laughed derisively and began to play again.

The men wanted to hear of the stranger's world travels, but he would not tell. The most they could get out of him was an account of an opium den he had been taken to in the San Francisco Chinatown.

Ralph thought, half enviously, of his mother and sisters. All summer plump letters and picture postal cards came to him and Molly from Yokohama, Tokyo, Shanghai, Canton. They gave the cards and envelopes to Magdalene who kept them on a shelf in the kitchen in a Roi-Tan cigar box which until then had only held an announcement of Grandpa Kenyon's funeral and the business card of a Watkins man named Edward P. Ottolengui. Leah and Rachel, in their letters, alternated between a formal essay style ("You will next want to know about the peculiar vehicle they have here which is called a 'rickshaw' and is the equivalent of the American taxicab") and a gushing coquetry ("our nice new suitcases have been just ruined by all the awful stickers the hotels put on them"), but Mrs. Fawcett always wrote in the same way; her tone was a combination of the sisters' two styles, half educational, half jocular. She wrote, "Luncheon has become a 'movable feast' for us since we never can tell what adventure is going to o'ertake us in the forenoon to keep us from our victuals. And, my dears, the victuals when we finally do get to them are just as strange. I'm afraid my persnickety Molly would have to change her habits if she came here. We have become very partial to bean sprouts! (How is Uncle Claude's garden, by the way? I hope you are both helping Mrs. B. in it, for that is a very nice way to show your gratitude to C.K.) What would the Orient do without bean sprouts and rice, I often wonder, but I dare say there is no danger of at least the rice giving out, as from every train window you see nothing but fields upon fields of it, dotted all over with coolies in their picturesque hats like those on the postal Leah sent you yesterday."

It was not the nonsense of the letters that disturbed him. Indeed, he was rather relieved to find that traveling had no effect upon his mother's silliness. What made him dread the daily mail was that each letter contained a passage on that happy future when the family would be reunited in Connecticut. There was an implication of ponderous finality in this reunion. Between the lines, he read that she would bury Uncle Claude as completely as she had buried Grandpa, and while this year he was often discontented and often wished to be elsewhere, whenever he thought of his mother and of Connecticut, he clung with passionate devotion to his uncle and to Colorado. He was, at these times, like someone who has been told that his lover will die soon and who, unable to conceive the metamorphosis of his habits and thoughts after her death, becomes the closer bound to the necessity of this love so that when the hour comes and she is gone, he feels that he has not been prepared at all. Such, he brooded, was the shape of the earth that the farther away the world-travelers went, the closer they came to the Atlantic seaboard and to their inexorable plans. In a short few months from now, his father's gravestone and Grandpa Kenyon's would be separated from him by the whole width of the continent, but Grandfather Bonney, portable, ubiquitous, reposing for the summer in a safety deposit vault, would always be at hand. And so, always at hand, would be Molly who could ruin him, blow up his world if she chose. He knew, but for no reason he could name, that she would do nothing so long as they were here, but in that bare wasteland where they were to live under the shadow of the trinity of fat men, he must guard himself against her weapon.

In the middle of the evening, Uncle Claude complained restlessly that the rain was getting on his nerves and that the wine was not doing him any good. Suddenly in the room there was a sense of fear and Ralph saw Dump look furtively at the stranger. The man, mean-mouthed and nasty-eyed, sat with his chair tilted against the fireplace. He had got over the nervousness Molly had caused him and had for some time been asking about the hunting in these parts. At first the men talked enthusiastically, blandly and casually interrupting one another, but bit by bit they withdrew and one by one fell silent. Uncle Claude for a while did not sense their dim suspicions, and having the floor to himself, told story after story. Then he said that he had not done much hunting this spring himself as he had in years past, but he told how many pounds of elk and deer the other boys had brought in, most of it hanging up out there in the icehouse this very minute. He recounted their adventures as if they had been his own.

"But you say you ain't got none of this meat yourself?" said the stranger. "How come?"

This was a question he had wanted to be asked and he smiled. "I'll tell you. Along here in April I was scouting around in the foothills having a look for a good fat beaver and one day I seen . . ." He paused. Now his men's distrust had made itself known to him. It was almost as if they were shaking their heads at him and even Winifred sat up straight, tense and waiting. He finished, "I seen something that took my fancy."

"And what in the world was that?" said the man. He let his chair down slowly and leaned forward, holding his wine glass in both hands.

"Well, that's a question I don't feel called to answer," said Uncle Claude.

Ralph was perplexed. He knew that what had stilled the men's tongues was that they had begun to wonder if the stranger were the Law in disguise and had come to collect evidence against them to settle their score with the game authorities. But why had they not wanted him to know that there was a mountain lion on Garland Peak? There was no bounty on them. Perhaps it was no more than a cumulative resentment of the man who had drawn their secrets out of them but refused to tell what the bet was that he had lost.

Hearing the thunder once again burst in the mountains, the thought of the lion enraptured him and he wondered where she was and if she were asleep now in her den. They had looked for her day after day but had never seen her, though twice they were sure they found the prints of her paws in the squelchy ground near the beaver dam. Then he knew that the reason Uncle Claude had not named Goldilocks by name was that she was his own property, his and Ralph's. The other men could know because they could be trusted not to hunt her. But you could not trust this ugly man who now, laughing out of his uneven mouth, said, "I wouldn't think you'd have to go to the mountains to hunt that kind of game. What's the matter with the little lady settin' here? Settin' right here with all us big grown men?"

Uncle Claude slowly turned his eyes to Winifred who had not even seemed to hear and he said reproachfully, "That's no way to talk." He sounded hurt like a misunderstood child. "I was talking about something else."

Soon after this, they all went to bed. Ralph lay for a long time listening to the rain and to the frequent thunder. Often the lightning shot like a flare through the curtains and illuminated the posts of his bed which ended in carved pineapples. There was too much noise outside for him to hear Molly in the next room, and for the first time in weeks he did not think of her, but only of Uncle Claude whom now he thought he understood. He had never grown up and his hunt for Goldilocks was a childhood game; his men indulged and protected him like an innocent. They wanted him to be happy and so they wanted him to have the mountain lion.

The day dawned in a dry brightness. But the stranger was gone before sun-up, leaving no trace but the marks of his horses' hooves in the mud of the lane. The sheriff came at noon with a posse and gave Uncle Claude a proper dressing down. "So, though he don't account for himself and he's drivin' twenty thoroughbreds, you don't catch on. By God, Kenyon, you must of got dropped on the head when you was a baby. And so must of your whole outfit here." He tapped his forehead with his finger and said, "To let." But all of them, including the sheriff and the mock-angry men who rode with him, were delighted that the stranger had been a thief. The Bar K outfit, at dinner that day, said they had known it all along. "I knew it from the start," said Dump. "I never let on but just played into his hand to watch the show. I knew from the start he wasn't no Law, he was an *out*law."

From that time forward, the summer was a rush of pleasure. In late July there was a forest fire in the mountains to the north and the unhealthy sun, remote behind the smoke, was as small and lusterless as a withered orange. People twenty miles away from the burning trees coughed and their eyes watered. All the men from the Bar K went to help fight it. They rapidly dug trenches in the soft ground, slippery with pine needles. Ralph's hands were blistered by the handle of his quick ax and his face was swollen with the heat. After twelve hours, when the fire was under control and there was nothing now but smoldering in the underbrush, Ralph and Homer Armitage and Uncle Claude went to the ranger's look-out where Ralph had his first drink of whisky. He did not enjoy the experience; he was hot already and the liquor set him ablaze. It was just dawn and he had had nothing to eat since the evening before. At first the light-headedness was pleasant; his ears rang as though he were holding shells to them and he heard the men talking as if from a far and golden distance. But in the next stage he was heavy-limbed and heavy-eyed and it was thus that he began the long walk home. He had to calculate each step before he took it lest he fall down. The other men had gone on ahead, and by the time they got home there was no one in the house but the womenfolk who were sitting at the table in the dining room drinking coffee and waiting to hear about the fire.

Ralph did not want to eat; he wanted only to lie full length on his bed and sleep, but he forced himself to lift his coffee cup with a sore hand to his parched lips and he ate part of a fried egg though it sickened him. He was aware that Molly was watching him, but he was too weary to care, and when finally, unable to sit up any longer, he excused himself and she said, half under her breath, "So you drink, too, Ralph Fawcett," he was not in the least afraid of her. He said crossly, "So's your old man," and joggled the back of her chair.

At haying, a whole new gallery of people came, Mormons

and people from Oklahoma with outlandish ways. A family named Prevost came to live in the house. The man was clumsy and once, out of simple awkwardness, fell off his rick. The woman, in unbroken silence, helped Magdalene with the cooking. They had brought with them a tow-headed girl of nine named Darling and a boy of three named Gasper. They had come on foot, carrying a shuck mattress and a couple of laundry bags which bulged with everything they owned in the world. They were from Muskogee and had accents so grotesque that not even Molly, an able mimic, could copy them. Although Uncle Claude offered them two rooms on the third floor, they preferred a small back bedroom downstairs off the kitchen, and they all slept in the same big brass bed. When their eldest daughter, Opal, lost her job in a café in town (a circumstance enshrouded in mystery) and came to stay with her parents, they still remained in one room. And then, in the last week of the harvest, three of Mr. Prevost's cousins, two women and a man, drove by to spend the night, and all of them slept in the same small room, eight of them together, six of them grown.

The cousins had come in a tall green Reo, as rusty and sorry as something left to perish on a dump. They left the next day at sundown, not even waiting for supper, taking the Prevosts with them. The Reo made loud gusty sounds and the driver, a dreary man they had called Cheesie, played the fool with the clutch so that the car shook back and forth in a paroxysm and with a racking cough until it died in the lane while the curious horses watched, hanging their long heads over the fence. Cheesie and Mr. Prevost got out and lifted up the hood and tinkered for a long while until

Ralph, who was watching from the porch, went to tell his uncle that they needed help. They worked uselessly until dark. The mute women, once the light was gone, got out of the car and built a fire in the middle of the road. Gasper and Darling went to the slough with a pan and they brought it back full of water and Mrs. Prevost made coffee, crouching over the small blaze like an unhappy gypsy woman. Uncle Claude gave the Reo a push with the pick-up over the bridge, but Cheesie had not understood his instructions and instead of turning down the road, he kept on straight ahead so that the Reo plowed up into the sage and stopped there, hugging the hillside for dear life.

They did not debate at all what they should do. The uncomplaining women and children stamped out the fire and joined the men and in the darkness they set out on foot, carrying their laundry bags, disappearing in the luminous sarvis berry. The Reo remained there, but the Prevosts, seen once in a strong light, were never seen again. The car disintegrated almost as one watched. The doors swung open and the hinges loosened until they all but fell. The tires collapsed; the running boards sagged and the top, on which the magpies impertinently sat, acquired blisters and dents. Whenever he looked at the car, Ralph remembered Opal, a yellow-haired girl with acne all over her face, who had spoken to him only once and had said, "Did you know my daddy used to raise goats?" Her dead voice was full of damaged pride; she had not asked a question but had stated a vanished fact. The Prevosts, like the downcast women of the train, existed lifelessly like the senile Reo in which the former animation, now quite gone, was unwilled.

When the quiet autumn came, inching redly over the

valley, and Winifred had gone to college and Uncle Claude had left for Missouri, Ralph roamed through the days like a sleeper, barely conscious of anything but the irrational feeling that if he could only figure out the way, he could make the world break open at his feet, even in spite of Molly.

CHAPTER NINE

IN THE WINTER, MOLLY WOULD GO ON SATURDAY MORNING up to the summit of Garland Peak where by chance one day, turning over a stone, she had found it red with hibernating ladybugs. No one at the ranch or at school had ever heard of this phenomenon and the president of the Nature Lore society, a boy of fifteen, told her it was something that ought to interest the people at the agricultural college. Accordingly, she sent the entymology department thousands of them, packing them into matchboxes and wrapping them carefully in heavy brown paper. She got no acknowledgment at all except for one typed postal card without a signature which notified her that her parcel—it was the eighth— had arrived. She was not at all disheartened and continued weekly to gather the sleeping bugs, sure that an investigation was under way and that in time her name would be mentioned in a monograph in a scientific journal. She went even on the coldest days when the snowdrifts were deep and the pine needles in the glades were ossified with ice. The shapes of the high blue trees were obscured by the snow that encumbered their branches and they looked like formless ghosts. Sometimes the wind came fiercely down the trackless slopes, blowing sharp pellets into her face. On the upland meadows the sun was blinding, and walking there was difficult because the crust was thin and the soft piles of snow beneath were deep.

Garland Peak had always been her favorite to climb. It was one of the lowest in the first range, lying to the north and west of the ranch. In the summer she went up the face if it, but since this involved scaling three chimneys, she had to change her route when the storms came and was obliged to approach it indirectly, first climbing half way up a higher peak and then cutting across a mesa, down a gulch, and up the opposite bank to the northern base. The ascent was not an easy one at any time of year, but it was worth all the fatigue. From the summit she commanded a view of the entire valley, of the range as far as the eye could see, and of Cuthbert Pass beyond which, disappearing finally in a gauzy blue, were the highest mountains of all, the Arrowheads, which seemed as far away as the end of the world. In the summer the mesa below was like a sheet of rusted metal with densely growing Indian paintbrush, and there was a part of it where columbines grew at the edge of a stream in which, down near the gulch where it broadened out just before it joined another stream, there was the largest beaver dam in all the hills around. In earlier summers, when Winifred or Ralph had gone with her, they had often seen deer grazing among the blue flowers, but she had never seen anything, not so much as a rabbit when she was alone.

She had been here in the fall when the aspens shone like money among the conifers on all the foothills and the high fields were dark green with the first shoots of winter wheat.

The hay had been up for weeks by then and the stubble in the meadow was short and even and had an itchy, barbered look. The highway, a narrow glitter, went between red banks until it vanished midway up Cuthbert at a pyramidal stone called the King's Tower. At that time, through Uncle Claude's field glasses which she took surreptitiously from his desk (Grandmother Bonney's eyes, each time she did this, seemed to follow her), she had been able to see the cattle moving down from the summer range, their white faces bobbing up and down like buoys as they ran; it was hard to see the bodies behind them for the soil up there was almost as red as their hides. She could clearly see Uncle Claude's place. One day she heard a shot ring out and she could see Homer running across the yard to a flapping turkey. She knew it was Homer by his black shirt. Another time she saw Mrs. Brotherman moving about in the kitchen garden and Molly, spying on her, said aloud, "Miz Budmanny's at the muskmelons."

Until she had found the ladybugs, Molly had gone to the mountain to be undisturbed at her writing. She carried her materials with her in a small knapsack on her back: three notebooks with glossy blue covers on the inside of which was printed the multiplication table and information about weights and measures; a pocket dictionary; pencils and a pocket knife to sharpen them with; a safety-match box full of paper clips and one of rubber bands; and, though she had no use for it, several sheets of carbon paper. She had found an ideal glade for her study. It was very small and surrounded so densely by trees and chokecherry that they were almost like walls, and right in the middle, as if planned for her, was a big flat rock.

The first thing she had written there was a long humorous ballad called "The Fierce Mexican" which she was able to admire for several weeks, rereading it nightly when she was in bed, but she turned upon it finally with such loathing that she tore it up into tiny little pieces and tried to forget it, but she could not. The imperfection of the rhyme of "Mexican" and "Mohican" stuck to her mind like paste. She had quit writing poetry after that and had simultaneously begun a detective novel called "The Mystery of the Portland Vase" and a short story about a leper colony. The novel was not successful because it was too short. Furthermore, the reading public would have immediately found her out because the article in the Sunday supplement of the Denver *Post* from which she had got the idea had said that the vase had just been found and had been put under lock and key in the British Museum, about which she knew nothing. But she was well pleased with the short story and thought of submitting it to the *Scholastic Magazine*. The hero was a man named Lord Garnsborough who had so wasted away that all that was left of him was one tooth; he and his close friend, Launfal Hottentot, who was all gone but the lobe of his right ear, traveled about together in a glass cage, visiting people in worse conditions than they. An especially pitiful case was that of Malachi Strattonbottle who had nothing left but a small spitcurl of oleaginous hair.

Now in the winter she wrote in her bedroom in the evenings and on Sundays and she kept a meticulously detailed account in a separate notebook of what she had seen on her ladybug trips. The ladybug place was very near her studio and she always looked in; completely covered in snow, it was as if it lay under dust sheets waiting her return in the spring. In some ways the view from Cuthbert was more exciting at this season than at any other. On a clear day it was possible to see the men on the ricks in the pastures, pitching down feed to the herd which appeared to be hundreds of small red blocks on the glaring snow, as small as her ladybugs. The Caribou was frozen solid and all the trees on either side of it were bare. Molly loved the snow. When she had seen her first snowfall, she pretended to have a sore throat and did not go to school that day but stayed in bed, watching the snow flurry in imperfect circles over the poplar trees.

Both Ralph and Uncle Claude thought Molly's enterprise was absurd and they said they imagined her boxes of ladybugs had given rise to all sorts of jokes in the laboratory. Uncle Claude said she called to mind a cranky friend of Grandpa's who had shot magpies for three weeks and had tried to sell the feathers to a veterans' hospital to use for burning out the sickroom smells. She did not care a red cent for the opinion of either one of them on this or on any other subject. She rarely talked to them, but now and again if she particularly did not want to talk to Mrs. Brotherman about plants—she was rather outgrowing her interest in them as a result of Mrs. Brotherman's preoccupation this winter with snakeroot which Molly found singularly unattractive—and if she had finished a book and did not want to start another, she would play Double Canfield with one of them or Casino with both. They were so stupid and slow-witted that there was no sport in playing with them, but it was fairly fun to watch them make mistakes.

It seemed to Molly when she was alone in the mountains

that she had been by herself for years now, really ever since Grandpa had died. It was as if Ralph and her mother and sisters were no blood kin to her at all, as if nobody ever had been except her father and Grandpa Kenyon who was really only what you called "a connection." She was entirely solitary at school which she disliked this year. She disliked the harsh mountain voices of the children and the teachers and the smell of winter clothes, and she hated riding Eye-Opener over the river and then two miles into town every morning when the sun was just barely up and then back in the late afternoon when it was already going down and the light on the snow-covered meadows was blue. The children in her grade were so backward that she had to be given extra work to occupy her and she made notebooks of advertisements clipped from magazines showing different types of "Houses," "Landscapes," and "Occupations." The motto for the Occupations notebook was "Give us, Oh, give us the man who sings at his work." When she was not unhappy, she was bored. The only things that really gave her pleasure were the ladybugs, her writing, and her plans for a horrible life for Ralph. She became so obsessed with the idea that he would turn into Grandfather Bonney that she almost believed that he looked like him already and on the flyleaf of her diary she drew a farcical facsimile of the portrait under which she wrote "Ralph Bonney, Jr."

Every Saturday she took her Brownie along. She did not have much luck with photography and in her pictures the sky took up more space than anything else and trees and buildings tended to be diagonal. But she hoped that she would one day see Goldilocks and could take her picture.

Uncle Claude and Ralph, timid of the snowy slopes ("Typical! Typical!" exulted her scornful heart), had left off their hunt and said they would find her in the spring. But just as always before, she never saw a living thing when she was alone.

And then, the very day they came with her, they caught sight of the mountain lion. On the Saturday before Christmas Uncle Claude decided that they must have a Christmas tree. They said they would go to Garland with Molly and on the way down would cut a big fir, and they took a sled along, leaving it at the foot.

There had been a big snowfall on Thursday and there had been no thaw. The sun was warm on the slopes and mesas and brilliant in the branches of the evergreens, but the air was cold and the wind was raw in the unprotected clearings. Uncle Claude said it might drop to twenty below that night. They had got the ladybugs—Uncle Claude scraped them up with his hunting knife to Molly's exasperation for she used a spatula which seemed more humane and also more scientific—and had started down. Uncle Claude was the first to get to the opposite bank of the gulch and just as Ralph and Molly began the ascent, he turned around and motioned them to come quietly. It was an easy climb and the path was deep in snow so that they made no sound. Once Molly broke off an ice-covered twig on a chokecherry bush but the noise was slight. Their uncle stood absolutely still, watching something. He had moved into the cover of a small deformed scrub oak laden with snow and he beckoned them to join him. They stepped carefully in his boot-prints, not seeing yet what he did. Then, when they were beside him, he pointed to the east side of the mesa and there they saw the mountain lion standing still with her head up, facing them, her long tail twitching. She was honey-colored all over save for her face which was darker, a sort of yellow-brown. They had a perfect view of her, for the mesa there was bare of anything and the sun illuminated her so clearly that it was as if they saw her close up. She allowed them to look at her for only a few seconds and then she bounded across the place where the columbines grew in summer and disappeared among the trees. Her flight was lovely: her wastless grace and her speed did not make Molly think immediately of her fear but of her power. When you saw a running deer, you were conscious only of its instinct to flee danger. The lion had sensed peril and yet they, the watchers, sensed peril in her, under her tawny hide, in the way her tail had moved against the glint of the snow, in the way she streaked across the flat land. Molly shivered to think she might now have climbed a tree like a tame cat and might be sitting there observing them with large green eyes.

"Goddamn," said Uncle Claude. "This would be the day we'd see her when we never brought our guns." His face, in the snow glare, did not show so much disappointment as anger, as if he really hated the mountain lion and wanted to kill her for that reason and not for the sport of it. Ralph did not say a word but continued to look at the place where she had been, smiling a secret smile. She was afraid and thought she could never come here again. The lion grew to huge proportions in her reflection. She imagined its claws, its teeth, the way it would hiss. She remembered a lioness in the zoo at Balboa Park who had stopped in her prowling now and then to lift her lips and grumble deeply; she had not reminded Molly at all of a cat with those heavy dewlaps and puppy-like paws, and it seemed incredible to her that their pansy-faced Budge belonged to the same species, though Leah and Rachel and Aunt Kathleen kept insisting that she see the close resemblance. Afterward, Molly often had a dream that she was being chased mile after mile through the streets of San Diego by the lioness who almost overtook her at every mailbox.

When they started down, she twice looked back over her shoulder and she kept close to Ralph. When they got home, she did not wait to help take the tree off the sled but went straight into the house, feeling unsafe until then. Mrs. Brotherman was in the living room putting up the holly wreaths and when Molly came in to warm her hands at the fire, she said, "A friend just sent me a box of Delicious apples and I do think they're quite the best I ever tasted. Let me finish this one wreath and then we'll go upstairs and have one." Molly looked at the scar on her hand and then she thought again of the golden cat and her fear left; in its place there came a soft, inexplicable sadness. On the way down, her arm had once brushed against her brother's and remembering this, she felt weak.

The warmth of Mrs. Brotherman's sitting room and the smell of the apples, the sight of the widow watering a pot of begonia with a small sprinkling can, the bright winter sunlight through the dimity curtains made Molly even sadder. She was full of wishes. She wished that she had yellow hair like Leah's and Rachel's and the lion's. She wished she could go to London and become a famous writer. She wished she did not have to wear glasses; she wished she were only four feet five.

Mrs. Brotherman, blowing up the fire with a pair of small red bellows, said, "I am always sad at Chistmas here, although your uncle does everything he can to make it a happy season." The statement must have come at the end of a long string of thoughts, but in that even, toneless voice there was no clue to their nature, whether Christmas made her conscious of her widowhood or whether she longed to be a child or longed to be in Salem. Molly was embarrassed and quickly said, "Oh, I forgot to tell you. We saw Goldilocks."

Mrs. Brotherman sat on a bench before the fire, clutching her hands together in her lap, and even though Molly could only see her profile, she saw fear arrive in the twilit face and remain there. Then, turning, she said, "There is nothing here but danger and there never has been, but this is the worst yet. I had hoped Mr. Kenyon had been mistaken."

"Oh, a mountain lion isn't dangerous," said Molly, courageous in the presence of this adult cowardice. "They're just as afraid of people as deer are."

"Perhaps. But I will feel safer when it is dead. I hope you will not go back there. If the men must go, they must, but it's not right for a girl to be alone in the mountains with a lion loose."

Molly threw her apple core into the fire and heard it hiss briefly. She, too, would not feel safe until the beautiful animal was dead. She would never be unafraid at Garland again because in the back of her mind she would always know that the big cat might be watching her from the crotch of a tree or from behind a rock.

She left the sitting room and went to her bedroom where she wrapped up the last of the ladybugs she would ever send. She could not keep her mind on anything; it kept darting around like a darning needle and she did not know what was the matter with her. If only she had yellow hair, she thought, she would be an entirely different kind of person; she would not be cross all the time. At the very thought of her crossness, she began to grow very angry and it became clear to her that Ralph and Uncle Claude had gone with her today, knowing they would see Goldilocks, just in order to spoil her ladybug project. They had *known* that she never saw any wild animals when she was alone and they had come today deliberately so that everything would be ruined. There had been absolutely no reason for them not just to stay at the foot and cut down their idiotic Christmas tree. She personally would have nothing to do with the tree as she thought the whole idea of it was too sentimental for words. In fact, she thought Christmas itself was bourgeois and she had never got anything she wanted but just things like a patent-leather hatbox or yarn flowers that you were supposed to pin on your coat, as if you ever *would*. There was going to be a piece of mistletoe hung in the door between the dining room and the living room and the thought of it gave her gooseflesh because she remembered once in Covina Mr. Follansbee had kissed Miss Runyon and Miss Runyon had squealed and said, "Of all things! Aren't you the foxy grandpa!" And besides that, Uncle Claude had bought a lot of grain alcohol and rotgut (*rotgut!* People ought to be put in jail for using words like that) and kept saying that they would all "get stinko and then I'm gonna trim every jack man of you at

Red Dog." It was not hard to imagine. They would all pile up to the gallery and clank their silver dollars together, acting as if they were in a movie.

And Winifred was coming home. She was coming on the evening train tonight, in fact, and there was no doubt at all that she had acquired insufferable airs. Molly knew because she had got a letter from her in which she sounded exactly like Leah and Rachel. "My sorority sisters are griped because I am the only pledge who has already got dated up for the Junior Prom." Molly had replied, "Personally, I have never heard of a Junior Prom. Possibly you are thinking of Promenade. I thought you went to college to study Cicero's essays and I must say, Winifred, that you do not sound as if you are making much effort to be an outstanding *bas bleu*." It had been a severe measure, but one thing no one could ever say about Molly Fawcett was that she was wishy-washy. Decisively she got out her diary and added Winifred's name to the list of unforgivables and then, because he had wrecked the ladybug business, she also put down "Claude (Club-Foot) Kenyon." Recently she had learned that Claude meant "lame," and she had decided to put a new character in the story about the leper colony called Claude Binks who only had one toenail left.

She lit the incense in the gilt incense Buddha burner which she had brought from Covina and very briefly prayed that the mountain lion would either clear out of the hills or would step into a skunk trap; she hoped neither Ralph nor Uncle Claude would get her. Molly had not decided yet whether she would be a Catholic or a Buddhist but she had narrowed the choice down to these two as she certainly had no intention of being either a Presbyterian or a Christian Scientist. Magdalene had told her about the Holy Rollers, but Molly did not think they were her style. Her final decision depended on what would make Mr. Follansbee the maddest, and now she sat down at the table and wrote him a letter, frankly asking him. She also wrote a letter to President Hoover and one to Henry Ford. They were identical and read:

Dear Gentleman:

I have been apprized of your outstanding munificence with regard to helping people along the highway of life and so I wonder if you have any typewriters that you don't need. I am very needful of one myself and if you could see your way clear to sending me one, I will be very grateful.

I think what you have done for other people is wonderful and hope it will come to pass that I will have first-hand knowledge anent this.

Respectfully yours,

Molly Fawcett

P.S. There is no Railway Express here so you will have to send it by freight.

These were quite useless, she knew. She had already asked ten other people of lesser importance—including Dr. Haskell—and had got only one reply (except for a comic postal from the doctor on which he wrote "If at first you don't succeed, try, try again," and so she had) and that was from Spencer Penrose's secretary saying that Mr. Penrose was out of town, was, in fact, in India, but would attend to her letter when he got back. Of course the blatherskite never did, and he had been in Colorado Springs for two months now and she had not heard a word from him. Furthermore, she had read in the Denver *Post* that he had bought an elephant to bring back to the Broadmoor (what for? thought Molly) which seemed really unfair considering how badly she needed a typewriter and how much cheaper they were than elephants.

She sealed her letters and then stood in front of the mirror with her teeth sticking out. "Clara? Clara?" she said. Then, without leaving the bureau but leaning on one elbow, she reached for her diary and her pencil and to the list of unforgivables she added her own name. She burst into tears and cried until she was hungry, and all the time she cried she watched herself in the mirror, getting uglier and uglier until she looked like an Airedale.

Easter came late that year. The pasque flowers were already paling on the mesas and the cactus was in bloom, smelling like melons. This time of year was full of wonders. Even the howling of the coyotes had a queer charm for Ralph, and after they had ceased, the meadowlarks sang freshly for an hour or so. The light lying on the meadows just at dawn and then again just before dark was a singular ominous yellow, giving to trees and to animals a submarine remoteness and ambiguity of outline. But then in the broadlight and then when the night came the shapes were separated. There was always a haze on the far mountains and sometimes it bedimmed Garland Peak. The evenings were cool and light; through the open windows came the smell of the first new leaves of the hop vines and the upturned dirt of the flower garden. There were clear, nocturnal sounds from the direction of the Caribou where the Negroes from the mines fished in the dusk and then when night came built fires on the river bank to fry their trout and to drink whisky and sing spirituals amongst the weeping willow trees.

Ralph dreamed of the mountain lion and thought, "Oh, if I don't get her, I will *die!*" He saw himself standing where they had stood before Christmas, taking perfect aim, shooting her through her proud head with its wary eyes, and then running across the mesa to stroke her soft saffron flanks and paws. Ralph had always loved cats and when Budge had died this spring of old age, he had been wretched for days, mourning the lost purr and the quiet feet. He would not skin the mountain lion, he decided, if he got her, but would have her stuffed and keep her in his room all his life. If he had to go to college, he would take her along with him. He wished that Uncle Claude were not so keen as he, for he felt, somehow, that he had more right to Goldilocks: he wanted her because he loved her, but Uncle Claude wanted her only because she was something rare. Besides, Uncle Claude would be here forever and could get another, but this was Ralph's last chance. Sometimes, indeed, he forgot that he was not her only hunter, and at such times he seemed to sink into a golden bath of joy.

They saw the mountain lion on Easter Sunday. This time she was beside the stream, nearer the gulch than the place where she had vanished before, close to the beaver dam. They had only a momentary glimpse of her and then she leaped away and was out of sight before they could even raise their rifles. They ran to the place where she had been and found that she had left her food, too startled by their voices to carry it off. A half-eaten woodchuck lay beside a tree stump, its entrails chewed but its silly head intact and twisted to a sheepish angle. It had been mauled and slobbered on and its grizzled hair was clotted. There was blood on some of the chips of wood left by the beavers when they had gnawed down the tree.

Uncle Claude, frustrated, angry, moved around the stump, examining everything as if he expected to find a clue which would lead him to her den. Sighing, he said, "Blast the yellow bitch."

And Ralph, feeling himself on the verge of tears, said desolately, "What'll we do now?"

"Go home, I reckon," said Uncle Claude, "but by damn, I'm going to get me my cat yet."

Ralph kept the edge out of his voice but his heart was rapid. He said, "You mean, I'm going to get *me my* cat."

Uncle Claude glanced sidelong at him but said nothing and they started down the creek bank. The creek was swollen from the thaws and there were places where the water sprayed like a geyser in the hollows between the rocks. Between two boulders at a widening, Ralph saw the points of a set of antlers sticking up out of the water and he waded in, not bothering to take off his shoes. But what he found was not just one set of antlers: he found the skulls of two deer with horns so tightly interlocked that he could not get them apart. They were wedged in between the rocks and he had trouble getting them loose. The water was cold and insistently flicked up his pants legs and once he lost his footing and slipped on a rock. When he came out with his trophy, he found Uncle Claude sitting on a patch of grass smoking, watching Ralph without the least interest.

"What'll you do with them now you got them?" he said.

Ralph did not immediately answer, but tried again to

get the horns apart. His heart constricted when he conjured up what must have taken place: the two bucks charging one another and then, by lunatic accident, being joined as one, toppling into the water to drown, still struggling to get free. But it was not so much the violence of this wilderness death that made him quiver; it was his uncle's indifference, the same indifference he had seen when he had looked at the sick bull. His passion for Goldilocks went over him like an ocean wave, for he was determined that she, at least, would be killed not out of this cold calm of Uncle Claude's but out of his own love for her golden hide.

Uncle Claude repeated, "What'll you do with them?"

"Why, I'll take them to Magdalene as a present," he said. "Or, no, I'll take them to Molly."

Uncle Claude laughed shortly. "You'd better take Molly a box of candy to sweeten her disposition. What's the matter with that kid anyway?"

Ralph took in his breath sharply. "Search me," he said.

Later, when he took the antlers up to Molly's room, he found her lying on her bed with the counterpane over her head. She pulled it down and stared at his present with terrible woe but without scorn. They exchanged, at last, after these months, a look of understanding and Molly said, "Thanks, Ralph. I'll shoot them with my Brownie."

Finally school was over. On the night of commencement, he sat in the hot auditorium where the June bugs bumbled foolishly against the window screens and the teachers sat among the baskets of gladioli and the potted rubber plants on the stage, listening to a boy in glasses deliver the valedictory. His voice broke twice, rising to a plaintive scream once on the word "emperor" and once on "romance." He used phrases like "elegiac cadences" and "poetic counterpoint" and he said that Vergil had been born to "the purple of classical literature." When he came to the end, he begged permission to finish with the lines of a "devotee of Roman literature more mellifluous than myself, *id est,* Alfred Lord Tennyson," and he recited *Frater Ave Atque Vale*. Ralph immediately saw the portrait of Grandfather Bonney and he was clutched by terror at the shortness of the time. He felt that his mother and sisters, who were now in Venice, were speeding, were about to overtake him, and there was no time to lose for he *must* have Goldilocks before they came. He looked for Molly who was to receive an eighth-grade diploma. She was sitting three rows away from him and when the boy had finished, she turned round and looked directly at her brother, puffing out her cheeks to look like a fat person.

The day after that they took the car, Ralph, Winifred, and Molly. Winifred drove and they went as far up Garland as the red road went. She and Molly climbed the face but Ralph could not manage the chimneys with his gun and went around the other way. Uncle Claude had taken a mare to stud and he had told them that when he got through, he would come looking for them in the hills and he would pack some food along so that they could cook out.

Ralph met them at the stream. Red dust had come off on their hands when they climbed the chimneys and they washed it off in the cold water, letting the fool's gold run through their fingers. All three of them lay down, crushing harebells, and looked straight upward. A chicken hawk lazily banked and coasted across the sky; behind them, in the forest, the chipmunks and the bluejays sent up their absent-minded racket against the wind which was always present in the pine trees like a voice. Hearing it, Ralph wished he were at the foot of a tree in the strange and smoky shade and were lying on the pinkish-brown pine needles; but the high, hot sun was too excellent to leave. Winifred held her arm over her eyes and Ralph noticed the tiny golden hairs on her wrists and on the backs of her hands. She was not going back to college next year; she was going to marry John Fulbright on the first of July and they were going to the eastern part of the state to start a truck farm. Mrs. Brotherman, too, was leaving the Bar K, now that her daughter was grown; she was going back to Salem. Ralph was sure that the odor of apples would cling to her rooms. He thought how lonely his uncle would be next winter and was sorry for him. The winter was an idle time for him and in this year Ralph had seen that idleness aged him. He did little of the feeding himself because, some years before, he had ridden into town without chaps, had been delayed, and coming back after the sun had gone down and when the thermometer registered twenty-five below, he had frozen both his legs and he was afraid thereafter of freezing them again. He hunted a little, emptied his traps, and took care of his beaver and ermine hides, gave a hand with the milking and gathered the eggs for Magdalene. The rest of the time he spent at his desk, studying the histories of his bulls and writing letters on lined paper with an indelible pencil to his foremen on the other ranches; playing a kind of Solitaire called "Once in a Blue Moon"; and reading books like *The Count of Monte Cristo, Graustark,* and *Beau Ideal*. Ralph pitied him so much at this moment that he almost wished Uncle Claude would get Goldilocks, but his generosity was brief-lived. Where was she now? How wonderful she must be in this hot sun!

The smoke from Winifred's cigarette went straight up and then opened out into a horn like a blue lily. Ralph thought somnolently: the lilies of the field are numbered. He saw in his mind's eye that wide, bare plateau at the glacier where the yellow orchids grew. Now, years after their expedition there, he thought how curious it was that he and Molly had not been tempted to eat the strawberry snow, for it had looked as delicious as sherbet. That was the day his friendship with Uncle Claude had begun and the day on which he had abandoned Molly. It had begun in a look of recognition.

He fell into a lazy meditation. He wondered if Montreux where the travelers were going next was similar to this and if the Alps were as tall as the Rocky Mountains; he wondered if their hotel would be like the Brown Palace. He pretended that he lay on the thick carpet in the center of the lobby looking up at the dome as if it were a motion-picture screen. He saw ladies in taffeta dresses and small velvet toques, mitts and pointed satin slippers, saw the gambling tables where the croupiers used heavy shovels because the money was all in gold bricks. In those days, the ladies had bathed in champagne in gold-plated tubs. Everything that presented itself to him was gold: the bark on the palm trees in Covina, the whisky in the glass that Grandpa had left when he went upstairs to die, Leah's hair above the tall chrysanthemums, the clasps on Grandfather Bonney's books. He did not will any of these images but they came in a stately promenade. There was a small gold brooch of two clasped hands in his mother's button box and in the same box was a tarnished heart-shaped locket on a fine chain. He remembered Jesus' halo on the cards given out at Sunday school, the gilt star of Bethlehem on the Christmas tree, his Tenderfoot pin.

Once they heard a freight train going out and once, from somewhere miles away, a blast of dynamite. Contented as he was with this present time, he was idly trying to think what it reminded him of and when at last, opening his eyes, he saw the chicken hawk again, he remembered the airplane those long years ago when he and Molly had lain on the lippia lawn, waiting for Uncle Claude to come and bury Grandpa.

He said, "Molly, do you remember the airplane that day of Grandpa Kenyon's funeral?" His voice sounded submerged and hesitant to him and he found he was trembling for her answer. She paused a long time and then, leaning across Winifred, she looked straight at him and said, "All I remember in the whole wide world is that I hate you and I hope you will get fat."

Winifred laughed. "You've got the worst temper in the county."

"I beg to differ," said Molly. "It is the worst in the state, in the United States, in North America, in the Western Hemisphere, in the world, in the universe." She said this rapidly, letting her voice rise powerfully.

"All right, be a bad sport," said Ralph wearily and closed his eyes again.

"You'd be a bad sport, too," she said to Winifred, "if you knew what he said to me."

"Molly!" he cried and sat up straight.

"What did he say?" asked Winifred, amused.

"Molly, if you tell, I'll . . ."

"You'll what?" She looked at him coldly. Then she stretched out her long thin arm and pointed in the direction of Cuthbert Pass and said, "If we had the field glasses, we could see the tunnel from here."

"What did Ralph say to you, Molly?" insisted Winifred.

"Oh, I don't intend to tell *you,* Winifred Brotherman. By the by, don't you think Ralph is getting fat?"

He jumped to his feet and picked up his gun. "I'm going now," he said tightly.

"What for?" Molly smiled at him teasingly, twirling a harebell between her fingers.

"Cat fur to make kitten breeches," he snapped and then was annoyed with himself for using the childhood joke.

"That is a very good pun, I'm sorry to say," said Molly. "I surely don't think you knew you were making it as I have never known anyone more unfurnished in the upper story."

He did not know what she was talking about; he did not understand the pun he had made. Striding through the harebells, he enjoyed the feeling of crushing the blue flowers under his feet. Winifred called after him, "Good luck," but he did not turn back. He could not have any luck, for even if he saw Goldilocks, he couldn't shoot until Uncle Claude came. He went downstream toward the beaver dam, making too much noise at first in his irritation with Molly and then treading lightly on the mossy, resilient ground. He passed the place where he had found the antlers and thought how wrong he had been the day he had given them to Molly and had thought they had understood one another

225

again. He felt suddenly that he was going along this stream for the last time.

Molly had spoiled everything and he could not even care about Goldilocks. Damn her, he said, damn her. It was only Goldilocks that had made him able to forget the tunnel. Now she had wrecked it all. It was possible that even now she was telling Winifred, but on second thoughts, this seemed unlikely: she was too smart; she would save up and use it when the right time came. She was always saving up something and always had; she saved her candy at Christmas until everyone else had finished and then, a day or so later, she brought all hers out and ate it in front of them and wouldn't give them a crumb of it. And she saved up all the jokes she heard and the things people had said and other people's dreams so that she had the reputation of being interesting, although no one could stand her because she was so sarcastic. She would, for instance, take the pun he had made and pretend it was her own.

He sat down finally on a lichen-covered rock beside the beaver dam. One day late in October he had come here by himself, not to hunt for Goldilocks but to escape Uncle Claude who had wanted him to go to look at the winter wheat. The day had been cold with a wind and a chill that crept along the skin, not quite penetrating. The sky was heavy and the leaves were all fallen and were all brown. The skinny trees were already gray with winter and the ferns underfoot crumbled, making a faint sound. He had seen a weasel and had thought how in just a little while its coat would turn white and it would be an ermine.

At the very moment he remembered the weasel, a sala-mander, black and orange, streaked through the fern brake beside his rock, making him think of Grandfather Bonney's snuff box. Was there anything in the world, he wondered, that did not make you think of something else? From the snuff box he went on to the night Miss Runyon had brought the flowers and he and Molly had sobbed silently for Grandpa on the floor beside his coffin. Nothing had ever been really right since then, but why? He perfectly saw the old man and perfectly heard him sing:

> Oh, we'll sit on his white hause bane,
> And I'll pyke out his bonney blue e'en,
> Wi' a lock o' his gowden hair,
> We'll theek our nest when it blaws bare.

"I'll never be happy again," he said softly and aloud. Neither would Molly, but Molly did not want to be happy and she wanted him to be as wretched as she. If she told his mother, if his mother gave him a moral lecture often using the expression "not quite nice," he would leave home. He would not just threaten, he really would join the Navy.

The decision made him feel better and he got up. He moved around the beaver dam, looking alertly through the trees. Just beyond this black silent pool there was a little glade he knew of with a flat rock in the center of it like a table. He thought he heard someone across the dam and stopped to listen, but he concluded that it had only been a bird rustling. It had occurred to him that it might be Uncle Claude, but he realized that he could not have got back from the stud farm so soon. Quiet as it was, there was, as always in the forest, a feeling of life near by and when, softly moving aside a branch of chokecherry, he saw Goldi-locks in the glade beside the flat rock feeding on a jackrabbit, he was not surprised. He had been certain, this last moment, that he would find her there. She delicately moved the rabbit with her paw and then savagely ripped it with her teeth. He stood, holding his breath, utterly motionless for a minute, debating, but he could not hold out against the temptation: Uncle Claude would have to forgive him; if he didn't, Ralph would go away.

As he raised his rifle, he heard another sound but this time from the direction of the face of the mountain. Goldilocks heard it too and lifted her heavy head; before she could find him with her topaz eyes, he shot and immediately he was stone blind. His blindness lasted for an exploded moment and when he was able to see again, to see the tumbled yellow body on the bright grass, he realized that he had not been blind but deaf, for there had been another gun, another shot a split second after his.

Uncle Claude came charging through the brush, hollering like an Indian. "By God, we done it! By Jesus Christ, we both done it." And he ran to the lion, throwing his gun on the ground. She had fallen toward Ralph on her wounded side and no blood was visible. Uncle Claude turned her over to look for the wounds and Ralph stepped forward.

"She's so little," said Ralph softly, as if Goldilocks were not dead but only asleep. "Why, she isn't any bigger than a dog. She isn't as *big*."

But what mattered was whose bullet had killed her. They looked together eagerly, pushing back the hair with their hands. Ralph was surprised to find how short and harsh it was. There was only one bullet hole, and it was not in the place where Ralph had aimed. He was sick with

228

failure, sick and furious with his uncle for coming so quietly and winning so easily.

Uncle Claude said, "No man alive can judge which one of us got her. I reckon we'll have to call it a corporation."

There was a sound in the chokecherry bushes beyond them, opposite where Ralph had stood to shoot. It was a sound that could come only from a human throat. It was a bubbling of blood. Uncle Claude and Ralph stood up and looked at one another in an agony of terror and for a moment they could not move but stood, hatless, the sun blazing down upon them and upon the lion at their feet.

"Somebody . . ."

Uncle Claude, bending almost in two at the waist, ran across the clearing and Ralph followed, his body a flame of pain. Molly lay beside a rotten log, a wound like a burst fruit in her forehead. Her glasses lay in fragments on her cheeks and the frame, torn from one ear, stuck up at a raffish angle. The elastic had come out of one leg of her gym bloomers and it hung down to her shin. The sound in her throat stopped. Uncle Claude knelt down beside her, but Ralph stood some paces away. He could as clearly see the life leave her as you could see fire leave burnt-out wood. It receded like a tide, lifted like a fog.

When Uncle Claude stood up, Ralph began to scream. He threw back his head and with his mouth as wide as it would open he let the sound flow out of him, burning up the mountains. Then he was too hoarse to scream any longer and he threw himself down on the ground and pounded the pine needles with his fists and with his feet, moaning, "I didn't see her! I didn't hear her! I didn't kill her!"

Uncle Claude came to him and seized him by the shoulder roughly and made him stand up. "Cut it out," he said sharply. "Get the hell out of here and go get somebody."

He stood with his arms hanging at his sides and said, "I didn't know she was there."

"Goddamit, I know *that*. Shove, now. Go on. *Get* somebody."

In a minute, he thought, just let me have a minute. He knelt down beside his sister and touched the blood on her forehead, stroked her cheeks, felt of her sodden hair. "Molly," he said. "Molly girl." He kissed her blood-salty lips as if like a dog he could lick her wound and heal it. Uncle Claude kicked him in the ribs and said, "When I say shove, I mean shove."

He had to go then. He stumbled across the clearing trying not to look at Goldilocks. At the head of the beaver dam he saw Winifred running toward him and knew that she had heard his screams. He stopped and waited for her, sitting again on the rock where he had seen the salamander. He pulled from its sheath a stalk of upland bearded barley and bit its succulent stem and chewed. There was neither a past nor a future to his life in this single, yellow minute.

When she came panting up, he said, "Go on through the clearing. They're on the other side," and though her face questioned him, she ran on without a word.

For a long time, he sat there muttering like a crazy man: Molly, Molly, Molly, Molly. He said it until they came back, Winifred carrying the guns and Uncle Claude carrying his dead sister with her ruined head. They had tied a handkerchief around her forehead so that you could not see the hole but the blood had soaked through; relaxed like that in Uncle Claude's arms, she looked like a tall, slim monkey.

230

By the time they got her down to the car, the sun was setting. Directly, Ralph thought, there would be that evil yellow light. Uncle Claude and Winifred sat in front and Ralph sat in the back beside Molly, whom they had propped up like a person. He looked straight ahead, watching the road being devoured by the car like an endless red noodle.

Magdalene was in the front yard picking mint and Uncle Claude called to her to come and help. She came to the car and looked in at Molly. There was no emotion at all on her pleated black face, but as soon as she spoke, Ralph was able to collapse. She said, "Lord Jesus. The pore little old piece of white trash."

Obelisk

The following is a list of Obelisk titles now available, each chosen as an example of excellent prose:

Donald Barthelme, *Sixty Stories*

Noël Coward, *Pomp and Circumstance*

Jane Howard, *A Different Woman*

Molly Keane, *Good Behaviour*

Peter Matthiessen, *The Tree Where Man Was Born*

Joyce Carol Oates, *A Sentimental Education*

Cynthia Ozick, *Levitation*
                 The Pagan Rabbi and Other Stories

Oliver Sacks, *Awakenings*

Raymond Sokolov, *Fading Feast*
                  Native Intelligence

W. M. Spackman, *A Presence with Secrets*

Jean Stafford, *The Mountain Lion*

Calvin Tomkins, *Living Well Is the Best Revenge*